22

V

8

BEST PRACTICES

BEST PRACTICES

Gwen Florio

SEVERN
HOUSE

First world edition published in Great Britain and the USA in 2022
by Severn House, an imprint of Canongate Books Ltd,
14 High Street, Edinburgh EH1 1TE.

Trade paperback edition first published in Great Britain and the USA in 2023
by Severn House, an imprint of Canongate Books Ltd.

severnhouse.com

British Library Cataloguing-in-Publication Data
A CIP catalogue record for this title is available from the British Library.

ISBN-13: 978-0-7278-5072-0 (cased)
ISBN-13: 978-1-4483-0759-3 (trade paper)
ISBN-13: 978-1-4483-0758-6 (e-book)

This is a work of fiction. Names, characters, places and incidents
are either the product of the author's imagination or are used fictitiously.
Except where actual historical events and characters are being described
for the storyline of this novel, all situations in this publication are
fictitious and any resemblance to actual persons, living or dead,
business establishments, events or locales is purely coincidental.

All Severn House titles are printed on acid-free paper.

Typeset by Palimpsest Book Production Ltd.,
Falkirk, Stirlingshire, Scotland.
Printed and bound in Great Britain by
TJ Books, Padstow, Cornwall.

To my colleagues at the Missoulian newspaper who, under the direction of editor Kathy Best, shined the strongest sunlight into the darkest places, enabling state Sen. Diane Sands to finally push through the changes in law she'd championed for years. Journalism matters.

ACKNOWLEDGEMENTS

This series owes much to the wise counsel of my agent Richard Curtis. Carl Smith of Severn House makes the editing process a joy. Thanks also to the rest of the Severn House crew who had a hand in Nora's most recent adventure – Anna Harrison, Natasha Bell and Jem Butcher. So much love to my partner Scott, for his unwavering support and for being my last best reader before the manuscript goes to the publisher. Finally, programs such as the fictional one in this book exist around the country. Of course not all are problematic. But no meaningful regulation applies nationally. Congress periodically considers it, and if this is the year it happens, I'll be grateful.

ONE

Nora Best was only two miles into her predawn run when the weak cry sounded. She whipped around to see two men dragging a teenage girl toward a panel truck.

A scream – her own – rent the air.

'Stop!'

She charged past the darkened homes, fumbling for her phone, memories of her own recent kidnapping and near-death propelling her forward, determined not to let anyone else suffer the same fate.

She extricated the phone from her tights and hit 911. 'Kidnapping in progress. Uh . . .'

Thankfully, a nearby house had one of those nauseatingly cute, grammatically incorrect, signs with a name and address: *The Smith's, 201 American Ave.*

'Two-hundred block of American Avenue. Hurry! Two men have a girl.'

'Your name? The full address?'

'Nora Best. And I have no idea. I don't even know what town I'm in.'

The dispatcher launched another question, but Nora clicked off, held up her phone, zoomed in on the van's license plate and snapped a photo.

'Let her go!' she roared.

The men spun to confront her, the girl dangling between them, struggling half-heartedly before her body went slack.

Nora stopped a few yards away, breathing hard, just beginning to contemplate the possibility that the men might be armed. Not to mention the fact that there were two of them and only one of her and that, despite her scream, no one in the surrounding homes seemed to be responding to the commotion. The windows remained stubbornly dark, the silence – but for her own ragged breaths – absolute.

She'd parked her Airstream the night before in a campground somewhere in the Midwest. Illinois? Indiana? The last time she'd paid attention, she'd been in Ohio. She was in a suburb by the looks of the winding streets adjoining the campground, full of aging but well-tended split-levels on neat, landscaped lawns and verging into an area of larger, older homes of brick or fieldstone set back from the street at the end of sweeping drives. Something so brazen as a kidnapping in such a setting seemed unlikely, but wasn't that the point?

'I've called nine-one-one.' Her voice shook. 'And I've texted the police a photo of your license plate.' She hadn't, but she would, as soon as she put a little more distance between herself and the two men in white coveralls. But for their ham-haunch musculature, they could have been house painters, electricians, their innocuous get-up part of their MO.

The girl's dark hair cascaded over her face, hiding her features. Drugged, most likely. Nora shuddered at the thought of the fate intended for her.

The men looked at each other.

'You'd better get them,' the shorter one said.

Oh, Christ. Were there more men in the van?

They tossed the girl, her body as limp as overcooked pasta, into the back of the van and slammed the door. The tall man took a few steps forward.

Nora tensed, poised to flee. Where were the goddamn cops?

But the man strode past her, breaking into a jog up a curving pea-gravel drive to a stone house with mullioned windows and an actual turret at one end. He banged a fist on the arched oaken door. It opened a crack. His voice barely carried down the length of the drive.

'You need to come out here. We've got a problem.'

Nora took one cautious step backward, then another. What if this suburban wannabe castle were the headquarters of some sort of sex-trafficking ring, a horror-movie dungeon next to the wine cellar?

She decided not to wait for the cops. Three sprinting steps away, a voice shattered the vitreous silence.

'Wait!'

A woman in a silk robe and mules advanced down the drive,

followed by a barefoot man in a T-shirt and sweatpants. Both were middle-aged, with the snarled hair and strained expressions that bespoke a sleepless night.

'Are you the one who called the police? There was no need,' the woman said as she reached Nora.

'Excuse me? These men threw a girl into that van. I saw them. She's in there now.'

The woman shook her head, her hair instantly arranging itself into the kind of layers signifying an expert cut. She tightened the belt of her robe, drew herself up and spoke in the sort of voice accustomed to commanding attention.

'That's our daughter.'

'No.' A few months ago, Nora might have accepted that explanation and backed away, scattering apologies in her wake. But she'd learned the most painful way possible not to accept bland explanations from reasonable-appearing people. The woman who'd engineered Nora's own kidnapping – Nora was even now traveling back to Wyoming to testify against her at trial – had seemed a friend right up to the moment Nora discovered she wasn't.

'Tell that to the cops,' Nora said. 'They're on their way.'

The woman and her husband aimed tense, tight smiles at one another. 'Happy to.'

Nora wished she'd downed more than a single cup of coffee before starting her run. This scene was making less sense by the moment.

A police cruiser, notably absent flashing lights or screaming siren, turned onto the street and pulled up beside them. The officer rolled down his window and leaned out. 'Everything OK here, Katherine?'

The woman nodded toward Nora. 'She saw them taking our daughter and misunderstood.'

Nora narrowed her eyes. 'That was really their daughter?'

The cop nodded. 'Unfortunate situation. We're well acquainted with her. This whole neighborhood is used to me showing up here. She's on her way to treatment. Hopefully, this time it'll take.' His expression showed he thought otherwise.

A junkie, then; probably overdosed. That would explain the

girl's lassitude. But why this unmarked van, rather than an ambulance?

The girl's father seemed to read her mind. 'It's a private program. Does all of this set your mind at ease?'

The tall man in the coveralls shifted from one steel-toe booted foot to the other. 'All done here? We'd like to get on the road. It's a long drive.'

The girl's mother's hand flew to her throat. Her eyes filled with tears. Her husband wrapped an arm around her.

'Come on, Katherine. This is for the best. Let's go back in.' He briefly released her, dug in the pocket of his sweats, and palmed a bill to the man. 'For the extra trouble. Thank you.'

The cop nodded a goodbye, rolled up the window, steered his car into a U-turn and drove off, following the van.

Nora stood alone in the street, wondering what the hell had just happened.

She glanced at her phone before sliding it back into its pocket. Her eyes widened and she broke into a run, hitting a new personal best on her return to her Airstream.

TWO

Nora fixed a fresh cup of coffee before looking again at her phone. She wanted to be sure she wasn't dreaming.

'Hope I didn't wake you,' read the text from her lawyer. 'I wanted you to see this first thing.'

'An hour from now.' She spoke aloud to the device in her hand. 'Or even two. For anyone else, that would have been first thing.'

Artie, an old family friend providing deeply discounted legal advice as a favor, was one of those people who arose at four thirty to get in a workout before going to the office and putting in a twelve-hour day, which is probably why Artie's wife had ended up sleeping with Nora's husband.

Ex-husband. And now – because Joe hadn't been nearly so lucky as Nora – dead husband.

'I heard last night from the prosecutor in Wyoming. He didn't want to contact you that late, even though I assured him you wouldn't mind. With just a week to go before trial, your assailant finally came to her senses. She's entering a guilty plea today. You won't have to see her until the sentencing hearing, which probably won't be for weeks, if not months. There's no reason for you to go to Wyoming.'

Nora fell back onto the bed.

It was about time she caught a break.

She'd stack her summer from hell against anyone's worst nightmare: husband caught cheating, then murdered (not by her, although she'd briefly and fervently wished him dead and at one point had been the prime suspect); herself kidnapped and left to die; and then, after fleeing to her childhood home on Maryland's Eastern Shore to recover, finding her own mother was not the person she'd thought – an understatement on par with the godawfulness of Nora's last several weeks.

'Murph. Mooch. It's over!' She tossed her phone in joyous relief, then leapt to grab it before it ricocheted off the Airstream's shiny riveted ceiling.

Michael Murphy, an aging Chesapeake Bay retriever, cowered beneath the dinette, safely out of the way of her inexplicable antics. Mooch, an orange tabby, arched his back and hissed his displeasure at such undignified, un*feline* exuberance.

By the time Nora hit the road, she'd forgotten all about the girl and the van.

Two weeks later Nora found herself navigating an increasingly narrow series of two-lane roads in far north-western Montana, on her way to what apparently was her sole surviving means of supporting herself.

She cast an anxious eye toward the sky. Luckily, even though the calendar had just ticked over into September, night still descended late in these northern latitudes. She calculated that she had an hour at most to get to Serendipity Ranch before dark.

Given her surroundings – mile after mile of unbroken pine forest, interrupted only occasionally by a gravel lane disappearing into the trees – she very much wanted to arrive before nightfall.

'We're remote,' Charlie Ennis, the ranch's affable director had told her in a job interview conducted via video call. He had a round pink face with the soft padding of fat that defies wrinkles, and a halo of cotton-candy flyaway white hair, looking for all the world like a benevolent, beardless Santa.

'Our isolation is by design, for two very good reasons. One, the extreme beauty of our surroundings works a healing balm on the troubled youngsters who comprise our clientele. And two, given their histories, the farther removed they are from their previous influences, the better.'

At the time, Nora had nodded enthusiastic comprehension. Now, that enthusiasm waned by the mile.

But really, what choice did she have? She needed work; more specifically, she needed a paycheck, and the job as housemother-cum-instructor had seemed as serendipitous as the ranch's name.

She'd quit her previous job in public relations in Denver to travel the country with her husband in the Airstream and write a book about their experiences, a plan that began to crumble upon her discovery of his infidelities on the eve of their trip and that went to hell completely when he was murdered in the mountains of Wyoming. When she'd recovered from the shock of those events, she'd thanked her stars for Joe's generous life insurance policy, only to be informed that a payout was still weeks in the offing.

She'd worsened her situation by deeding her family home on Maryland's Eastern Shore to recently discovered relatives, a guilt-driven act that at the time had saved her conscience but proved ruinous to her financial stability, two words that no longer applied to her life.

The elation stemming from the news that she wouldn't have to endure testifying at a trial was short-lived. She'd celebrated by bypassing Wyoming and indulging in a real vacation in Seattle, where she spent her days on a whale-watching trip, taking the ferries to various islands, and gawking at Mount Rainier's postcard majesty, and her nights applying for jobs.

But the series of lightning-fast rejections to the increasingly wide net of applications she'd cast revealed that – surprise, surprise – a fifty-year-old woman whose recent unwanted notoriety could be discovered with a single keyboard click was nobody's idea of an ideal hire.

When Charlie Ennis contacted her via a LinkedIn account she'd hurriedly refreshed, she was so desperate she'd have volunteered to shovel cow shit on his ranch. He explained early in their conversation that it wasn't that kind of ranch.

'Troubled children,' he'd explained. 'Teenagers, actually, but from some of their behaviors, you'd think they were barely out of kindergarten. It's sad. By the time they come here, they've spun so far out of control their families are frantic. About those families. They're among the country's most prominent. You'll recognize some of the names. For that reason, we require all of our staff to sign nondisclosure agreements. You can imagine how the press might feast upon some of the tales of these children's, ah, misbehavior. That's not a problem for you, is it?'

Nora, who'd had more than one brush with the press in the past summer, didn't care if she never spoke to a reporter again, although she put her assurance to Ennis more tactfully.

She'd tussled briefly with her conscience, which to her dismay won out. 'But I don't understand how I could possibly be qualified for this job.' Goddammit. How had those words come out of her mouth? Now that a job had seemingly fallen in her lap, she was pushing it away. Just as she'd resigned herself to spending the rest of her life asking people if they'd like fries with their burgers, Ennis spoke again, leaning close to the screen.

'We have a professional counselor to deal with the matters that seem to be most concerning to you, as well they should. But our children can't be in therapy twenty-four hours a day. They need normalcy, routine, role models.'

Nora thought of the girl she'd seen on that early-morning run, being dragged away to a treatment program that – given the two thuggish men, the creepy van – was probably more

like prison. Why couldn't her parents have sent her to a
place like this?

'That's where you come in,' Ennis continued, 'as a responsible, well-adjusted adult who's not their parent.'

Nora congratulated herself for restraining an eye-roll at
'well-adjusted'. Charlie Ennis had no idea how very far from
well-adjusted she was.

'Most of our applicants for these jobs are young people,
often just out of college. They have romantic ideas about the
adventure of it all. And many are skilled outdoorswomen,
which dovetails with our program of physical challenges as a
way of coping with emotional issues. We hire several, for that
very reason. But they're so close in age to our students. It can
create issues with, ah, boundaries. Our clientele needs to learn
to respect the authority of adults; adults they can look up to.
Sometimes, unfortunately, their parents don't always model
the best behaviors. Someone of your mature age' – Nora, still
adjusting to being in her fifties, winced – 'and your professional background is a rare find. We only have one other
housemother of similar age. You'll be a welcome addition.'

The earnest lines creasing his face smoothed. He tilted back
in his chair. 'Besides, you come highly recommended. Your
former supervisors couldn't say enough good things about
you.'

They couldn't? Nora had left her university job on good
terms, but unless every last one of her former colleagues had
been whisked away by space aliens, she couldn't imagine they
hadn't heard about her recent troubles. On the other hand, HR
guidelines would have prevented any allusions to those issues.
Was it possible Charlie Ennis hadn't Googled her? If so, that
was an abundance of mercy from the hiring gods. But . . .

'The job said houseparent. Am I expected to live with them?
Because I have a travel trailer and I'd much prefer to stay in
that. I have a dog and a cat, and I can't imagine bringing them
into a dormitory.'

Nora wished it had been a simple telephone interview
without the scrutiny afforded by video. Then she could have
silenced her phone while she discreetly slammed her head
against the wall for her own ill-advised honesty.

'We call it a bunkhouse,' Ennis gently corrected her. 'And to expect someone to spend every single night with a group of teenage girls – well . . . Our salaries are excellent, but no amount of money would be adequate compensation. We rotate housemother duties among the female staff.'

Nora chortled along with him, even as she thought, Is it possible I did not actually blow this?

She hadn't, which is how she found herself glancing repeatedly at the directions to Serendipity Ranch, glad she'd printed them out from Charlie Ennis' email. Cell reception had gone spotty a few miles back. She turned off the paved road onto one of those mysterious gravel tracks.

She eyed it with some concern. Her truck, a Chevy with high clearance and four-wheel drive, could easily navigate a rough road, but the trailer she hauled behind it was another matter. The truck jolted across a section of washboard, rousing Mooch and Murph, snoozing in the backseat. Mooch leapt into the passenger seat and commenced an outraged yowl, while Murph, elderly gentleman that he was, limited himself to a low mutter.

The trees crowded closer, low branches scraping the sides of the truck and her beloved Airstream. Panic fluttered in Nora's throat. This couldn't possibly be the road to the sizeable operation Ennis had described. But now she was trapped; her only way out to back truck and trailer down the half-mile she estimated they'd traveled so far, and backing up was not at the top of her skill set. The trailer might end up crunched against one of those infernal pines and she wouldn't even be able to call for help. She'd have to leave the animals in the truck and walk to wherever she last had cell service, along a road where she'd seen no other vehicles for miles, and with night coming on fast. Her only hope was to keep going and pray she'd come to a clearing where she could somehow turn around.

As though her very thoughts had conjured it, the trees fell away and Nora steered into just such a clearing, where an elaborately lettered wrought-iron sign swung from an overhead crossbar: Serendipity Ranch.

THREE

Nora set the emergency brake and lifted shaking hands from the wheel.

Mooch's yowls subsided into a skeptical meow and Murph's tail began a slow sweep.

'We made it,' she said, as much to herself as to the animals. 'I've never been so glad to see a place in my life.'

Except, the place looked deserted. She sat a moment longer, taking it in. Serendipity Ranch consisted of a large lodge at the far end of a clearing and another building, nearly as large, near the entrance. Several smaller log cabins edged the circle. All were dark, and only a single light glowed in the lodge. Nora didn't even see any vehicles, though she supposed a long shed behind the lodge might house them.

She climbed out of the truck and opened the rear door to help Murph, whose aging joints no longer permitted a leap to the ground. She snatched up Mooch before he could escape and walked him back to the trailer, where she unlocked the door and deposited him in front of his litter box, earning another screech of outrage when she closed the door behind him.

She stood a moment, rubbing her bare arms. Despite her long years in Denver and its environs, she'd forgotten the way temperatures plunged at night in' the mountains. She checked her watch – it was barely nine o'clock. Surely people weren't sleeping yet. She'd warned Ennis in an email that she'd arrive late. She started across the clearing toward the lodge, when the door to the largest cabin creaked open and a teenage girl ran toward her, blonde ponytail swinging.

'Wait! Wait!'

She stopped in front of Nora, wrestling her arms into the sweatshirt she'd pulled on over a nightgown. She was tall and slender, with features so model-perfect that Nora, thinking back to what Ennis had said about the ranch's wealthy clientele, suspected minor plastic surgery – a tiny bump in a nose smoothed away, cheekbones emphasized, and surely those pillowy lips owed a debt to Botox.

'Are you the new housemother?'

Nora nodded, unable to speak, overcome by her own imperfections – the fast-graying hair whose disguising highlights had grown out, the lines digging their way across her forehead and fanning from the corners of her eyes and mouth, an incipient crackle in her knees that made her sympathize with Murph. Just you wait, my pretty, she thought spitefully. Although this girl would probably look as good at fifty as she did at – what? Fifteen? Sixteen?

'I'm Nora,' she finally managed.

'Mackenzie. But we have to call you by your last name.'

'Best.'

Mackenzie's smile could have sold a pauper on the benefits of expensive orthodontia. 'Cool name, Mrs Best.'

'Ms,' Nora corrected. 'Why can't I go in there? Have they shut down for the night?'

Mackenzie stepped close and lowered her voice. Nora sensed a riveted attentiveness from the large cabin nearby, an occasional twitch of a curtain hinting at the watchers behind the windows.

'Sort of. I'm to tell you to just pull in your trailer beside our bunkhouse and get settled for the night. You can talk with Director Ennis in the morning. Is that your dog?'

Murph trotted to her and happily submitted to this new source of affection.

'What a sweet boy.' Mackenzie stooped and bestowed a kiss on his graying muzzle. 'How old is he?'

'Ancient. Listen, could you help guide me as I back my trailer into a spot? I want to do it before it gets any darker.'

Mackenzie wrapped her arms around Murph for a long hug. When she straightened, Nora was surprised to see tears in her eyes.

'Sorry. No PDAs allowed here. This is the closest I've come to one since I got here.'

Nora got back into the truck and rolled down her window. 'PDAs?'

'Public displays of affection.'

As she followed Mackenzie's clumsy signals to position her trailer beside the cabin, Nora contemplated the girl's remark. Wouldn't troubled kids need affection even more than normal ones, she wondered, even as she reminded herself not to use words like 'normal' at Serendipity Ranch. But then she thought of all the stories about teachers and counselors and other adults abusing kids in their care. Such policies were probably standard everywhere now.

'Thanks, Mackenzie.' Nora turned off the ignition, got out her checklist, and set about leveling the trailer and unhitching it, Mackenzie dogging her heels.

'What's with the airplane?' She pointed to the large decal on the side, depicting an old-timey silvery airplane soaring into a bright blue yonder.

'Ah.' Nora switched off the buzzing cordless drill she'd used to lower the stabilizers and straightened. 'I named my trailer Electra, for Amelia Earhart's Lockheed Electra. That's the plane in the decal.'

Mackenzie's smooth young brow furrowed. 'Didn't something bad happen to her?'

Which is pretty much what everyone said when Nora explained Electra's artwork.

'Yeah. She disappeared somewhere over the Pacific. But before that – my God, the things that woman saw and did. She was fearless.'

'Is that good? To be fearless?'

Nora tried to push through her exhaustion to give her answer the thought it deserved. Whatever she said would be the first lesson she'd impart in her new job. She didn't want to get it wrong.

'Usually.' She thought of the last summer, when she'd knowingly brought the wrath of a community upon herself. 'But,' she rushed to add, 'sometimes fear is the thing that saves you. When you get that bad feeling in your gut, the one that all girls and women know?'

She waited for Mackenzie's nod, which came so quickly it saddened her.

'When you feel that, pay attention.'

She mentally patted herself on the back for what she'd hoped was exactly the right mix of wisdom and tact. She'd never had kids of her own, but she'd been a teenage girl herself. She could do this job.

'Your trailer's awesome. Can I see the inside?'

Nora hesitated. She hadn't expected Lesson No. 2 so quickly. But . . . boundaries.

'The trailer is my private space. Maybe, after I've been here a while and we all know one another better. Now I just want to feed the pets and myself and get a good night's sleep so I can get an early start tomorrow.'

Mackenzie's next words stopped her on the trailer's step.

'No need to get up early. We won't have any classes or group sessions tomorrow. We're all in individual therapy, one after another, all day long. Irene, one of the girls, took a header into the gorge last night.'

Nora thought of her own header off a forest bluff a few months earlier, when her kidnapper jabbed her with a knife and shoved her over the edge. Her hand strayed to her side, her fingers tracing the raised scar through the thin cotton of her T-shirt.

'Oh, no. Was she badly hurt?'

Mackenzie gave her the patented teenage eye-roll that conferred maximum stupidity upon her.

'No. She wasn't *hurt*. She's dead.'

FOUR

The knock at Electra's door interrupted what Nora had hoped would be a late sleep. She checked her phone, confused. Six a.m. But the girl had told her classes were canceled for the day.

Murph gave a warning bark, then looked to Nora for approval. 'Good boy,' she assured him as her whereabouts slowly reasserted their place in her consciousness.

'Ms Best. Ms Best.'

The same girl. Mackenzie. That was her name.

Nora stumbled the few steps to the door, wishing a bathrobe had been among the things she'd squeezed into the trailer's small closet. Somehow gym shorts and the same T-shirt she'd worn the previous day seemed inappropriate, given her new position. She cracked the door and feigned dignity.

'Good morning, Mackenzie. How are you?' Although, it barely seemed to be morning, the sky still more gray than blue. The surrounding pines were a single black mass.

'I'm fine.' But Mackenzie didn't seem fine. Her eyes were red, her voice hoarse. She glanced over her shoulder, then lifted a hand to her mouth and chewed on a thumbnail.

'Director Ennis wants to see you right away.'

'As in now?'

Mackenzie gave the thumbnail a break and put all her energy into an eye-roll, her second of their brief acquaintance. 'That's generally what right now means.'

'Of course. Sure. Tell him I'll be right there.'

'I'm supposed to wait for you.'

She peered past Nora into the trailer, her expression hopeful.

Boundaries, Nora reminded herself.

'Give me a few minutes to make myself presentable. You can keep an eye on Murph to make sure he doesn't run off after doing his business.'

She shooed the dog outside and Mackenzie brightened. Nora shut the door and turned the lock, in case Mackenzie got it into her head to escort the dog back inside when he was done.

She'd have preferred a shower and shampoo, a blow-dry, some make-up, all in the interest of making a good impression on her first day. She settled for washing her face, brushing her teeth, and running a wet comb through her hair. She buttoned herself into a long-sleeved cotton shirt and pulled on some khakis – the program's dress code forbade jeans as a way, it said, to help the students reacquire pride in their appearance; staff were expected to follow suit – and called it good.

She opened the trailer door to find Mackenzie seated cross-legged on the ground with Murph lying across her lap, a look of pure bliss on his face as she stroked his head and spoke softly to him.

She scrambled to her feet when she saw Nora.

'He's so sweet. He may be the nicest dog I've ever met.'

'Murph?' Michael Murphy, whose care she'd assumed after her mother's death, was a very good boy but Nora largely took his amiable presence for granted. Now she added that dismissiveness to the long, long list of things about which she felt guilty.

Murph climbed into the trailer with a longing backward glance at Mackenzie.

Nora faced the lodge that loomed ghostly within the morning mist.

'Let's do this.'

She'd assumed Ennis had summoned her for an introductory chat, to go over the information in the manual he'd sent her and maybe launch some sort of orientation.

But the unshaven man pacing the spacious office just off the lodge's great room bore little resemblance to the one who'd lounged behind his desk in an open-necked shirt and blazer during their interviews, deflecting her doubts with his confident, reassuring responses to her questions.

He'd seemed tall during those video encounters, perhaps a trick of lighting and staging. In person he was little and lumpy, a tooled leather belt cruelly cinching his squashed-bread torso. His shirt, so crisp in the video, looked as though he'd slept in it.

He spun on his heel and greeted her without preamble. 'Ms Best. You're the PR expert, correct?' He flicked a glance toward Mackenzie. 'You can go.'

Nora waited until the door clicked shut behind Mackenzie before responding to his question. 'I worked in public relations for a number of years. I don't know if that makes me an expert.'

Ennis waved away her hesitation.

'We have a, ah, situation here. An unfortunate situation.' He hesitated and Nora rushed to fill the silence.

'The student, yes. The one who fell.'

A purple vein wormed to prominence across his forehead. 'How did you know that?'

'Mackenzie told me last night.'

The vein wriggled. 'And she was doing so well.'

He picked up his desk phone and punched in four digits. 'I'm afraid we're going to have to knock Mackenzie Masterson down a rung. Insubordination.'

'I think she was just trying to be helpful.'

He kneaded his forehead and shook his head. 'Didn't you read the manual?'

Nora had skimmed it at night in her trailer, taking note of things that would immediately apply to her, such as the dress code, and vowing to review the rest more completely later. She knew the program relied on a series of steps – it styled them as rungs up a ladder – of privileges earned as rewards for certain achievements. But she hadn't yet committed those to memory just as she'd forgotten the infractions that could impede a student's progress. To her relief, Ennis didn't wait for an answer.

'We'll deal with that later. For now, we need to craft a letter to all the program's parents. A very carefully worded letter. This sort of thing can be so damaging. Parents tend to panic. Their first reaction often is to pull their children – already overly sheltered, the cause of so many of their problems – back home, right back into the situations that saw their children end up here in the first place. We need to send it quickly, nip that sort of thing in the bud. And don't worry. Our lawyer is on standby, waiting to review it. He's awaiting our call.'

Nora spoke in a rush, eager to get the words out before he cut her off again. 'It's a tragedy, the worst sort of one. But from what little I understand, it was an accident. Surely they'll understand.'

Ennis regarded her from beneath knitted brows. 'It was no accident. Irene Bell killed herself.'

Despite Ennis' stress on the need for haste, it was well past noon when Nora finally drafted a letter on her laptop that met both his, and the lawyer's, specifications.

The missive stressed the troubled nature of the program's clients, adding that sometimes, by the time they arrived at Serendipity Ranch, their problems were already too far advanced for reversal – a notion that, to Nora, sounded uncomfortably like blaming the parents or even the children themselves, but that set Ennis nodding with undisguised satisfaction after he'd tweaked her wording several times.

She tried a final time to soften it. 'If there's the least bit of doubt that it was an accident rather than a suicide, wouldn't it be smart to mention that possibility?'

Ennis blanched.

'This girl's parents are both attorneys. How many words do you know for nightmare? Believe me, if there's even a hint that this was an accident, something that might have been prevented, they'll own this place.'

'But couldn't a suicide have been prevented?'

He shook his head sorrowfully. 'You have no idea the devious determination of our students. We do our best to watch every child twenty-four/seven, but it's impossible. They act out sexually, find ways to get high despite our most stringent precautions, even leave the premises.'

It took Nora a moment to mentally translate 'leave the premises' as 'run away'.

'We spend so much time trying to keep them from self-destructing that it's a wonder we make the progress we do. We accomplish miracles here, Ms Best. You'll soon see.'

He'd shaved, showered and dressed after ordering Nora to fetch her laptop and set it up in his office, a process that had required a summons to one of the cabins for a girl – not Mackenzie, who presumably was in some sort of time out – to escort Nora back across the clearing to the trailer she could see from the lodge's front window.

'Is that necessary?' she'd asked.

'Best practices,' came Ennis' tight-lipped response. 'The students don't go anywhere unaccompanied, so neither do we. Everything we do here involves modeling.'

The girl was equally uncommunicative, answering Nora's carefully generic pleasantries with equally generic 'mm-hmms', finally muttering, 'You got Mackenzie in trouble,' before ceasing to speak altogether.

'But why my own laptop?' Nora ventured when she returned with it tucked under her arm.

'Our computers are down for maintenance. The timing couldn't be worse.'

Nora's stomach rumbled. At some point during the morning, she'd detected the scent of bacon, but when she asked about breakfast he merely lifted the phone and summoned one of the girls, who arrived with two slices of toast and orange juice.

'Coffee?'

'If you've indeed read the manual, you know our policy on caffeine. These children arrive with their systems full of all manner of drugs, legally prescribed and otherwise. Our goal is to send them home clean in mind and body. As we clearly state. In the manual.'

Nora bit her lip. She'd read that part but assumed it applied only to students. Thank God she had plenty of coffee in Electra. She remembered the last town she'd driven through on her way to the ranch. It was at least ten miles away, a dot on the map. She had vague memories of a gas station, a café, a scattering of modest homes. She suspected it was the sort of place that offered only Folgers in cans, but the minute she got a break, she intended to drive there and buy enough industrial-size cans to power her through the school year.

She choked down a bit of toast – dry! – and tried to banish sarcasm from her mumbled thanks.

'If you and the attorney are satisfied with this version, I think it's ready. May I go ahead and email it to you so you can send it out when the computers are back up?'

'Unfortunately, our system will be down until tomorrow. Under the circumstances, this needs to be sent right away. Tell you what.' The easygoing attitude she remembered had returned with the attorney's approval of the letter. 'I'll e-sign it, and have the attorney send you our email list. You have my permission to send it out yourself. Of course, this is above and beyond your job description. There'll be something extra in your first paycheck. I can't tell you how grateful I am.'

He stood above her, his early-morning agitation gone, radiating the good will she remembered from their interviews. 'I've always handled the public relations for the ranch. The newsletters, the social media and the press. It's a strain, given all my other duties, but it needs to be done. Now, watching how quickly and well you work, I see that was a mistake. I wonder – just tossing out an idea here – would you be willing to handle those responsibilities? Given that you don't have a teaching degree, I'd envisioned you as a classroom aide, but this would be a much better use of your talents.'

The stack of rejections Nora had accumulated in response to her job applications had led her to assume she was unemployable, at least in her former profession. Now, Ennis was offering her a chance to ease back into that line of work, to hone skills dulled by trauma, to rehabilitate herself. And, despite Serendipity Ranch's ban on jeans, its location deep in the forest wouldn't require the rotation of tailored suits, uncomfortable shoes and understated jewelry that had been part of her previous life.

'You don't have to decide right now. And obviously, because this would come in addition to your duties with the students, there'd be a raise in pay. Say . . .' He named a figure.

Nora's eyes widened.

He held up his hand. 'Don't answer now. It's something we counsel our students: never make impulsive decisions. Sleep on it and get back to me. Deal?'

Nora nodded, too dazed for more than a single word.

'Deal.'

Ennis told Nora to take the rest of the day to get settled.

'This has been so stressful for everyone. As bad as it is for us, you might imagine the effect on our students. We'll start fresh tomorrow with a tour of the facilities, and then you'll begin in the classroom the next day. I've assigned you to the art therapy room.'

'But I'm not a therapist. And I'm even less of an artist. I never got past stick figures.'

He laughed, seeming positively giddy now that she'd emailed the letter.

'Now, now, Ms Best. I saw that beautiful painting on the side of your trailer.'

Nora started to protest that she'd paid someone to do it, but he waved her words away. 'Relax. It's an hour and a half of our students working on various art projects – painting, ceramics, even sculpture. We call it a brain break. They spend all day in group and individual therapy, as well as traditional schooling – some go on to Ivy League universities – and strenuous physical activity, so they need that time to simply work with their hands. Some of their projects are quite good. You'll be impressed. The more adept students help the others. You're there mainly to keep order. A few students, especially the newer ones, can be quite volatile.'

'Volatile?'

Nora awaited reassurance. When none came, she tried again. 'Verbally? Or –' she gulped – 'physically?'

'Oh, verbally. Mostly.'

Which wasn't reassuring at all.

FIVE

Nora made a simple dinner: salad, pasta with butter, wine, garlic and Parmesan, along with a healthy grind of pepper, and the heel from a ciabatta that she'd grabbed on her way out of Seattle two days earlier. She poured herself a crisp Pinot Grigio and reviewed the school's manual with a fresh eye as she ate.

Serendipity Ranch operated on a 'rung' system, something common to such programs, as Nora had learned in her cursory research about them.

All students came in at the First Rung: no communication with families, spartan meals and a ban on talking with fellow students during classes and meals. Through good behavior and progress in therapy and schoolwork, they earned their way into higher rungs with more permissions.

Violations of program policy could see those privileges revoked, as well as various consequences, such as extra exercise sessions, unspecified chores and an ominous reference to isolation.

Ennis had termed Mackenzie insubordinate. Nora searched the manual for what, specifically, comprised insubordination, yet remained unenlightened. The manual was, however, quite specific in its no-drugs-or-alcohol policy.

Nora poured another glass of wine, defensively reminding herself that, as with the restriction on caffeine, the manual said nothing about those same restrictions applying to staff.

Mooch purred beside her on the dinette. Murph lay at her feet, occasionally opening one rheumy eye to check on her and, thus reassured of her continuing presence, reward her with a thump of his tail before falling back into slumber.

For all its frustrating vagueness, Serendipity Ranch's manual was explicit in what the school wasn't. For starters, despite the log buildings, split-rail fences and overhead gate with its swinging wrought-iron sign depicting ladders flanking the Serendipity Ranch name, it wasn't a real ranch in any sense.

'Many programs such as ours incorporate animal care into their programs,' Ennis had explained. 'But we determined that would take too much time away from academics and therapy. The "ranch" in our title mainly refers to the outdoor nature of several of our activities.'

That said, despite day hikes and overnight backpacking excursions, it wasn't a wilderness-survival type program. Nor was it a boot camp, although military-style rigorous exercise and adherence to rules was also part of the program. And it wasn't rehab, though the manual noted that many, if not most, of its clients arrived with a wide experience of drugs, frequently walking right up the line of addiction.

'It is therapeutic in the sense that through a series of steps, guided by long-tested best practices, our students come to *willingly* change the behaviors that brought them here and return to society, ready to fully participate and lead purposeful and productive lives,' the manual stated on its first page.

The program's 'rungs' aimed to further that progress, the manual explained in a chapter illustrated by a sketch of a tall ladder. At the bottom crouched a defiant girl, arms folded across her chest, glaring at the reader. Off to the side of each rung, a thought bubble enclosed the privileges involved – things such as writing letters home (but not receiving them); checking out a book from the ranch's library – 'all of our titles are designed to help our students in their journey and as such are screened as appropriate and inspirational; nothing overtly sexual or violent', the manual stressed – or an hour of computer time (albeit with no internet access); and so on.

Each privilege seemed to come with a caveat. Nora made a note to visit the library, although she shuddered to think of the pap that might line the shelves. She congratulated herself for filling a recent moment of boredom by downloading several e-books onto her phone and resolved to read them slowly, rather than in all-night binges, until she could make a trip to a town with a bookstore or library.

She returned to the illustration. The ladder reached into an azure sky dotted by cotton-puff clouds. At its top, a jubilant girl stepped from the final rung onto one of the clouds, a beatific smile on her face. Nora wouldn't have been surprised to see a rendering of St Peter peeking from behind one of the clouds, so closely did the drawing resemble a child's Sunday School version of heaven. She wondered if the unfortunate Irene Bell had pictured such a forgiving destination when she soared into the gorge.

Thoughts of Irene reminded her of Ennis' request that she take on additional duties as Serendipity Ranch's public relations person. God knows, she could use the extra money, at least until Joe's life insurance came through. But Ennis had mentioned dealing with the press, and Nora had already faced far too much press scrutiny due to her own arrest in her husband's disappearance (she was painfully aware that despite being quickly cleared, the taint lingered) and the exposure of her mother in connection with a decades-old murder.

The more she thought about it, the less she liked the idea. Besides, as financially lean as her immediate future appeared, the job at Serendipity Ranch provided all of her meals, if she wanted them, and a place to live rent-free. Best to stick with her original plan of using her year at the ranch to regroup.

She resolved to tell Ennis in the morning that she appreciated his offer but would prefer to throw herself into her duties as housemother and instructor.

As it had the previous night, Serendipity Ranch shut down early.

Nora set the manual aside, turned out the lights in the trailer and peeked through a slit in the curtains as, one by one, the cabins went dark and the lights in the lodge finally went out. She gave it fifteen more minutes, then summoned Murph – her alibi – and crept behind the cabins, skirting the clearing until she neared the lodge. She listened hard but heard nothing but a few sleepy chirps as birds settled themselves for the night. Soft scurrying sounds on the forest floor briefly ceased at the hoot of an owl, aloft on its nightly foray. The moon edged above a nearby mountain, silvering the landscape. She ducked into the generous shadow of a towering Ponderosa pine and pulled out her phone, dimming the light until she could barely read its screen.

A twig snapped nearby. The birds fell silent. Nora held her breath, waited a moment, then returned her attention to her phone. Her trailer was parked in a dead zone for cell reception. But she'd been able to send the email from her laptop that morning in the lodge and sure enough, two bars showed on her phone indicating a good-enough signal. Nora clicked through to her email and began deleting the come-ons from companies from which she'd made a single purchase years earlier, along with the occasional mention of her own name in a news story. She'd set up an alert for her name during the dreadful aftermath of the revelations about her family, figuring that it was marginally better to know what was coming her way than be taken by surprise.

Usually, the appearance of one story meant phone calls from reporters eager to write their own version. But the only story she saw on this day was a wire service brief on her assailant's guilty plea, and her voicemail was mercifully free of calls. Maybe she was finally beginning to escape her own unsought infamy. By the time her one-year contract at Serendipity Ranch expired, she might be able to resume something resembling a normal life.

Delete.

Delete.

Delete.

Nora's inbox steadily diminished, her actions so rote that she nearly deleted another email from her lawyer, probably a follow-up, maybe saying that her assailant's sentencing date had been scheduled. A relieved sigh escaped as she anticipated the update. She'd always been skeptical of the concept of closure but seeing her assailant sent off to prison would at least end that particular chapter of her life. She squinted at the screen. Then:

'Holy shit. Are you freaking kidding me?'

Once again, the surrounding woods went silent. A cloud slid across the moon, wrapping the ranch in a woolly blackness.

A hand grasped Nora's wrist and wrenched her arm behind her back. Another clamped over her mouth, deadening her scream.

An unshaven face rasped her cheek. A voice echoed harsh in her ear.

'What the fuck do we have here? A little runaway?'

Her captor jerked her arm so hard she feared it would break. Her knees gave way. He went to the ground with her, his other hand still over her mouth. She tried to bite him but couldn't gain purchase.

He pinned her with the weight of his body, edging a leg between hers, letting go of her arm and sliding his hand beneath her, cupping her breast. Squeezing. Nora howled into his hand.

Murph growled, deep, terrifying and gratifyingly brief.

'Fuck! Something bit me!'

The hand vanished and then she was free of him, scrambling to her feet, backing away.

Another growl, a thud, a piteous yelp.

'You got it!' A new voice. 'Where is it? I'll finish it off.'

Dear God. There were two of them. No winning against those odds. Murph whimpered somewhere nearby.

'Don't hurt my dog!'

A blinding light raked her face. She froze.

'What the fuck? An old broad. Who the fuck are you?'

Nora ducked away from the light. It followed her, so close now she could see the dark bulk of the man behind it.

'I repeat the question.' Thug One again. 'Who are you? What are you doing here?'

An old broad. So they'd been after the girls. Would the men let her go, then? Or drag her off into the forest and finish what her assailant had started?

'That's more than one question.'

The light jerked. Nora ducked. The swish of the flashlight past her head told her it was large and heavy. She hastened to answer.

'I'm Nora Best. I work here.'

The crackle of a walkie-talkie stopped the panicky runaway train of her thoughts. One of the men spoke into it.

'We've got a trespasser. Right behind the lodge. Says she works here. Yeah, we'll hold her for you.'

SIX

Lights flared within the lodge. The back door flew open. Ennis stood silhouetted within.

'Ms Best? What on earth?'

Nora offered the excuse she'd practiced when she'd left the trailer.

'I was taking the dog out for his walk.' Her voice wobbled. She braced a hand against a tree trunk for support, nearly undone by the knowledge that she was safe. 'Then these two jumped me. One, uh, assaulted me. And they hurt my dog.'

She twisted to look at her erstwhile captors, but they'd stepped back into the darkness. She rushed toward the sound of Murph's whimpers and nearly tripped over him. She stooped beside him, gently flexing each leg and running her hands over his torso. He yelped at the pressure on his ribcage, but with a little help, clambered to his feet and stood panting, head down.

'You sonofabitch. What did you do to him?'

'Bitch yourself. That mutt took a piece out of me.'

'Now, now.' Ennis broke in. 'Let's dial down the language. Allen, are you bleeding?'

The big flashlight clicked on again, shining up and down a length of heavy canvas pants. A small tear showed in one leg. Its owner reached down and pulled the fabric apart, revealing a long scratch.

'There, there.' Ennis spoke as if to an injured child. 'The skin is barely broken. Come into the lodge and we'll put some antiseptic on it.'

Nora inserted herself into the conversation. 'You know these people?'

Ennis sighed. 'I thought it best to hire security for a few days after Ms Bell's, ah, departure. This sort of thing can cause a disturbed youngster to take it into her head to try and leave. We can't let our charges put themselves in that sort of danger. It's for their own safety.'

'That's who we thought she was. One of the girls,' Thug One said. 'Then, once we saw how old she was, we didn't know what was going on.'

Nora's outrage ramped up on two fronts: how *old* she was? And, would they have treated a teenager just as they'd treated her?

'He grabbed me. Fondled me. I can't imagine the sort of trauma that would have inflicted upon an already troubled young person. Especially a girl.'

'My hand slipped,' Thug One mumbled. 'You were wriggling around so much I couldn't help it.'

'Bullshit!'

Ennis' silhouetted shoulders stiffened.

'Once again, let's dial down the emotion. Gentlemen' – Nora snorted – 'Ms Best has a point. Heaven forbid this situation should arise again, but when apprehending a girl, please refrain from physical contact. That way, you don't have to worry about your hands slipping and any resulting misunderstandings.'

Nora could still feel his thumb and forefinger closing around her nipple, his knee jammed against her crotch. 'It was no misunderstanding.'

'And Ms Best,' Ennis continued, 'you might want to confine those nighttime walks to the area around your trailer. Our students can be . . .'

He paused, sighing so deeply that even Murph stopped whimpering and swung his head toward him. 'Serendipity Ranch is such a change from their previous lives of privilege and permissiveness. Some try the most desperate measures to return to those deeply damaging lives. An event such as Miss Bell's unfortunate incident may awaken those impulses in even our more advanced students. Unlike you, Vance and Allen are trained to deal with such situations. They come highly recommended by our local sheriff.

'They'll patrol the grounds for the next few nights. Students who try to vacate the premises without permission don't realize just how remote the ranch is. There are miles of dense, unsettled forest in all direction. There are mountain lions, black bears, even grizzlies. Why, we've heard wolves howling at night! We do our very best to keep the girls safe.'

He spread his hands before him. 'But sadly, as you now know, sometimes a determined student defeats our very best efforts. You should keep in mind that some of our students – as you will find – can be tremendously manipulative. But Vance and Allen are impervious.

'As to your dog . . .' He glared into the flashlight's beam. 'That was uncalled for. I hope there's no serious injury to him. If there is, we'll find the nearest veterinarian and of course will cover the bill. Good night, Ms Best.'

He closed the door behind him, leaving Nora alone, casting nervous glances about for the two hulking men who'd seemingly vanished into the darkness.

She looked over her shoulder the whole way back to her trailer but saw only shadows.

The unsettling event had succeeded, if only briefly, in pushing from her mind the email she'd opened while poaching the lodge's Wi-Fi.

It remained open on her screen and she scanned it again in the safety of her trailer, hoping maybe she'd misread it in the gloom beneath the trees, groaning aloud when it became clear she hadn't.

'Heads up,' Artie had written. 'Charlotte's suing.'

He'd thoughtfully pasted in the document informing her

that, unlike the women Joe had harassed at the law firm –
actions Nora had learned about only after his death – Charlotte
wasn't going after the firm.

No, her target was Nora, who she claimed had heaped
considerable public humiliation upon her when Nora had
displayed on a big screen, to the shock of all the guests at her
send-off party, the surreptitious photo she'd snapped of
Charlotte fucking Nora's husband just moments earlier.

'Severe emotional distress . . . cessation of income due to
inability to face coworkers . . . months of counseling . . .
marriage of two decades shattered.' All the standard phrases.

'Blah, blah, blah,' Nora muttered at the screen. That last
part especially. Nora knew the decision to end the marriage
had been Charlotte's. Artie was such a wimp he'd have taken
her back, despite being cuckolded by his best friend.

She scrolled down, coming to the part that elicited the 'holy
shit' that had revealed her presence to the two thugs. 'Security
guards, my ass,' she muttered as she read on.

Charlotte was going after Joe's life insurance policy, the
money Nora was counting on to sustain her while she regained
her professional footing. In some ways, it was immaterial
whether Charlotte would succeed. As Artie noted in his brief
email, the suit would tie up the money for the foreseeable
future. 'Try not to worry,' he wrote. 'Our aim will be to settle
out of court. But if I were you, I'd withdraw as much cash as
safely practical from your accounts. Charlotte could move to
have them frozen until this winds up.'

Nora's vow to decline Ennis' offer to take over as Serendipity
Ranch's public relations specialist dissolved in the face of this
new reality. Her discomfort in dealing with the press was
suddenly the least of her worries.

She shut down her phone for the night and crawled into
bed after first giving Murph an antihistamine to help him sleep
through the pain. And she reminded herself as she drifted off
that other than Irene Bell's tragic death – the sort of thing that,
as Ennis had pointed out in the letter she'd helped him fashion,
was not unheard of among all teens, especially those as
troubled as the ranch's clientele – what could possibly turn
the attention of the press to a place like Serendipity Ranch?

SEVEN

On her second morning at Serendipity Ranch, Nora Best was ready. She wouldn't start her classroom duties until the following day but she'd begin to ease into the program's routines, starting with breakfast.

This time she set her alarm for five forty-five, to allow plenty of time for a shower and a cup or three of forbidden coffee.

What she hadn't expected was the ear-splitting recording of 'Reveille' blasting through the compound at six thirty, causing her to spill half a precious cup of Robusta across Electra's dinette, splashing Mooch, who'd been snoozing in a patch of sun across from her and sending him hissing to the far end of the trailer, where he licked himself clean while throwing the occasional poisonous glance her way.

Nora checked herself – by some miracle, her freshly pressed khakis had avoided Mooch's fate – took a deep breath, and patted Murph goodbye. He banged his tail on the floor with his customary enthusiasm, with a little lingering stiffness the only evidence of the previous night's encounter.

'Here goes nothing,' she told him, and trailed the group of girls walking in brisk, silent, single file across the clearing toward the lodge.

Morning sunlight streamed through the clerestory windows in the lodge's high-ceilinged dining hall, splashing onto small round tables set with snowy cloths and small vases of pink carnations. Five teenage girls and a young woman – an instructor, Nora guessed – stood at each table.

A raised platform at one end of the room held a long rectangular table. Ennis sat in the middle, an empty chair to his left, to his right a gray-haired woman who looked up as Nora approached, setting aside knitting needles and a skein of red-and-black yarn. A man in a chambray shirt, his dark hair clipped just short of military-severe, sat on the other side of the empty chair. He stared vacantly across the room's expanse, his face a blank mask, his expression not changing at Nora's arrival.

She scanned the room again. No sign of the two men who'd assaulted her. Maybe, after the previous night's misadventure, Ennis had reconsidered and sent them home.

He beckoned her toward the waiting chair, and Nora crossed the room's expanse, her footsteps echoey in the silence, uncomfortably aware of all the eyes following her progress. Was anything worse than the scrutiny of teenage girls, all quick cool assessment, mercilessly judging and inevitably finding the subject of their attention wanting?

The girls stood behind their chairs, waiting until Nora settled herself.

Ennis cleared his throat.

'Let us take a moment of silence to contemplate the day ahead and the progress we hope to make by discovering strengths we never imagined; the wondrous things we wish to achieve: the respect and trust of our families, of our peers, of our community and the world at large. As we all know . . .'

He paused and quirked a meaningful eyebrow at the girls below him, apparently a cue of sorts because the girls chanted in unison, 'Trust takes years to build, seconds to destroy and forever to replace.'

Ennis smiled benignly. 'Enjoy your breakfast. Because . . .' Another prompting pause.

'Today is the first day of the rest of your life,' the students recited with no more enthusiasm than before.

Had Nora eaten anything yet, she might have barfed it up. During her initial job interview, she'd been relieved to find that Serendipity Ranch's program was nonsectarian. Now, she thought she might have preferred an overtly religious message to the sort of psychobabble she'd just heard.

Ennis must have caught her expression. He leaned toward her. 'I know,' he whispered. 'It's almost insultingly simplistic. But everything we do here is broken down into a series of steps, starting with the most basic concepts of acceptable behavior and expectations. And it doesn't get more basic than what you just heard, right?'

Nora felt her face redden.

'Trust me, it works. You'll see. These girls come here so tangled in their own excuses and justifications that they barely remember how to function in polite society. By the end of their time here, you'll hear them utter these same mantras, the ones you find so corny, in utter sincerity.'

She nodded, shamefaced, if not entirely convinced. Wasn't it possible to mend one's ways without becoming a Hallmark-sentiment-spewing robot?

But then student servers arrived bearing platters of buckwheat blueberry pancakes, sausage patties, and bowls of sliced strawberries swimming in their own garnet juice.

Another student moved among the tables, pouring herbal tea into china cups. Nora eyed it suspiciously, glad for her early dose of caffeine.

Ennis lifted his own cup to his lips and inhaled, beaming. 'Nothing sets a calming tone for the day quite so much as our tea. It's a blend I've designed just for us. A company in Denver ships it here.'

Nora ignored the tea and cut a small wedge of sausage.

'It's vegetarian,' Ennis announced, just as she bit into it. 'Just like our bacon. Although our evening meal features meat, usually chicken and fish, we prefer to start our days as cleanly as possible.'

Nora choked it down. It didn't taste . . . bad. Just not like sausage.

Her tablemate made a dry sound in his throat. She turned her head in time to catch a twitch of his eye that could have been a wink, but when she looked again, she thought she must have been mistaken. Despite his perfunctory smile, the man had the saddest eyes she'd ever seen, the whites threaded with red, the skin beneath them papery and pouched with fatigue.

He held out his hand. 'Luke Rivera. I'm the counselor here.'

That explained his appearance. He'd spent the previous day in individual counseling sessions. His voice, even scraped by exhaustion, reminded Nora of the nighttime FM deejays of her youth, low and soothing, letting listeners know they were in good hands. Did those people even exist anymore? She couldn't remember the last time she'd listened to an actual

radio station instead of apps that compiled and shuffled play-
lists for her, efficient but devoid of that human touch.

'Aren't you forgetting to tell her something?' Ennis broke
in, his twinkle a jolting contrast to Luke's funereal mien.
Without waiting for an answer, he added, 'Today's Luke's
birthday. We're having cake tonight, a rare treat. Remind us
again, Luke. Which one is it?'

'Forty-five.' Luke mock-grimaced and Nora automatically
noted the acceptable math – only five years younger – even
as she chided herself. Given her husband's literal in-your-face
infidelity and subsequent death, and a disastrous subsequent
flirtation in her hometown, a lifetime of celibacy seemed to
be in order.

'Happy birthday.' She willed her renewed blush to subside.
'I'm Nora.'

It prompted a flurry of introductions. The older woman, who
also served as the program's receptionist and intake coordin-
ator, was June Ennis, as plump and pleasant as her husband.
'It does the children good to see a happily married couple,'
she said, smiling fondly at her husband.

June added in a stage whisper, 'So many of them come
from broken homes, or less than healthy unions. Or they're
mostly raised by nannies and housekeepers as their parents
gallivant around the country on business trips rather than giving
their children the loving guidance they deserve. It's no wonder
they end up here.'

At least she'd said parents. Nora would have bet she meant
mothers. Somehow fathers who gallivanted around the country
on business trips always seemed to see praise heaped upon
them for being such good providers.

June reached across her husband's plate, took Nora's hand,
and gave it a friendly squeeze. Nora winced as June's wedding
band, its gold nearly obliterated by diamonds the size of small,
sharp pebbles, dug into her flesh. 'Do you have children,
dear?'

Nora had long ago become familiar with the judgment that
accompanied a simple negative. 'I'm afraid not.' Her standard
response meant to imply regret, perhaps a sorrowful inability,
rather than a choice.

June squeezed her hand tighter. Nora bit the inside of her cheek, willing the tang of blood to distract her from the pain in her hand.

'We don't, either. For years, it was a sadness that defined our existence. We thought about adopting or becoming foster parents. But that would have been so limiting. Now look at us!' She freed Nora's hand with a sweeping gesture and picked up her knitting. 'Over the years, we've helped hundreds through our program here, all of them in desperate need.'

Nora rubbed at the marks left by June's perilous ring. She could think of children in far more desperate need than the girls who sat before her, straight of teeth and perfect of skin, with long shiny hair and practiced posture. Certainly none – unless by choice – had ever lacked for a meal or a roof over her head.

She gestured toward June's knitting. The woman's hands dipped and spun, somehow looping the yarn without catching it on her ring. 'What are you making?'

'A scarf. I make them in the Serendipity Ranch colors to give to each girl when she graduates, in the hope that she'll remember her time here with all the warmth and love that I knit into these scarves.'

'Mother spends every free moment knitting,' Ennis said. 'You see those girls at the nearest table? They're all Level Five. If you'd seen their behavior when they arrived, you wouldn't know they were the same girls. Soon, each will be going home with one of Mother's scarves. I'm so glad you'll be able to be part of our ceremony.'

'I'm looking forward to it.' Nora looked to a table off to one side of the room with only two girls. She recognized Mackenzie, whom she'd met upon her arrival, and a willowy girl with dark hair falling to her waist. Not for them the pancakes studded with glistening blueberries, the stacks of fake sausage patties, the glass bowls of strawberries that caught the sunshine, rendering their contents jewel-like.

Instead, a single small bowl of what looked like oatmeal sat before each girl, along with a glass of water. They weren't even afforded a cup of the mossy-tasting herbal tea. Mackenzie spooned up her oatmeal, making an exaggerated grimace with each mouthful, but the other girl merely sipped at her water, eyes downcast.

Luke Rivera followed her gaze.

'That's the First Rung table. Mackenzie's there because she violated a confidence in speaking to you about Irene's death before Director Ennis could tell you. Girls like Ashleigh, who arrived recently, spend their first few weeks on First Rung. It helps them adjust to their new environment and gives them an incentive to follow the rules, work on their issues, and earn their way up the rungs so they can have more privileges. Look at Ashleigh. She should know by now that if she doesn't eat this morning's oatmeal, she'll get it again for lunch and for dinner, too, until it's gone. Actually, for all I know, that's yesterday's oatmeal.'

'I thought the whole philosophy here was based on positive reinforcement.' Cold, day-old oatmeal sounded like the very definition of negative to Nora.

Ennis broke in. 'The positive reinforcement is the delicious hot and healthy meal she'll get as her reward for complying with the rules.'

But first, the gray congealed mass that sat like wet cement in the girl's bowl. Nora opened her mouth and closed it again before she could voice an objection. She reminded herself that these people were the experts, and this job was saving her bacon – even if she'd be denied literal bacon during the length of her contract.

Luke offered a welcome distraction. 'Look around. What else do you notice?'

Nora wrenched her gaze away from the First Rungers, whose silent misery reminded her of something out of *Oliver Twist*. The other girls talked quietly among themselves. No. Not all of them. Those at two tables were silent.

She turned to Luke. 'Lower rungs?'

'You catch on quick.' His expression softened, his eyes crinkling at the corners, deepening lines that remained even when his smile faded. Strands of gray glinted in his hair. 'Talking at mealtime is a privilege. What else?'

She forked up a piece of sausage and ran it through the maple syrup, which added enough flavor to make her forget that first, nondescript mouthful. She chased it with a bite of the pancakes, which truly were good.

A girl got up from one of the talking tables and went to the kitchen, returning with another large bowl of strawberries. All the girls at the table helped themselves.

Nora cocked her head and thought. 'Seconds?'

Luke raised an eyebrow. 'Remind me never to play charades if you're on the other team. Exactly right, although it's a little-used privilege, unless it's fruit or salad. Overeating isn't an issue with most of these girls. They're all so concerned about image. A bigger problem is bulimia. With some girls, it's so bad that whoever's on housemother duty accompanies them to the bathroom to make sure they're not throwing up.'

'Speaking of whom.' Nora looked around again. 'Where is the other housemother?'

'It's Miss Hanford's day off. Poor thing.' June brushed a lock of silvery hair, escaped from the bun at her nape, away from her face. 'She took the news about Irene Bell hard. We told her to take some extra time. What do they call it now? Self-care?'

Nora scanned the room again, this time noting the empty chair at the table with Mackenzie and the other girl. 'How long had Irene been here?'

'Just six months.'

'She was still on the First Rung?'

Luke spoke up, his voice clipped. 'She was *back* on the First Rung.'

A long look passed between Luke and Ennis. June stared down at her empty plate, her lips crimped.

Ennis clapped his hands three times. All the girls leapt to their feet.

'Fifteen minutes until sessions begin. Today we move from individual to group counseling. Please check the bulletin board for your time.'

The girls picked up their plates and silverware and carried them toward the kitchen. Nora started to do the same, but Ennis stopped her.

'The First Rungers clear up after us. We try to give them as many responsibilities as possible. No idle minds here, especially on a day like this, when they might otherwise be given to brooding. The time slot for your art class is being used for a group session today. We won't start a full schedule of classes until tomorrow. You might want to use this time to commit the manual to memory.'

'I went over it again last night,' she began.

She spoke to his retreating back.

She hesitated, wondering if he'd assigned her an escort. But the mass of girls heading into the clearing apparently rendered such caution unnecessary. Once again, she followed them, but halfway across the clearing she heard running steps behind her.

'Ms Best! Ms Best!'

Mackenzie stopped beside her, pressing a hand to her side. 'Mr Ennis wants to speak with you.'

Nora had planned to wait until the end of the day to tell him she'd decided to accept his offer.

'The answer is yes,' she said as soon as she walked through his office door. 'I'd be happy to help with public relations. Just let me know what you've done until now and we can talk about the best way for me to transition into those tasks, and how to work them into the schedule with the rest of my duties here.' Office-speak. It came back to her so easily, all the bland phrases designed to buttress the rightness of Ennis' impulsive offer.

'What? Oh. That. Good. Fine.' Ennis had the distracted air she'd seen the previous morning. She wondered if he was already getting feedback to the letter. Would Irene Bell's parents have announced a lawsuit so quickly?

He handed her a sheet of paper.

'I just got this. It's from Miss Hanford, the other housemother.'

He'd printed out an email, brief and heartbreaking.

'I just can't anymore. I'm sorry. Carolee.'

Ennis lowered himself heavily into his chair, positioned his elbows on the desk and laced his fingers together.

'This business with Irene Bell has left her utterly devastated. Programs such as ours tend to have a high staff turnover. They naturally attract empathic people who feel too keenly the distress of their charges. It takes a toll. We're far more successful than most in retaining staff, due to our unwavering insistence upon best practices. I just wish you'd had more time to get acclimated.'

'I'm so sorry,' Nora said. 'Is there anything I can do to help?' Her knee-jerk reaction elicited a response that was anything but expected.

'Why, yes. There is. Quite a bit, actually. At least until we can hire her replacement.'

'Excuse me?' Nora took a step back.

'We'll start a national search right away. After all, it's how we found you. Mother will take a weekend night, but that's all she can manage. We're older, you know,' he said, with a bit of his characteristic twinkle returning. 'We need our rest.

'For all practical purposes, at least for the time being, your housemother duties just doubled. I'll give you a quick tour now, but after that, you should take the remainder of the day to rest up. You start tonight.'

EIGHT

As they set out from the lodge, Ennis again reassured her, as he had during her video interview, that her classroom duties were merely supervisory. She'd be on her own in the art room, and eventually transition into serving as something of an aide to the regular instructors in the academic courses.

'Serendipity Ranch received the highest rating from the governing body of such programs, in part because we require our instructors to have teaching certificates, even though as private programs, that's not a legal mandate. We meet the state teaching standards as well as those of the supervisory organization. Each of our six instructors has her own living quarters.'

Small cabins lined one side of the clearing, each labeled with a sign designating a Western tree or flower – Columbine, Aspen, Yarrow – with a skillfully rendered woodcut of same.

'They're basically free-standing one-bedroom apartments. Each has a small kitchen, even though people eat most of their meals in the lodge. But these jobs carry so much responsibility that we think it important for our staff to have their own space where they can rest and regroup.

'You having your own trailer saved us from a bit of a dilemma. It can be hard to recruit people to work in such a remote location. But word of our program's excellence has gotten around, and we have a full complement of instructors, a rarity for us. We were going to put you up in the lodge, but I understand that you might be more comfortable in your own space. And of course, until we find a replacement for Miss Hanford, her cabin is available should you change your mind.'

Nora looked wistfully at the cabins, with their tiny front porches, each with its own Adirondack chair, and their stone chimneys denoting cozy fireplaces within. She loved Electra but the cabins held an undeniable appeal.

Ennis led her across the clearing toward a line of larger cabins. 'These are our classrooms, for math, literature and the like.'

He knocked at Cabin B and pushed open the door a bit without waiting for an answer, gesturing for Nora to step in. A dozen young female faces peered at her, momentarily looking away from a room-length whiteboard filled with calculations. Nora saw triangles and rectangles and mysterious calculations and guessed geometry, a hypothesis confirmed by the chirpy instructor standing before the board. Ennis introduced her as Miss Whaley, then whispered her first name to Nora, 'Loraine. She's our lead instructor.'

Loraine aimed a laser pointer at the whiteboard and a green dot moved across one of the formulas: $A = bh$.

'Care to identify this one for the class, Ms Best?' A question that transported Nora back to her freshman year of high school. Now, as then, her palms grew clammy. Her brain went blank, leaving her barely enough presence of mind to shake her head.

'Class?'

The students shared a collected smirk.

'Area of a parallelogram,' they sang out, perhaps louder

than necessary. Nora wiped her damp hands on her pants and crossed her fingers against the possibility that she might be assigned to one of the math classes, relaxing only when the door closed behind them.

'And here –' Ennis led her away to the next cabin – 'is literature. What are we studying today, Miss Lawrence?'

The young woman – surely she had graduated from college only a week earlier? – nodded to the class and they obediently held up dog-eared paperbacks: *The Scarlet Letter*.

'We try to tailor our reading choices to our program,' Ennis said sotto voce. 'For instance –' he inclined his head toward a girl at a desk far removed from the rest, who hadn't looked up when they entered – 'she's dealing with the fallout from some of her actions. This book underscores the importance of consequences.'

Nora bit her lip against a smile. Clearly Ennis had never read more than the jacket copy of Hawthorne's classic novel. She herself had always been enamored of Hester Prynne's rejection of the shame the town heaped upon her, of her outsize, gold-embroidered scarlet 'A' for adultery, of her adoration of Pearl, the little girl born out of wedlock.

She wondered who among the girls would delve beneath the unfamiliar prose style, stultifying to present-day readers, and discover the sly subversion within. She scanned the room. Most of the girls were fidgeting, whispering among themselves, or looking to her as though grateful for even such an insignificant distraction. But the girl sitting apart flipped each page with avid expectation. That girl – she got it. When she lifted her head briefly, Nora wasn't surprised to recognize Mackenzie.

Ennis touched her elbow. 'There's more.'

He hurried her past the art and science cabins without looking in – 'you'll see them soon enough' – although they did step into a spacious gym equipped with state-of-the-art treadmills, exercise bikes and rowing machines, and a wall of Bowflex-type equipment, as well as a half-basketball court.

'We originally had a free weights program but eliminated it when we realized the weights could be used as weapons. We were so naïve in those early days,' he said with a rueful shrug. 'The same with our science classes. So much of basic chemistry involves mixing dangerous substances. You won't believe this, but the girls immediately tried to make alcoholic drinks, or concoct something they could snort.'

Nora, harkening back to high school and the hideous party punches comprising a combination of every type of alcohol she and her friends had been able to swipe from their parents' liquor cabinets, absolutely could believe it.

'And biology! Those little scalpels needed for dissections?' He didn't elaborate, but the look of horror on his face told Nora all she needed to know. 'All of our dissections are done virtually now.'

Once again, unease flickered like a lighthouse beacon, warning of treacherous shoals below.

Girls clobbering each other with heavy free weights? Slicing their classmates – or themselves – with scalpels? And, once those implements were removed, resorting to leaping from cliffs, a weapon-free form of destruction?

Ennis hurried to reassure her. 'Don't worry. This was years ago, when programs such as ours were just coming into being. For years now, we've achieved the highest safety rating from our supervisory organization. I constantly receive queries from other such programs about how best to incorporate our methods.'

He clapped a hand to his head. 'I almost forgot that now you'll be the one fielding those queries. Ms Best, I can't tell you how much of a relief it is to have you on board. Your work will free me up to improve and refine our program still further, so that it can serve as a model worldwide, not just nationwide.'

He bounced on the balls of his feet. 'Forgive my enthusiasm, Ms Best. The Serendipity Ranch program you see now – the one that has evolved after so many years of research – is the culmination of my life's work. I'm so glad you're part of it.'

For weeks, Nora had been the subject of criticism, suspicion and anger. She'd been accused, arrested and freed without apology; been termed both a racist and too sympathetic to black people; and had seen her reaction – she still thought it entirely understandable – to her husband's infidelity turned against her in the form of Charlotte's lawsuit.

Moisture wobbled behind her eyelids at Ennis' approval, the first she'd experienced in far too long. She turned her head away and blinked hard as she pointed to the cabin, smaller than the others, they were passing.

'What's that?'

'Storage. Let's go back to the lodge. It's almost time for lunch. The cook has made a wonderful Niçoise salad and she came in at two in the morning to bake fresh sourdough baguettes. You're in for a treat, Ms Best.'

Nora followed him into the lodge with renewed enthusiasm, her incipient tears vanquished. As far as she knew, unlike with the bacon and sausage, no one had found a way to fake tuna.

NINE

I t could have been worse, Nora told herself as she prepared for bed.

She'd envisioned a narrow bunk bed, sleeping cheek by jowl with the girls, a throwback to summer camps of old. Except those had been lighthearted experiences, the nights filled with delicious post-lights-out whispering about the cutest counselors, comparisons of limited sexual experience and speculation about what it might be like to go further.

But a roomful of girls seething with anger and anxiety and God knows what other roiling emotions? She doubted she'd get any sleep at all.

It turned out, though, that the housemother had her own room at one end of the bunkhouse, with its own half bath and – hallelujah! – a lock on the door. Serendipity Ranch had a sparkling bathhouse with long sinks and a dozen showers, but in the bunkhouse, bathroom facilities for the girls consisted of a doorless room next door to her own, with a single toilet and tiny sink.

'That way,' June Ennis had explained as she'd showed Nora around the bunkhouse, 'you can hear them if they're throwing up or – this is the most dangerous thing – if they're in there for too long. If that happens, you must check immediately. Don't be shy. You could be saving a life.'

Nora shuddered. She'd envisioned herself as sort of an exalted babysitter, not someone with life-and-death responsibilities. Her brief fantasy of locking her door and enjoying a good night's sleep vanished.

But the girls, thirty in all, filed into the dorm in the same sort of silent lockstep with which they marched to and from the dining hall and their daily activities. They changed out of their daytime clothes – khakis and red polo shirts with the black Serendipity Ranch logo – and into identical long white nightdresses of heavy cotton, fluttering about silently as moths in the near-darkness.

Nora pulled her door to, hovering with her ear to the crack until her eyelids grew heavy, then climbed into bed and, despite missing the customary warmth of Murph snuggled against her back and Mooch purring on the pillow beside her, fell fast asleep.

A soft tapping, barely perceptible, woke her.

She crept from bed, shivering in a penetrating cold, no less shocking for being expected. Serendipity Ranch deliberately kept the bunkhouse largely unheated to discourage, as June Ennis put it, 'nighttime wanderings'.

She cracked the door wider and saw Mackenzie in the faint glow of the night light – another hedge against illicit activities under cover of darkness.

'Ms Best?' The girl's breath hung in a cloud between them. 'I'm sorry to wake you.'

The figures on Nora's watch glowed three a.m., which made Mackenzie's previous six a.m. wake-up call look positively civilized.

When Nora didn't respond, the girl tried again. 'It's Ashleigh. She's been crying for an hour.'

Nora sifted through the list of trendy female names she'd tried to memorize – MadisonBaileyOliviaIsabella and more, including two Sierras and three variations on Sophia – and tried to retrieve an image of Ashleigh's face from the blur. There. The girl with the long dark hair sitting at the First Rung table, poking her spoon disconsolately into the mess of oatmeal, but conveying precious little to her mouth.

'Irene was her mentor. They pair us up with longer-term students when we arrive. Ashleigh's having a hard time with this.'

Mackenzie took Nora's hand – Nora was pretty sure even such innocuous physical contact ranked somewhere on the forbidden list – and pulled her from the room. 'Here. Take this.'

The girl had wrapped herself in a blanket, which she transferred to Nora's shoulders. 'You'll need it. I'm going back to bed. Lower bunk, third from your door. Ashleigh's all the way at the end. Bottom bunk.'

Nora quick-stepped barefoot between the twinned rows of bunks, the blanket trailing behind her, until she stood beside the shuddering form in the last bed. All around, the other girls inhaled and exhaled audibly, a deep regular chorus of sleep real or feigned. Ashleigh's breath came in shallow gulps, muffled by the blanket over her head.

Nora knelt and put a hand on her shoulder. Ashleigh flinched away.

'It's OK. It's me, Nora. Ah, Ms Best. Are you all right?'

Stupid question. Nora wondered if Ashleigh rolled her eyes through her sobs.

The girl didn't answer but gradually relaxed against her hand. Nora rubbed her back in slow circles – did that count as a PDA? – and hummed a tune, a song her mother used to sing to her when she had trouble sleeping. 'Simple Gifts', the old Shaker song, an odd choice given her mother's staunchly Episcopalian background, but lovely nonetheless.

She hoped Ashleigh didn't know the lyrics. ''Tis a gift to be free'– something Ashleigh might find insulting, given her present circumstances.

The girl's juddering sobs slowly stilled. She sighed, swallowed and slowly lowered the blanket, whispering something so low that Nora didn't catch it. She put her ear close to the girl's face. 'Again, please?'

'She didn't kill herself. Irene. She didn't suicide.'

Nora couldn't think of a single thing to say that wouldn't get her in trouble, given Ennis' legal concerns. 'Maybe she slipped,' she finally offered, though even that seemed fraught.

Ashleigh shook her head. 'No way. She was afraid of heights. They took us on a hike and when we came to a cliff, she stayed way back from the edge. She was . . .' She began to sob again. 'She was . . .'

'Hey.' A sharp voice sliced into the room's half-darkness. 'Shut the fuck up before we all get in trouble.'

Ashleigh jerked away from Nora and dove back beneath the blanket.

Nora couldn't tell who'd spoken. She stood and sought to sound the way she imagined a housemother might.

'That language is unacceptable. Everyone back to sleep. I'm leaving my door open, so if there's any commotion, I'll hear it.'

But she couldn't stop herself from leaning over and giving Ashleigh's hand a squeeze before she headed back to her room, dropping the blanket on Mackenzie's bunk along the way.

Whatever the girl had been about to tell her would have to wait.

TEN

Nora lay awake much of the rest of the night, unnerved by the prospect of the day ahead – her first in the classroom – and also by the unfamiliar sensation of sleeping again in a room.

Except for a brief sojourn back in her childhood bedroom, she'd spent much of the summer in Electra, whose aluminum walls curved around her like a cocoon. Within them, and with Mooch and Murph pressed close, she felt sheltered, safe.

She'd have preferred to think the animals likewise restless and agitated without her in the trailer, but knew they were probably sprawled across the bed, luxuriating in the extra space. She writhed within the rough cotton sheets until they wrapped her like a straitjacket, then kicked herself free and lay atop them despite the cold, taking long, deep breaths to calm herself and prepare for her first day in the art studio. It turned out to be a surprise.

Nora, who hadn't taken art since high school, had envisioned a throwback to those long-ago classrooms supplied only with watercolors and posterboard, maybe some modeling clay, and charcoal pencils that necessitated constant warnings against using them for fake mustaches and tattoos.

The interior of the cabin that housed Serendipity Ranch's art studio looked like Nora's imaginings of an atelier. A semi-circle of easels stood in one corner, backlit by floor-to-ceiling windows with a sweeping view of the forested mountains beyond, their peaks disappearing into low clouds. Nearby, a tall cabinet held dozens of compartments for tubes of oil paints, wide sticks of pastels, and charcoal pencils of all widths. Soapstone sculptures-in-progress lined a workbench that ran the length of one wall. The room held potters' wheels, racks of bright fabrics, even a letterpress.

Nora paused before a wall of framed paintings, some of them clumsy landscapes, others angry dark abstractions. A collection of portraits with a shimmering, luminescent quality caught her eye. A girl gazed somberly from each, not a single smile to be seen. But something about the individual images – a quirk of the lips, a lifted eyebrow, a tilted chin – conveyed intense emotion, from mischief to defiance to despair so acute that she flinched away. She turned back and studied that last portrait, belatedly recognizing Ashleigh of the midnight weeping.

'That's Mackenzie's work. She paints us the way we see ourselves,' said a voice at her shoulder.

Nora turned to see one of the Sophias – this one, she reminded herself, spelled it Sophie – whose auburn ringlets and ethereal pallor defined the term pre-Raphaelite.

'They're incredible. Where is she?' Nora looked around for Mackenzie, wanting to compliment her. Ennis had said Serendipity Ranch ran on positive reinforcement. In this case, it would be easy.

Sophie shrugged, her shoulders bony as a hanger within her polo shirt. Nora wondered if she was among the girls who specialized in surreptitious upchucking.

'She's back on First Rung. So, no art. She'll have to earn her way back in.'

So much for positive reinforcement, Nora thought once again. But given the girl's obvious love for her craft, perhaps the possibility of returning to it was the most effective carrot.

'What's she doing instead?'

Sophie nodded toward the window. 'There.'

Nora turned away from the portraits. A figure in a red T-shirt and baggy gym shorts circled the clearing in a slow jog, not much faster than a trudge.

'A hundred times,' Sophie said. 'Look. Mama June is counting.' June Ennis sat in a webbed lawn chair beneath a swaying pine, her knitting needles rocking rhythmically in her hands, the scarf now the length of a hand towel. As Mackenzie rounded a turn toward her, she put down her knitting and picked up a plastic clicker to note another lap. She made a circling motion with her other hand and Mackenzie picked up the pace.

'You can bet we'll be having potatoes for dinner,' Sophie said. 'Which nobody likes.'

What in the world did potatoes have to do with Mackenzie's punishment?

Sophie correctly read her confusion. 'She'll have to peel them. And we'll have to eat them, no matter that they're the last thing we need.' She patted her improbably concave stomach, which even the baggy red polo shirt failed to disguise. Her forearms were mere twigs between the knurls of elbow and wrist; her cheekbones so sharp Nora feared they might razor through skin.

'Eat the potatoes,' she said before she could stop herself, although she managed not to add, 'with as much butter and sour cream as they'll hold.'

Sophie mimed a retch too realistic for Nora's comfort. 'You sound just like Mama June and who wants to end up like her?' She puffed her cheeks out in an impossible imitation of plumpness.

'There has to be a happy medium.' But the look on Sophie's face told Nora she believed no such thing.

Nora glanced through the window again. Despite her tedious assignment, Mackenzie made a pretty picture, her red shirt a striking contrast with a backdrop formed by the green of pines and the mellow golden logs of the cabins and lodge. Nora slid her phone from her pocket and snapped a photo.

Sophie sucked in her breath. 'You'd better delete that. No photos.'

'It's fine.'

Part of Nora's duties on the public relations front included compiling a newsletter for parents. But when she explained as much to Sophie, the girl's face darkened. 'That photo will never make the newsletter.'

Nora didn't want to get into a discussion about what was and wasn't allowed. She ignored Sophie and clapped her hands. The dozen chattering girls in the morning art session fell silent. They stood bunched together across the room, arms folded, feet planted wide, scowling like the girl in the bottom rung sketch in Nora's lightly perused manual.

'Be seated.' Nora stayed on her feet, hoping to project an image of authority. The girls sank into chairs but maintained the same challenging pose, their lovely brows creased, arms crisscrossed over chests, pouts pronounced beyond even what Botox had achieved.

Nora tried for an upbeat, encouraging tone. 'Let's get to know each other. I'm Nora – Ms Best. Until recently, I spent most of my working life at a college.' No need to tell them her interaction with students had been nearly nonexistent. 'You . . .' She nodded to a petite girl who'd tortured the hem of her polo shirt into a tight knot, exposing an inch of midriff. For whose benefit, Nora wondered?

'Tell us a little bit about yourself. And untie your shirt, please.'

She held her breath, but the girl complied, albeit with a gusty sigh and what could have been a muttered epithet, which Nora pretended she hadn't heard.

'Sybil. From River Oaks.' Identifying herself by neighborhood rather than greater Houston, Nora noted. 'Been here four of the longest months of my life.'

'Thank you, Sybil. Next – and please forego any embellishments.'

Aliana from Kalorama, three months. Sophia with a 'p-h' from Buckhead, eight months. Sophie-no-a from the Upper East Side, five months.

With each neighborhood, among the toniest in their respect-
ive cities of Washington, Atlanta and New York, Ashleigh slid
a little farther down in her seat. 'Ashleigh. Two weeks.
Meridian Hills,' she whispered after everyone else had spoken,
her voice falling lower still on the last two words.

'Where?' Sophie-no-a demanded.

'M-m-m-meridian Hills.'

'Where the hell is that?' Sybil leaned forward, a sudden
avid gleam in her eyes.

'Language,' Nora said. 'Ashleigh, you don't have to answer
that.'

'Yeah, she does.' Aliana, with a conspiratorial wink
toward Sophie. 'Because who the—whoever heard of
Meridian-freaking-Hills?'

Nora cleared her throat.

'No way *freaking* counts as language,' Aliana said with
great authority.

Nora hadn't expected pushback so immediately, on such an
innocuous subject.

'If I say it counts, it does. Do you all want to end up out
there with Mackenzie?' She had no idea if she had the sort
of power to order an entire class to run laps, but figured if she
didn't know, the girls didn't, either.

'It's in Indiana,' Ashleigh muttered miserably.

Sophia and Aliana exchanged tight, triumphant smiles.
Indiana! They didn't have to say it. Lips curled in sneers.
Ashleigh's eyes begged her to change the subject. Nora
hastened to comply.

'Thank you for the introductions. Whatever project you
were working on, please resume.'

To her relief, they positioned themselves around the room,
donning paint- and clay-smeared red aprons printed with the
Serendipity Ranch logo and setting to work.

Nora breathed normally again. She wandered the room,
complimenting a painting of a girl's pink-and-white bedroom, a
charcoal sketch of a mare protectively nuzzling her foal. The
potter's wheel spun, a bowl taking shape under Sybil's wet,
clay-fattened fingers. Nora thought that when she felt more firmly
in control, she could ask the girl to show her how to use it.

She looked at the clock. Just a half-hour to go, with only a minor rebellion and resulting cooperation to show for her first day. She allowed herself to hope she'd make it through. Too soon, too soon.

'Ms Best! Sofia—'

Nora looked to the speaker and then to Sofia-with-an-f, who stood smirking at the sculpture table.

'She's sculpting a dildo. I mean, can you blame her? We're all cooped up here without sex. But that's not allowed, is it?'

Nora said all the bad words she could think of under her breath during the long, long walk across the room to examine Sofia's sculpture. She'd expected the job to be challenging. She'd even considered the possibility that she might not last the length of her yearlong contract. She hadn't expected something that could get her fired on her first day.

The knot of girls who'd rushed to the sculpture table obligingly pulled apart at her approach. They watched, something feral in their avid expressions as her eyes fell on Sofia's creation, which indeed looked like . . .

'A mushroom! Swear to God, Ms Best, that's what it is. My dad's a hobby mycologist. That's someone who studies mushrooms.'

'I know what a mycologist is.' Nora took another look and failed to choke back a guffaw.

'Mushroom, my ass,' she blurted unprofessionally.

Faces cracked into smiles.

Sofia looked at her with big round eyes and a solemn expression. 'It's a *member*' – Nora grimaced as she emphasized the word – 'of the family Phallaceae. People call it . . .' She paused, playing to her rapt audience. 'A stinkhorn.'

That did it.

Nora bent double, helpless with laughter, the girls joining in after a shocked second.

She got herself under control and reached for Sofia's 'mushroom', yanking her hand back just before she touched it, prompting another gale of laughter.

'All right, everybody. Calm down. Sofia, you've had your fun. And I've no doubt this is an authentic replica of a . . . stinkhorn.' Laughter burbled up again.

'But it's also inappropriate, as you well know, and it's going to have to go.' She glanced around and spied a small hammer in a well-supplied tool rack. She retrieved it and held it out. 'Would you like to do the honors, or shall I?'

The room fell silent again. Nora thought she'd crossed so many lines that she might as well leap over one more.

'Go ahead.' She thrust the hammer toward Sofia. 'If you're anything like every other woman in the universe, you've met a stinkhorn or two that could use a good whack with a hammer. It might help to think of one in particular. Come on. Give it a go.'

'Yeah, Sofia,' one of the girls urged. 'You know who to think of. We all do.'

Sofia's smile was not something Nora would soon forget. She raised the hammer high and brought it down so hard the table bounced. The sculpture broke in two, pieces spinning across the table.

'Me, too! Let me! I want to hit him!'

The girls pushed and shoved to get at the hammer, yanking it from one another and pounding the bits of soapstone until it was little more than powder, leaving Nora shaken and wondering just what – or who – had unleashed such universal rage among the well-brought-up young women of Serendipity Ranch.

ELEVEN

Nora didn't get fired.

The girls seemed to have reached a tacit agreement not to rat her out, just as she in turn said nothing about Sofia's artistic endeavors to Ennis.

Which didn't mean everything was kumbaya between her and the girls, who continued to push her on a daily basis.

They sniped at one another with sly, sidewise glances toward Nora to make sure she'd heard. They did their damnedest to transform their utterly asexual polo shirts and khakis by tying the shirt in ungainly knots under their breasts and shoving down the pants' waistband to reveal tanned, taut midriffs and more than one belly button ring. And they frequently did such a piss-poor job of clean-up at the end of each studio session that she held them late to redo it, keeping a constant count of all the materials: the sculpture tables' hammers and rasps; the paintbrushes with their hard plastic handles that could be sharpened into tiny spears; the cans of turpentine and tubes of paint with their intoxicating fumes. Every day after they left, she made the rounds of the room, inventorying the equipment, bargaining with God against the day when something potentially lethal might go missing.

But nothing carried the same barbed undertones of that first day. Instead, she and the girls performed a daily pas de deux of trespass and rebuke, the girls expertly dancing up to – but never crossing – the line that would have required busting someone back a rung. Nora, with no children of her own, found herself employing her own mother's 'look', the flash of narrowed eye, the tuck of chin that signaled, 'Knock it off this minute,' cowing the girls into sullen submission.

'It's exhausting,' Nora confessed to Luke Rivera.

She'd run into him one evening in the free hour after dinner, as she walked Murph in the woods behind her trailer. The forest, gilded by late-day sunlight, was a different animal than the menacing tangle of trees where the two thugs had jumped her that first night. Birdsong burbled in concert with the urgent whisper of water sliding fast over smooth stones.

Nora had tried to find the stream on one of her early walks, but following the sound only led her to a high bluff with the water rushing far below. She gauged the distance – probably not so high that a fall could be fatal – and couldn't help but think of her own forced tumble from a low cliff in the seemingly forever-ago early days of summer, as well as the loftier leap Irene Bell must have taken. She'd backed quickly away and hadn't returned.

On this day, she rounded a bend in a faint trail that led into the trees and found Luke on hands and knees in a small clearing, scooping pinecones into a tarp.

'For Thanksgiving decorations,' he said. He looked skyward,

where the sun radiated a mellow cheer. 'It seems far away, especially in these warm fall days, but it'll be on us before you know it.'

Nora stooped to help him, rolling cones from the duff onto the tarp. Murph chased a couple of errant cones, showing an unexpected youthful friskiness.

Luke gathered the tarp's corners together, then slid down with his back against a tree. He gestured to one nearby, inviting her to do the same. She nearly fell in her eagerness to join him, so starved was she for adult conversation that went beyond mealtime chitchat. The instructors had proved nearly as cliqueish as the girls, seemingly viewing her as someone from another century, and all of her dealings with Ennis involved program business.

She said as much to Luke.

He gave a short laugh. 'I know what you mean. When I first came here, I made an effort to get to know the instructors. But they rotate through here so fast it's barely worth it. I mean, they're fine in the teaching department. But most of them are outdoors enthusiasts who come here for their big Montana adventure. They live for backpacking trips on their days off and move on to some other place like New Mexico or the Cascades when they're ready for new terrain. From what little I know, it's not uncommon for them to cycle through several of these types of programs, picking them by location.'

Murph flopped beside him and lay his grizzled head across Luke's legs.

Luke pulled a single cigarette and a safety match from his breast pocket. 'You mind?'

'I thought we weren't allowed to smoke.'

'We're not.' He grinned and flicked his thumbnail across the matchhead. It flared obediently and he touched it to the cigarette, inhaled, and sighed with eyes shut.

'The longer I'm here, the more I sympathize with the girls. Something about all these rules – you just want to break them. Even if it's just for a smoke.'

He opened his eyes and held out the cigarette to Nora. She waved it away along with the thoughts of her glass – or two, or three – of wine on the nights she slept in Electra. She nodded toward the mound of pinecones.

'Shouldn't the girls be doing this? That whole mantra about fresh air and exercise?' She'd finally committed the manual to memory. 'Especially while the weather's nice?'

'Oh, bad weather won't stop anything. They'll have those girls out running when it's twenty degrees.'

Twenty? She tried to imagine a line of girls with zero body fat struggling through the snow – surely there would be snow, the air so dry and crystalline that each breath seared the lungs and the snow squeaked underfoot – no parka bulky enough to retain sufficient heat.

'That's crazy. How does subjecting kids to frostbite help anyone?'

His lips tightened. 'They run around the clearing. They can duck into the lodge or bunkhouse if things get too bad.'

He'd opened the door for her to ask the questions she hadn't dared pose to Ennis.

'But they said this place isn't a boot camp. That sure sounds like one to me. And if it's so exclusive, how come I've never heard of it?'

'There's a reason you don't hear about these places. Discretion is part of the deal. Do you have any idea how much they cost? We're talking six figures a year and insurance doesn't cover it.'

Nora thought of the owners of the faux-castle she'd seen on her cross-country trip, the ones sending their daughter off to God-knows-what sort of program. Clearly, they had resources to burn. If that sort of program catered to such clients, how much more must Serendipity Ranch cost?

'Jesus! You said places.'

'Programs like this are scattered all over the West. A lot of it has to do with the landscape – remote locations are part of the mystique. But regulations in these western states tend to be a lot more lax.'

He hadn't answered her question about boot camps and he apparently wasn't going to. 'How are you doing so far? Settling in? How's it going with the girls?'

Nora gave him a vague outline that omitted the stinkhorn

incident. He didn't seem as though he'd pass it on to Ennis, but you never knew.

'That sounds about par for the course. You've already lasted longer than some. I always thought Carolee had found the sweet spot, but even she burned out. The girls, as you've already found, can be a handful.'

He scratched behind Murph's ears and the dog groaned in pleasure.

'You've made a friend. He doesn't take to everybody. How long was Carolee here?'

He moved his fingers, silently counting. 'Six years? Long before I got here.'

'When was that?'

'Closing in on a year. My contract's up in December.'

A sliver of sunlight found his face. He closed his eyes against it and Nora took the opportunity to study him, the set jaw, the bristly not-quite-high-and-tight hair, brow as creased as her own. He sat close enough that the occasional breeze brought her whiffs of tobacco and sweat and shaving cream, refreshingly masculine after days among the girls and their fruity shampoos and lotions. Ennis, the only other male at the ranch, wafted musty, old-man scents. Nora hadn't spent so much time in an all-female atmosphere since her college dormitory days and had almost forgotten how male presence, for good or ill, rearranged the ions in the atmosphere.

She eyed the hair again. 'Military?'

He smiled without opening his eyes. 'What gave it away?'

She dropped her gaze to his bare forearm, only just noticing the tattoo.

'The Semper Fi on your arm? Where'd you serve? Were you stationed here at home? Or . . .?'

His smile vanished.

'Iraq. The Marines basically funded my college education.' He opened his eyes and added, his tone mocking, 'Now look at me, a gen-you-wine psychologist. Except it turns out we're a dime a dozen. That's how I ended up here. You?'

Nora took a pinecone from the pile and tossed it from hand to hand, wincing as the sharp scales jabbed her palms. She'd taken the advice she used to give clients and applied it to her own situation: *write up talking points. Memorize them. Say them in front of a mirror until they feel natural.*

'I spent most of my career in public relations, the last few years at a college in Denver. Then my marriage went bust and I needed a change, a big one. So here I am, living in an Airstream in the wilds of Montana. I couldn't be a bigger cliché if I tried.'

She held her breath, letting it out in a whoosh when he threw back his head and laughed. It had worked.

'Good for you. My own marriage went down the drain before I'd been back from Iraq a year. Speaking of clichés. But that was a long time ago.'

She wanted to hear more, but he took a last, long drag on the cigarette, cheeks hollowing, then pinched it out. He rose, rolling the butt between his fingers, tobacco and bits of paper flaking onto the ground. He stomped them deep into the duff and kicked pine needles over the telltale spot.

He bent and took two ends of the tarp. 'This'll go easier if you take the other side. Really appreciate the help.'

She was laughing at something he'd said as they came out of the woods, swinging the laden tarp between them, Murph dancing around them, chasing the occasional stray cone that bounced from the tarp.

Ennis stood in the middle of the clearing, arms crossed, head cocked. Surveying his backwoods kingdom, Nora thought. She waved and he returned it with a small, clipped gesture.

'I'll drop these off in the art studio,' Luke said. 'Thanks again for the help.'

She turned toward Electra, but Ennis hailed her.

'Stay,' she said to Murph, and jogged over.

'Ms Best. I'm glad to see you're enjoying your time here.'

She held out her arms, as if to share all of the good feeling from her late-day walk.

'How can you not enjoy a beautiful afternoon like this? I wish fall could go on forever.'

'Yes. As do we all. Enjoy it now. Winters here can be intense. It's hard on the girls. We do as many outdoor activities as possible, but they're naturally limited. When people are cooped up together, tempers can fray. Behaviors deteriorate.

It becomes even more important that we model impeccable conduct.'

'Of course.' She wondered if Ennis ever relaxed his vigilance. But maybe, as director, he couldn't.

'Among the behaviors we discourage' – Nora had already learned that 'discourage' was simply a gentler term for 'forbid' – 'is attachments among staff. They happen. Carolee and Luke, well . . .' He gave a helpless shrug. 'Mother spoke to them more than once. Each insisted they were just friends. But apparently whatever was between them meant more to poor Carolee than any of us imagined. I can't help but wonder if that's why she's chosen not to return.'

He walked away, shaking his head, leaving Nora standing alone in the middle of the clearing, absorbing the message she'd just received.

During art class the next day, Nora drifted over to the corner of the studio set up for painting.

Mackenzie, who'd served her First Rung penance, was back in the class, furiously sketching the outline of a face on a piece of canvas.

'Your work is amazing,' Nora offered.

'Thanks.' Mackenzie never took her eyes off the canvas. The charcoal pencil moved quickly across it, outlining a long jaw, tousled hair.

'Where did you learn?'

'My parents paid for lessons with Maria di Maiori.'

Nora blinked at the name. 'That sounds familiar. Who is she?'

'Ever been to the National Portrait Gallery?'

Nora smiled at the memory. 'I waited in line to see the Obama portraits. Yes, I've been.'

'That's how. Some of her work hangs there.'

Nora blinked again, harder this time. 'You actually studied with her?'

Mackenzie sketched the eyes, then rubbed the charcoal lines with the meat of her thumb.

'I actually did.'

'Wow. Your parents must be . . .'

'Rich. That's the word you were thinking, right?'

It was, though she hadn't intended to put it so crassly.

'They're not just rich, they're stupid rich. Wish they weren't.'

'But then you wouldn't have learned how to paint so beautifully,' Nora pointed out.

'But then I wouldn't be here,' Mackenzie countered. 'I'd be in a public school somewhere, just a normal juvenile delinquent like everyone else.'

She selected several tubes of paint and smeared some onto a palette.

'I recognize some of the girls in your portraits,' Nora said, easing the conversation toward the reason she'd approached Mackenzie. 'But do you ever paint any of the staff? Mrs Ennis or, um, Carolee? I mean, Ms Hanford?'

Her voice caught a little on Carolee. She hoped Mackenzie hadn't noticed.

The girl barked a laugh. 'Mother Ennis? Not a chance. I see enough of her as it is. As for Ms Hanford, I never got around to it. Wish I had.'

A perfect opening.

'Why? What was she like?'

Mackenzie picked up a brush and daubed a dark gray, almost black, onto the canvas and began blocking in the background with short, angry strokes.

'Nice.' She thought a minute. 'Fair. Sort of like you in that regard.' She flashed a smile so rare that Nora suppressed a gasp. 'I miss her.'

'I guess Luke – Mr Rivera – misses her, too.'

Mackenzie returned her attention to her subject's eyes, leaning in close and catching her lip in her teeth. 'I guess,' she mumbled. 'Maybe.'

Which didn't make it sound as though there'd been anything special between Luke and Carolee.

Mackenzie stepped back and studied her canvas. The eyes bored into Nora, anguished, imploring.

'God. Who is that?'

Mackenzie gave her an odd look.

'Irene. Of course.'

She threw down her brush and walked away, leaving Nora alone with the dead girl's unspoken plea.

TWELVE

On Nora's day off, a dump truck ground to a clanking halt beside her trailer at seven a.m., her plans to sleep in foiled yet again.

She'd heard reveille a half-hour earlier, but luxuriated in rolling over, wrapping a pillow around her head, and sinking back into slumber.

But there was no sleeping through the series of piercing backup beeps, screeching gears and rolling crashes only feet from the window above her bed. She joined Murph and Mooch in peering out just as the last rocks from the truck's load tumbled onto the small mountain now standing beside Electra.

A gritty dust filmed the air, veiling her view of a man in a hard hat holding out a clipboard to Ennis, who signed with a satisfied nod. The man got back into the truck and, taking more time and making more noise than Nora could have imagined necessary, finally got it turned around and departed, leaving Nora wide awake and cranky.

At least she didn't have to rush to the communal breakfast, she told herself, as she prepared coffee and real bacon, hoping spitefully that the scent carried to the dining hall. She let Murph out to do his business – he knew not to wander far from the trailer – and put some kibble down for Mooch, who turned his back on it and crouched, tail twitching and eyes fixed firmly on her bacon.

She ignored him, savoring both the bacon and her plan for the day. She'd squandered her first day off by remaining at the ranch, but this week she'd vowed to drive into town in search of decent coffee, perhaps a lunch out involving a real hamburger, and a visit to a library or bookstore. And if the nearest town offered only some of those options, she'd drive until she found a town that had them all.

No matter where she ended up, she wanted a strong Wi-Fi signal. More than anything, she looked forward to the homework she should have done before coming to Serendipity Ranch. She wanted to find out everything about the place she could.

The town of Ponderosa was . . . enough.

Even though it was hardly the oasis she'd hoped for. On the drive in, she'd fantasized about a coffee shop, one that made tiny, intense macchiatos with a single dollop of foamed milk, not the giant bastardized versions favored by chains. She wanted a bookstore with the musty scent that indicated a robust used-book section; a café with, please God, organic selections that went beyond vegetarian.

What she got was a main street with small log buildings reminiscent of those at Serendipity Ranch, housing a gas station, a grocery/hardware store, a city hall and sheriff's office next door to a volunteer fire company, a café and a small park with outdated metal playground equipment, the kind that sent kids home with chipped teeth and broken bones. A low brick elementary school anchored one end of the street. At the other – Nora turned in excitement to Mooch and Murph, crowing, 'A mirage!' – a tiny library, in the same log-cabin style as the other buildings.

She stopped next to the park, under the shade of a generous cottonwood, the first non-pine tree she'd seen since arriving at Serendipity Ranch. She didn't realize how oppressive she'd found the thick stands of pines, the way they leaned into one another, blotting out the sun, until she saw the cottonwood standing defiantly on its own in the open, its summer-dry leaves clacking in the light breeze, glinting gold in a final blaze of glory before drifting to the ground.

She let Murph out for a few leisurely ball-tosses and pondered her next move. Books? Food? Coffee?

Murph lurched toward her, panting, signaling the end of the game. She sloshed water from a bottle into his bowl, gave him a treat and put him back in the truck with the windows down. His eagerness for the treat helped her make her own choice: food first.

While Arlo's Restaurant – she supposed there might be some sort of copyright issue with Alice's – didn't tout the sort of locally sourced, all-organic meal she'd dreamed of, it

boasted a steak and eggs combo that arrived with the eight-
ounce steak a tender, perfect medium-rare and the poached
eggs with the whites fully cooked, no mean feat, and toast –
'homemade bread?' she asked the server, who hovered nearby,
coffeepot in hand.

'Mom comes in early every morning to get it started.' The
server glanced toward the open window into the kitchen,
where a woman with the same high forehead and sloping
stance tended the griddle.

Nora checked her watch – nearly ten. 'She must be dead
on her feet by now.'

The server refilled Nora's coffee mug. 'She would be if we
didn't have the kids to help.'

Nora glanced again at the woman in the kitchen. She had
to be at least seventy. 'You mean grandkids?'

The server, whose nametag identified her as Marian, straightened her apron and laughed. 'Oh, no. I'm the only one of her
kids she conned into working here, and the grandkids left
Ponderosa as soon as they got out of high school. I was talking
about the kids from the school. They're a big help.'

Nora took a sip of her coffee, which was strong and hot,
the two things she valued most. She lifted her mug toward the
server in a sort of toast. 'Is there a high school here? I only
saw the elementary school.'

Marian shook her head. 'No, I mean the place out in the
woods for juvies.' She misread Nora's look.

'I guess that's not the right term. I don't know what they
call them anymore. Girls gone wild, I guess. A bus brings
some of them down in the afternoon. Of course, they can't be
around the customers. We found that out the hard way after
one sweet-talked a truck driver into helping her run away in
exchange for God-knows-what kind of favors. But they do the
dishes, mop the floors, take out the trash, sweep the parking
lot – we'd have closed years ago if it weren't for them.' She
tugged a tea towel from her waistband and flicked a crumb
from the table and turned to go.

Nora tried to keep her, hoping for more information.

'Sounds like the kind of job I did when I was in high school.'

Marian laughed. 'Bet you got paid for yours. These kids,

it's all volunteer. A town this size, business this small, we don't make the kind of money to pay a bunch of help. Serendipity Ranch saved our bacon, pun intended.' She looked at Nora's half-empty mug. 'Be back in a jiff with more coffee. I'm going to brew a fresh pot.'

Nora had seen an SUV with the Serendipity Ranch logo leave in the afternoons. When she'd asked Ennis, he'd said simply, 'Volunteer work.'

She didn't know what she'd thought – maybe picking up trash along the side of the road, mowing lawns for the elderly, the sorts of things that were supposed to build character. For sure, she hadn't imagined free labor for a local business.

She paid for her meal and tipped generously, though she guessed none of the money would find its way to any of the girls from Serendipity Ranch.

The grocery store had coffee beyond Folgers. Sort of. A few brown paper bags of whole beans lined up next to a grinder, though there were only three varieties, none espresso, and when Nora ground them, the scent was disappointingly faint.

She wondered how long they'd been sitting there and entertained herself with the notion of buying out the entire selection, forcing the store to order fresh. Or, maybe it wouldn't order any at all, she told herself, with a reminder that she couldn't afford such a stunt anyway, not with Charlotte's lawsuit hovering like a malevolent cloud overhead, its destructive funnel beginning to take shape.

Which reminded her. The store had an ATM. Artie had advised her to empty her bank account. She hovered in front of it, finally taking out five hundred dollars in three separate transactions. It was only a fraction of her savings yet it still seemed excessive, given that Serendipity Ranch covered her living expenses. Other than gas and the occasional meal at the café on her days off, she couldn't imagine what she'd need money for. Besides, she hoped the suit would be settled well before her yearlong contract with Serendipity Ranch ended.

She stashed the coffee in the truck and let Murph out again. From there, it was a short walk to the library, past the municipal building and the fire company, its giant garage door raised to let in the breeze, revealing two men at a card table set up between a pair of hulking trucks gleaming a modern lime-yellow rather than the shiny red version so beloved by children's books.

The men hunched over a cribbage board, cards scattered beside it, languidly moving pegs, glancing up at the distraction of her approach. They raised big hands in greeting.

She smiled back. 'Slow day?'

'Every day,' said the younger of the two. 'And a good thing. Can you imagine if someone dropped a match in these woods?'

'Nobody around here anymore to drop a match,' his partner huffed. His gray bottle-brush mustache hung over his mouth, muffling his words. Having established dominance, he turned to Nora. 'Lightning's our biggest worry.'

The younger one, wiry arms so roped with lean muscle that Nora guessed he pulled double duty on a wildland crew, grinned at her. 'Don't mind Fritz here. He's our resident curmudgeon. I'm Paul. Just guessing you're from the school.'

'Nora.'

Paul extended a hand and she took it, then turned to Fritz, who shook after a moment's hesitation. 'How did you know?'

'Because we know everyone in this town and we don't know you.' Fritz, still combative.

'And because the school is the only thing around that brings in anyone new,' Paul added.

Nora fought a temptation to linger, to stand in the sun and chat with two strangers. The simple conversation was such a nice change from the charged atmosphere of the school, where even the most innocuous remark bore a hint of challenge or defensiveness, everything subject to layers of interpretation.

But morning had already edged into afternoon, and her mission at the library would take some time.

'Nice meeting you. I'll probably see you again sometime, given that I'll be here for the next year.'

Fritz barked a laugh layered with sarcasm. 'That'll make you the oldest of old-timers.'

Paul offered an apologetic smile along with his goodbye. But he didn't contradict him.

*　　*　　*

The trepidation launched by Fritz's remark vanished as soon as Nora stepped into the library.

It made up for the grocery store, with more stacks than she would have thought possible squeezed into its single room and a display of just-published novels, their covers bright and inviting within their cellophane protectors. Apart from a burly man at a desk across the room, punching at a keyboard with his index fingers, she was the room's only occupant. Dust motes tumbled undisturbed through the sunlight slicing through tall windows and the silence was the tranquil sort long uninterrupted by human voices.

The man broke off his laborious typing with evident relief when she approached. 'I'd like to get a card.'

He tilted his head toward a stack of papers on one corner of his desk. 'Just fill out one of those.'

Dust sifted from the application when she lifted it. She bent to her task, noting a pair of computers at a desk beneath a window as she did so.

'Are those for the public?'

'Yes, and a good thing. More people come in here for the computers than for books. Along with the sheriff, we've got the best Wi-Fi in town. Here's the password.'

He handed her a small piece of paper, pinching it between thumb and forefinger. The rest of his hand ended at the knuckles.

'Got into an argument with the saw at the mill,' he said when he caught her looking. 'The saw won. Although, with the mill shut down now, I guess it lost in the end.'

Nora blushed at her unseemly curiosity as she took the paper, with its printout of the Wi-Fi password: ReadAllTheBooks. Despite his mangled hand, his powerful physique looked far more suited to his previous job than the light lifting now required. Nora pictured him in a hard hat and canvas coveralls, in a haze of sawdust, surrounded by screaming machines. No way a publicly funded library job in such a down-on-its-luck town could compete with what must have been union wages in a sawmill.

'When did the mill close?'

His muscled shoulders lifted in a shrug. 'Ten years ago? Eleven? Seems like forever. Damn near killed this town. Most of the workers packed up their families and left. A few of us are hanging on, trying to scratch out a living as best we can. Damn environmentalists.'

Nora opened her mouth, but she was too late to stop the inevitable rant.

'They found one of those stupid endangered birds here and the next thing you know, these woods –' he gestured toward the window, which looked out onto the forest that ran right up to the edge of town – 'weren't a job site anymore, one that supported who knows how many families for who knows how many generations. Now they're *habitat*,' he sneered, making a curse of his final word.

Nora waved the piece of paper he'd given her, hoping to distract him. 'I like the password.'

She couldn't believe it worked. But he brightened. 'My idea. Generally, we limit people to half an hour on the computers, but it's not busy, so unless two more people come in wanting to use them, it's yours until at least three thirty. We turn them off then.'

'Why then?'

'Come afternoons, those kids from the school who work at the café are always trying to sneak in here and use them. They're not allowed on the Internet and they know it. I usually shut down the computers when they're around. It's not fair to everyone else, but what can you do?'

He glanced at her card application and raised an eyebrow.

'I see you work there. You know the drill, then.'

Nora nodded. No need to tell him that this was one more drill she didn't know.

'Here's your temporary card. You can take out two books today, and up to five a week when your permanent card comes in.'

Nora headed for the fiction section, found a unicorn – a James Lee Burke book she hadn't read – and then made a beeline for the computers, wondering what else she might discover about Serendipity Ranch.

'Ma'am? *Ma'am.*'

The unlikely librarian stood beside her. He cleared his throat. 'We're about to turn off the computers.'

Nora blinked and looked at the wall clock. How was it already three thirty?

She leapt up, remembering Murph back in the truck.

'Thank you!' She hurried for the door.

'See you next time,' he called after her. His wistful tone made her wonder just how many people – how many adults – used the library every day. No one else had come in during her lengthy sojourn; at least, she didn't think anyone had. She'd been so deep in her reading about Serendipity Ranch she probably wouldn't have noticed.

There was little actual information about the ranch itself. But its name cropped up in years' worth of newspaper stories about attempts, always futile, by the state legislature to regulate such programs.

Every two years, Charlie Ennis traveled to the capital to testify that his program's tenets were more stringent than anything proposed for state law.

'Not only do we follow best practices, we helped develop them,' he was quoted as saying in one story. 'Serendipity Ranch's model is now the nationwide standard for such programs' – the same thing he'd repeatedly told Nora and apparently everyone else.

The stories, at least the early ones, also noted that a foundation named for the ranch donated generously to the charitable causes favored by lawmakers on the committee that oversaw legislation affecting such programs. Nora knew what she'd read next, and she was right: those politicians reliably voted against tightening regulations.

More recent stories were shorter and lacked any mention of the donations. Nora supposed that was due to the same sort of cutbacks that plagued news organizations around the country, putting investigative journalism on life support, but a boon for public relations specialists.

Indeed, she noted an uptick in feel-good features about Serendipity Ranch – more donations to local causes (though no mention of the 'volunteer' work at the café); an occasional tearful testimonial from an alum who praised the Ennises for helping turn her life around; a photo display – though no accompanying story – from what was termed a character-building river-rafting trip, the spray of water as the raft careened through rapids serving to hide the students' faces, thus dispelling any concerns about privacy.

Exactly the sort of pablum she herself had fed news outlets when she worked in her college's public relations department, praying nobody had combed court records and stumbled over the embezzlement charges filed against a former provost.

She erased 'Serendipity Ranch' from the search field and typed in 'Irene Bell,' only to discover exactly how common Irene's name had been. She tried the name and 'Serendipity Ranch.' Nothing.

Then she tried 'Irene Bell' and 'obituary' yielding a crop of unfortunates. At least, this list was manageable. She clicked past teachers and accountants, a small-town mayor and a centenarian, until she found a short notice in a California newspaper: 'Irene Bell, 16, beloved daughter of Daniel and Melissa of Hidden Hills . . .'

No mention of suicide, which wasn't unusual. Such deaths still carried a considerable stigma and families often worded those obituaries in code: 'died suddenly' for someone who'd shot himself; an 'automobile accident' for the woman who'd pointed her car at a concrete bridge abutment and stomped the accelerator to the floor; 'a long illness' for someone who'd finally succumbed to years of agonizing depression.

Irene had died, according to the newspaper, in a hiking accident – exactly the scenario Nora had proposed for the letter to the Serendipity Ranch parents, only to see it shot down. Nora narrowed her search by adding 'Hidden Hills' and came up with a few mentions:

Irene as a little girl, blonde braids peeking beneath a riding helmet, winning gymkhana ribbons on a fat roan pony named Pepsi.

Irene balanced on the physical and emotional tightrope between child and teenager, flashing a little-girl grin as she hoisted a spelling bee trophy, her hair out of braids and tumbling over her shoulders in perfect waves.

Irene looking far older than her age as the freshman on her private school's Homecoming Court, elegant in a slip dress whose pale fabric showed off an enviable tan that bespoke hours in a booth, her long hair wound into an elaborate up-do.

After that, nothing.

Nora unlocked her truck and helped Murph out. He scampered into the park as fast as his arthritic joints would allow, and lifted his leg against the cottonwood, drenching its rough bark. Still lost in her thoughts, she barely noticed.

What had happened in the intervening year or two to turn a smart, athletic, seemingly cheerful girl into such a problem child that her parents had packed her off to this hidden place deep in the forest in the hopes that the golden girl they'd known would be returned to them?

And what had happened at Serendipity Ranch to send Irene into such despair that a leap from a cliff onto the jagged rocks below seemed the only solution?

THIRTEEN

A voice hailed her.

Nora turned to see a man in uniform, a pointy star flashing importance from his chest pocket.

'Ma'am?'

The librarian had likewise addressed her. Nora wondered when she'd gone from Miss to Ma'am. Probably a long time ago.

'Is that your dog?'

Murph, sensing attention, trotted over and held up his head for a pat.

The sheriff obliged, even as he directed a disapproving look at Nora from beneath a Stetson that shadowed his square face. 'Dogs need to be on leash in town.'

'I'm sorry.' Even though she wasn't. 'He'd been in the truck for a long time so I was in a hurry to let him out.' She didn't see any need to tell him that she didn't have a leash with her.

'Do you always leave your dog in your vehicle for a long time?'

This wasn't going well.

Nora might have been relegated to ma'am category, but she still remembered how to mount a charm offensive.

She tossed her hair, tilted her head and smiled past her inward grimace, forcing a bright tone as she held out her hand.

'I'm Nora Best. I'm new here. I work at Serendipity Ranch. This is my first trip to town. If I'd known it was so nice, I'd have come sooner.'

'Foley.' He didn't bother with a first name. But at least he took her hand, albeit with the bone-crushing, male-dominance grip she'd expected. She hadn't expected him to step in quite so close, so near that she rounded her shoulders protectively against a possible chest-bump.

'Today's my day off. I'm just exploring, trying to get to know the area,' she chattered along. 'Any advice about things to see?'

She used Murph as an excuse to back out of range, hustling him into the truck like a responsible citizen.

His answer was so long in coming that Nora wondered if the area offered any attractions at all. 'You could try the falls,' he said eventually. 'They're usually pretty puny this time of year, but we had a lot of snow last winter, so the creek's running high, even this late. Head on about five miles down the road. There's a turn-off with a sign. Just be careful. The rocks are wet and it's a long way down. Every few years, we lose somebody there.'

'Thanks. I'll check them out. Nice meeting you, Sheriff Foley. I'll be sure to keep Murph on his leash next time I come to town.'

He raised a hand and started to turn away.

But his words had raised a question.

'Sheriff? What you said about the falls and people slipping?'

He waited, big hands hooked in his duty belt.

'There was a girl at Serendipity Ranch who . . . fell . . . recently. They said it was suicide.'

He dipped his head. 'I was the coroner on that case. A tragedy, young girl like that, her whole life ahead of her.'

'Any idea why she might have taken her own life?'

'Those girls up there . . . You work there, so you know. Charlie and June Ennis perform miracles with them, but they just can't save all of them.'

Which didn't tell her anything she didn't already know.

'But her friends said she was afraid of heights. Are you sure it was suicide?'

Someday, thought Nora, she was going to learn not to blurt the first words that came into her head. This wasn't that day.

'Ma'am.'

Again with the ma'am.

'I had the sad task of examining that poor child's body and her injuries were consistent with a fall. Those girls may have a lot of problems, but they're none of them murderers, if that's what you're saying.'

'I didn't mean to imply . . .' she began. Yet, how else was he to take her question?

She backed toward her truck, her face red with embarrassment, not fast enough to escape a final 'ma'am'.

'Count yourself to be lucky to work at Serendipity Ranch. Now that the mill has shut down, they're our largest taxpayer. They're good citizens. Those girls – and honestly, it feels wrong to call them that, given that most of them are sixteen going on forty – do volunteer work all over town, learn responsibility, all the values that come with our way of life out here. If that young lady could have just held on for a few weeks, she could have turned her whole life around.

'You be careful when you go to the falls, ma'am. I don't want to see anything like that again in a long time.'

Nora stood at the lip of the falls, albeit with her feet firmly planted on dry ground, well away from the rocks that glistened from the spray, staring into a torrent as roiling as her own thoughts.

The overlook was about midway down the length of the falls, which roared from a precipice high above and plummeted into a churning pool below. Nora supposed the creek was the same one that ran through the gorge where Irene had plunged to her death. She shivered at the thought, wondering if the girl had still been alive when she hit the water, sucked down into

a maelstrom from which there was no escape. She hoped for
Irene's sake that the girl had hit her head on a rock straightaway; that the death she so desired had been mercifully quick.

She turned away from both the falls and her grim thoughts
and headed back to Serendipity Ranch, little more knowledge-
able than when she'd left.

FOURTEEN

Nora timed her return to arrive at the ranch after the
group dinner hour, aiming for a quiet meal in her
trailer while dipping into her library book, actions
that increasingly comprised her idea of the perfect evening as
she adjusted to the notion of a future alone.

A few times, after the spectacular flame-out of her marriage,
an exceptionally brave soul had asked whether she'd ever
remarry.

'Doubtful,' she'd answered, but never for the reason they
thought, although she kept that to herself. People assumed it
was because she'd been so badly burned, but in truth, she was
discovering the quiet pleasure of her new life on the road,
with just the company of the animals. She savored the luxury
of an evening involving a good book and a glass of passable
wine and thought that if she'd had to choose between that and
a date – whatever a date might involve these days – the book
would win every time.

Disappointment lodged in her throat as the truck rolled
beneath the Serendipity Ranch sign swinging from its crossbar
and she beheld a clearing full of people, all of them turning
at her approach.

She'd forgotten about the free hour between dinner and
lights out, when the girls were released from studies
and chores, their only limits that they spend the time
outdoors, weather permitting, and that no one roam the grounds
unaccompanied.

'Solitude breeds selfishness,' Charlie Ennis had explained

when she'd confided that, as an introvert, she'd have found that last rule difficult.

'For much of their lives, these girls have always gotten their own way. Almost without exception, their sojourn at Serendipity Ranch is the first time they've had to accommodate other people. Also, people tend to get despondent when they're alone.'

He'd left it at that, but the reality hung dark between them: Irene had gone off alone and look how that had ended up.

Nora gazed upon a vista of girls strolling in pairs or perched on the split-rail fence that flanked the clearing, or just sitting quietly together beneath trees, reading or writing home, those last two activities privileges granted only to those who'd achieved the top rung. Charlie and June Ennis walked hand in hand among them, stopping occasionally to talk with one of the girls, or admire another's backflip.

It made for a pretty tableau, and she stood for a moment beside the truck, admiring the way the setting sun, having relinquished its summer fierceness, washed the clearing with gold. Even the fast-darkening forest looked benevolent, encircling the ranch in a protective embrace. It discouraged the girls from escape, yes, but it also barred intrusions from the outside world that had proven so confusing, full of the enticing dangers that had turned out so ruinous to impressionable young girls.

'People throw the word "heal" around so much it's become a cliché,' Ennis had told her. 'But in addition to everything else we offer, the very physical environment has a reassuring effect. None of the things that so damaged them can hurt them here. They're safe here.'

Nora raised her phone and snapped a photo, capturing an image perfect to headline the next week's newsletter. What parent, trying to cope with a daughter spinning out of control, wouldn't feel at least a fraction of their torment eased by the sight of such an environment?

'Ms Best!' Mackenzie jogged across the clearing toward her, Ashleigh shuffling behind.

The girl's summons meant further delay before she could crack open her book, not to mention the bottle of wine. But Mackenzie's voice was so lighthearted, so different from the

sulky drawl she sometimes affected, that Nora couldn't help
responding with a smile.

'How was town?'

There's more going on here at this very moment than there
was all day in Ponderosa, Nora wanted to say. But Mackenzie
probably already knew that.

'I had a nice meal at the café.'

She'd wondered on the way home how to approach the
subject with the girls. For heaven's sake, they already had
plenty of chores, without adding swabbing the café's dusty
floors to their load.

But Mackenzie's face lit up. 'Didn't you just love it? Isn't
Mrs Foley the best? And her mom! Did you have the pie?'

'No pie. I had her bread, though.'

'Next time, have the pie,' Mackenzie said with authority.
'Mrs Foley bakes it special and knows all our favorites. I can't
wait until it's my group's turn to go again. She always makes
huckleberry for me.'

So much for Nora's fears about an exploitive set-up. Which
it remained, but if the girls liked it so much, who was she to
judge?

'Foley? Like the sheriff?'

'His wife.'

Ashleigh hung back during their conversation, glancing
wistfully toward Mackenzie, who turned to her with an apology.
Nora made a note to tell Ennis – the girls' selfishness was a
familiar refrain, but Mackenzie had flashed genuine concern
for Ashleigh's feelings.

'I keep forgetting you can't go yet,' she said. 'It's a Second
Rung privilege,' she told Nora.

Maybe, after months on the ranch, a trip to town – even
one so desperately clinging to that status as Ponderosa – would
seem a relief; and scrubbing the gunk from the griddle and
scouring a day's worth of dishes at least meant a change of
scenery from the same chores they did at the ranch.

'When will she get to Second Rung?'

'Any day now.'

Nora jumped at the sound of Ennis' voice. He stood behind
her, as usual hand in hand with his wife. The pair smiled

at Ashleigh, who offered a tentative twitch of her lips in return.

'Ashleigh came here during a particularly stressful time, but she's making great progress. We're doing everything we can to help her succeed. I, for one, have full confidence that soon she'll find that strength she never dreamed she had.'

They moved off, hailing Sofia, who'd added a twist to her backflip.

'Brava, brava!' June patted her soft hands together.

'We'd better get going,' Mackenzie said. 'You probably want to get back to your trailer. She calls it Electra. That's the kind of airplane on its side,' she told Ashleigh. 'Bet it's really cool inside.'

Nora ignored the broad hint. 'Good night, you two. I'll be back in the bunkhouse tomorrow.'

But as much as her original plan for the evening tugged at her, she lingered at her trailer door, looking back out over the clearing, at the girls enjoying a moment of peace in their until-now chaotic lives; at the Ennises wandering among them, offering encouragement.

Ennis and the sheriff were right, she thought. Given the high-risk nature of the ranch's clients, tragedies such as Irene Bell's death were likely unavoidable. She was painfully aware of her own inadequacies as a mentor, but that could change. She'd borrow the books in Ennis' office, chat up Luke about the best methods for dealing with such troubled youngsters, model her own behavior on that of the Ennis' supportive example.

Maybe, once she got out from under Charlotte's lawsuit, she'd go back to school, get a master's in psychology or social work. Far from being the last-ditch job she'd imagined, Serendipity Ranch might be the thing that set her life on a whole new course, just as it aimed to do with its students.

She shook her head at the irony of it all and took a final look at her young charges, vowing that not a single girl would die on her watch.

FIFTEEN

The girls were always slipping treats from the dining hall to Murph, despite Nora's frequent admonitions, which was probably why she awoke to the ominous sound of the retching and wheezing *on her bed.* 'Murph, no!'

Nora came fully alert just in time to grab the dog and pull him from the bed and through the door and perform the fancy footwork that kept most of the vomit from landing on her bare feet.

She hopped from one foot to the other, the grass brittle with frost, feeling sorry both for herself and Murph, who hunched, ears low and eyes sorrowful, in a few final heaves.

'Poor guy.' She stroked him, mentally crafting a far sterner lecture to the girls than she'd previously delivered. She looked around. She hadn't checked her clock on her rush from the trailer, but from the faded quality of the darkness guessed it was about four. Still two hours before the obnoxious reveille would sound. But the cold had brought her fully awake and she knew that if she managed to go back to sleep, she'd wake groggy and cranky. Best to mainline some coffee now and power through the day.

She felt Murph's belly for signs of further upheaval within. None. His tail began its characteristic slow sweep and his eyes brightened.

'Let's go back in and get warm.' She started up the steps, but the sound of a car engine stopped her. She hustled back into the trailer, eager for its warmth, but peeked from behind a curtain in time to see a white delivery van pull beneath the gate, killing its lights just before it entered the clearing. It drove around to the back of the lodge, out of Nora's field of vision. A few minutes later, light blazed from one of the windows in the lodge.

Nora brewed her coffee in the dark, not wanting to alert anyone to the fact that she was awake and watching, peering occasionally out the window, awaiting the van's reappearance. She thought she saw people moving in the trees beyond the lodge, but in the still-dark couldn't make them out and anyway, the next time she looked, they were gone.

Charlie Ennis dropped his spoon when she asked him about it.

Breakfast was oatmeal, but not the bland gray mass served up to the First Rungers. This was dense with walnuts and raisins and a generous splash of real maple syrup. It was, Nora had to admit, delicious.

'You saw a van? In the middle of the night?'

'No. Early this morning. Probably around four.'

'What were you doing up then?'

'The dog was sick. I need to remind the girls not to feed him. Could you please reinforce that?'

'Happy to. Ms Best, what exactly did you see?'

Nora signaled one of the girls for seconds of oatmeal. 'Not much. Just the van. It was weird, though – driving with no lights.'

June Ennis' knitting needles stilled. She put her latest scarf aside and lay a hand on her husband's arm.

'I asked them to, so they wouldn't wake anybody. Especially you. You've been working so hard lately.'

She picked up the mass of red-and-black yarn, pursing her lips as she counted the stitches on the needle, then nodded with satisfaction and looped the yarn anew. Within seconds, her needles were clicking away at their characteristic blur.

'It's that special hard red spring wheat flour we ordered from Seattle a few weeks ago. I meant to tell you, but I forgot. We're so far from their regular delivery route that this was the only time they could make it.'

Nora watched, her oatmeal momentarily forgotten, mesmerized by the woman's ability to talk and knit at the same time.

June cocked her head at her husband. 'Should I have woken you? If so, I'm sorry. But I just didn't have the heart.'

'You work just as hard as I do, dear. But I'm grateful.'

They beamed at one another. Nora, her own marriage having descended into perfunctory routine long before it went completely south, gazed at them with a mixture of appreciation and envy. How did people maintain that level of affection for decades?

But she had another question. 'There were some people – at least, I think there were – in the woods this morning after the van drove in. Would that have been the delivery men? What were they doing?'

June and Charlie Ennis looked at each other, shrugged, and then at Nora.

'It can't have been them,' said June. 'They were so efficient. They were here and gone in a flash.'

'Maybe a moose,' Charlie Ennis offered. 'They wander through occasionally. They're so tall. If you couldn't get a clear look, I can see how you might have mistaken one for people. I'm surprised you haven't seen one yet. Last year, one actually gave birth right behind the bunkhouse!'

Nora thought back to the shadows she'd seen, trying to assign them the shape of a moose. *Maybe. Probably.*

She was far more certain of one thing. She'd never seen the van leave.

But when she'd detoured around the back of the lodge before breakfast, it was gone.

The run of beguiling, sun-soaked days fled over the weekend.

Nora set out for the dining hall on Monday morning to an angry gray sky spitting occasional drops of what couldn't possibly be snow, she told herself, even as she ducked back into the trailer for a jacket as protection against the cutting wind. The pines bent before it, branches creaking in protest.

The girls were tense and restless at breakfast, complaining about their polo shirts that saw them arrive goose-pimpled and purple-lipped. Ennis assured them that 'Mother' would unpack winter clothing immediately after breakfast, but they remained fretful, calling for more of the oddly flavored tea, wrapping their hands around the cups and bending their faces to the steam.

Even Ashleigh, who was supposed to be celebrating her last day on First Rung, slammed her hand on the table when the girl pouring more tea passed her by.

'Come on. I'm freezing here!' she called, and the room fell

silent at the double violation – speaking during breakfast and complaining besides.

Ennis' head snapped up and he shot her a gimlet-eyed stare. She returned it, eyes narrowing.

'One more day on First Rung,' he announced, and even from the distance of the staff table, Nora could read the silent f-bomb formed by Ashleigh's lips. She caught her breath, but Ennis had pulled a pad and stubby pencil from his breast pocket and jotted a note to himself, and so missed the additional defiance that might have earned Ashleigh another whole week rather than a single day on First Rung.

The mood continued into art class, something festering beneath the surface, freed by the tiniest emotional cut or scrape, its poison oozing into view.

Sophia and Sofia got into an argument over, of all things, which was the correct spelling of their shared name that ended with Sophia yelling, 'Everyone knows what the "f" stands for, you stupid fat fuck.'

'Fat fuck is two f's. You can't even spell, bitch,' Sofia responded before Nora thrust herself between them, grabbing each girl by the scruff, barely restraining herself from giving them a good shake.

'Knock it off, both of you. Do you want to end up like her?'

Heads swiveled toward the window overlooking the clearing, where Ashleigh, bundled into a too-big parka, bent to pick up sticks and debris as a sanction for her breakfast outburst.

The unease permeated the whole program, Luke told her at lunch.

'Group today was a nightmare. All kinds of old shit, stuff I thought they were long past, bubbled up again. I was looking at the clock every five minutes, praying for it to be over.'

Nora recalled her own rose-hued imaginings of a future as a counselor. Just as she was beginning to reconsider, Luke added, 'Luckily, days like this are rare. But when they are – whew. It really takes it out of you. Times like this, I wish we had a bar nearby.'

Nora cut her eyes toward the Ennises, deep in conversation.

'What's your drinking pleasure? Wine? Whiskey? I've got both. Sorry, no beer.'

His eyes widened. 'Really? I ran out a week ago.'

'Happy to share.' She bit her lip against a grin, recalling his remark about feeling a kinship with the girls, gleefully plotting to skirt the rules. 'But I've been cautioned against even the appearance of forming, uh, friendships.'

Because friendship was all she wanted from him. Right?

'So, no casual conversations in the clearing while sipping doctored tea from go-cups, I guess.' He was already two jumps ahead of her, laying out a plot for something as simple as a drink together. 'One of the instructors has housemother duty tonight, right? How about if I come by after lights-out? And if you change your mind, just don't answer your door.'

She dipped her head in appreciation. Very mannerly of him to give her an out.

Which she didn't intend to take.

SIXTEEN

'I have so many questions.'

She and Luke sat facing one another over Electra's dinette, sipping whiskey from coffee mugs by the tiny glow of her phone charger.

He was barely more than a shadow, darkness coalesced and given form. They spoke softly, lending a sense of intimacy to an otherwise innocuous conversation. The last time she'd whispered in the dark with a man, she'd been with her old high school boyfriend. To venture into the realm of wild understatement, it hadn't ended well.

This was different, free of the sexual tension that had charged those encounters, although the possibility fizzed at the edges of her awareness. But for now, just friendship offered, friendship gratefully accepted. Not to mention that Luke was a potential font of information.

'Are we being paranoid? Sneaking around like this? We're almost as bad as the girls. In my brief experience, they're always pushing limits.'

'Come on. Don't kids push limits from the minute they're born? Not to mention probably half the adults you know.'

She thought of her husband, who'd apparently hit on every woman between twenty-two and forty in his office for years, pushing things to the limit and beyond.

'As for paranoia, can you imagine the fuss they'd make if they found out we were drinking?' He splashed a little more Jameson's into their coffee cups, binding them in a subversive pact. 'I haven't seen anything forbidding alcohol to staff, but it goes against that whole we're-here-to-set-a-good-example thing.'

Nora took a grateful swallow. 'No example seemed to work today. Yesterday, I was so taken with this place that I was actually thinking about going back to school when I'm done here, maybe getting a degree in social work or psychology. But I'm not sure I could handle many days like this.'

His shadow shifted as he leaned back against the wall and stretched his legs across the dinette seat. 'Think twice about that degree. Remember, this is the only job I could get, and I even had preferred status as a veteran. But quit kicking yourself about today. Do you honestly think it would be any different in regular high school? Or even in any household with teen-agers? They're kids on the cusp of adulthood, acting out, testing their limits. Do you have kids?'

'No.' Nora didn't bother with her usual fake regret. She wasn't sure it would register in the darkness anyway. 'You?'

'A son. Twelve. He's with his mom in Albuquerque. I see him four times a year. Charlie gives me extra time off.' The pain in his words hung spectral between them.

She leaned away from it – she'd had enough pain of her own in the last few weeks to want to take on anyone else's – and turned the subject back to the students. 'I know that all kids act out, but these girls must have been really over the top to end up in a program like this.'

The ice in his mug clinked as he took a long sip.

'Maybe. My guess is that some of them were just what you'd call a handful, in households where money always solved every issue. Got a problem child? Throw your money at Serendipity Ranch.'

Ah. They were finally getting around to the things she wanted to know.

'Define problem.'

His cup rapped softly against the table. 'That's not my place to divulge. Confidentiality is something I take seriously. But you'll find out soon enough. Charlie's called a bonfire for tomorrow night.'

The word bonfire landed with a hard edge. He stood. 'Thanks for the snort. It really helped take the edge off a tough day.'

Nora held the door for him. 'What's a bonfire?'

'Big fire, lots of wood.' He stood so close his arm brushed hers.

'Hah. Seriously. You made it sound like something official.'

'Seriously? It's sort of a reset button. Just wait. You'll see.'

Charlie Ennis announced the bonfire after dinner the next night.

'Tonight's free time is suspended.'

A groan ran around the room.

'We'll be lighting the bonfire in about half an hour.'

The girls fell silent, the ones who'd been there longer stiffening in their seats as newbies like Ashleigh looked around for an explanation that never came.

'I'm really curious about the bonfire.' Nora nudged Ennis as they followed the girls out of the dining hall. Luke's reticence, the girls' reactions, all puzzled her.

'It's a full-program session. Usually those are done in small groups. This is a way of holding each girl accountable to all the others for her past behavior, helping her to put it behind her and setting her on the path to her future success, with every girl in the program opting into every other girl's journey. It's an intense experience, so much so that we only do it a few times a year.'

He held the lodge door open for her, casting a glance at the sky, already darkening, a little earlier each evening. 'Yesterday's weather was a warning. This is probably our last chance for a bonfire this year. And it's not all serious. The girls roast marshmallows, make s'more.' He chortled. 'It's a way to lighten – pun intended – the stress of group.'

Nora liked marshmallows and s'mores as much as the next person. Still, she looked longingly toward the solitude of her trailer.

'Group?'

'As in therapy.'

Whew. An out.

'I appreciate you wanting to include me. I really do.' She really didn't. 'But when it comes to therapy, I'm not qualified. Thank you, though.'

She turned toward her trailer, anticipating with relief a night to herself. Before dinner, she'd sneaked behind the lodge for a quick phone check, only to see an email from her lawyer. 'You might want to consider some sort of settlement with Charlotte,' he'd written. 'Yes, it will cut into the insurance payout, but the cost of prolonged litigation could be prohibitive. Settling at least would give you something, albeit a far smaller amount, more quickly.'

She didn't want to settle with Charlotte, the memory of the woman fucking Nora's husband in her own house at her own goodbye party forever seared into her brain. If anything, she should be suing Charlotte! Artie's email left her spiteful and discouraged, and the last thing she wanted was to attend some sort of quasi-therapy session with a bunch of teenagers who'd never known a moment of financial insecurity in their pampered lives.

But Ennis called her back. 'Ms Best.' The smile held, but the tone was steely, an invisible trap snapping shut. 'You've proven your worth as a housemother and in the art studio. Tonight's group therapy will move you more deeply into Serendipity Ranch's program, give you more insight into the girls, make you a more effective mentor, able to better help them recover and shed their destructive behaviors. That *is* why you came here, correct? To help these girls?'

She remembered the seemingly endless stream of rejections from potential employers that had stacked up in her inbox like planes over O'Hare.

'Of course it is.' Her leg twitched, as though straining against metal teeth. 'Just let me grab a fleece. It's already getting cool.'

'See you in half an hour behind the lodge.'

SEVENTEEN

Nora had taken 'bonfire' as an exaggeration, imagining the kind of campfire she herself built, small and easily contained, just a few sticks of wood at a time.

She rounded the corner of the lodge to see flames leaping five feet into the air from a carefully constructed pyre nearly the size of a Volkswagen Beetle.

She cast a nervous glance at the forest beyond. The fire flung exuberant handfuls of sparks into the blackened sky, landing who knew where. It had been a dry summer and devastating wildfires were routine in this part of the world. She noticed several plastic gallon milk jugs filled with water among the circle of students surrounding the fire, as well as two garden hoses snaking from faucets in the rear wall of the lodge. The girls had been saving the milk jugs to make bird feeders in art class. They'd apparently been repurposed for the night. They seemed inadequate.

Queasiness mingled with curiosity at the thought of being included in some sort of group therapy session. While she couldn't imagine herself divulging anything she might hear, she'd not taken a professional oath not to betray the girls' confidences. What if she accidentally let slip something damaging? Then she laughed at herself: Who would hear it? Her world was so cloistered now that any potential damage was contained by default.

Anyway, as Ennis was always reminding her, Serendipity Ranch set the national standard for such programs. He wouldn't have invited her if there'd been anything improper about including her. And, this might give her fresh insights into the girls, who so far had talked little to her of anything other than their art projects.

The higher-rung girls hastened to take their spots on logs arranged around the fire, sitting as far away as possible from the director's chairs reserved for Ennis and June, Luke and Nora. The young instructors initially grouped together, but at a tight-lipped headshake from Loraine, spaced themselves among the girls.

Nora pushed her chair back a couple of feet. The predictable night-time chill had fallen, but the fire threw off so much heat her fleece was unnecessary.

Ennis reached beneath his chair and pulled out a bag of marshmallows, followed by a box of Graham crackers and a stack of Hershey bars. 'Girls, pass these around. You can just roast plain marshmallows if you wish, or you can make s'mores.'

Luke extracted a bundle of sticks from beneath his own chair and distributed them. He leaned toward Nora. 'We actually have long forks, but the last thing we need is to put implements of destruction in these girls' hands.'

She thought the sticks only a marginally better option – memories of Every Mother Everywhere: 'Quit waving that thing around before you put your eye out' – but kept that to herself. After all, how else was one supposed to roast marshmallows?

The girls extended their sticks, some containing two and three marshmallows, toward the fire. Beside Nora, Luke gently rotated his marshmallow above the flames, browning it evenly. She herself had always been a marshmallow-into-the-fire aficionado, yanking it out as soon as the flames caught, twirling it as it burned, then blowing it out and sucking the hot melted interior, saving the delicious contrast of the charred shell for last.

Luke glanced over and raised an eyebrow. 'Interesting.' He drew the word out mockingly, as though to pronounce judgment.

'I suppose this tells you something about me.' She slid another marshmallow onto her stick and jabbed at the flames.

He stroked an imaginary beard and delivered a diagnosis. 'Hmm. A woman in a hurry. One who knows what she wants and doesn't want to wait for it.'

Nora popped the marshmallow in her mouth and fanned herself against its blistering heat. He had no idea how very wrong he was.

'Meanwhile,' she pointed out, 'I've already had two marshmallows and your first isn't even done yet.'

'Ah, but mine –' he lifted his stick from the fire and spun it to show off the marshmallow's lovely caramel hue – 'is perfect.'

'If you call half-baked perfect. I suppose you like your eggs runny and your coffee lukewarm.'

'Better than getting burned,' he observed. A message of sorts? Had he, unlike Ennis, researched her background?

Ennis cleared his throat. He ate his marshmallows uncooked, Nora observed. Who did that?

'Shall we begin? I'm Director Ennis and I'm the founder of Serendipity Ranch. I'm here because my highest goal is to see all of you succeed in life.'

Nora nearly dropped her stick. She hadn't expected the Twelve-Step model.

'I'm Luke Rivera and I'm the counselor at Serendipity Ranch. My job is to ensure that your stay here is as short as possible.'

Ennis cleared his throat and turned toward Nora. 'Ms Best?'

I'm Nora Best and I'm here because apparently a fifty-year-old public relations specialist with some recent public relations issues of her own is unemployable.

Nora fiddled with her stick. 'I'm Nora Best and I'm a housemother here at Serendipity Ranch. I'm here because . . .'

She searched the stars overhead. Save me, she implored silently, as though expecting them to blink a coded answer her way.

'. . . because I was a teenage girl myself once.'

Ennis awarded her an unexpected nod of approval.

The girls ran through their own lines in a well-rehearsed monotone. 'I'm Graciela and I'm here because my mom went through my stuff and found E and weed.'

'I'm Sofia and I'm here because my dad walked in when I was having sex.' Pause. 'With my girlfriend.'

Snickers all around. Ennis' eyes flashed a warning.

Sophie: 'I'm here because I called my stepmom a slut when I found out she was screwing her personal trainer.'

Caroline was a self-declared shoplifter.

Jennifer ended up at Serendipity Ranch after her second abortion.

Andrea threw a party for fifty of her closest friends while her parents were away that did several thousand dollars' worth of damage to their home.

So far, so typical teenager, Nora thought, although Andrea's party went well beyond the more typical kegger in the woods. Not that their issues were insignificant, but did such troubles merit shipping a girl off to the ends of the earth and paying astronomical sums for the privilege? And what, in fact, would their money get them? A compliant, vacuously smiling daughter, back on the honor roll and on track for an Ivy League acceptance letter?

They continued their recitation, until only two were left.

Mackenzie half-rose from the log and issued a proclamation. 'I'm Mackenzie and I like to fuck.'

The girls sat up straight. Anticipatory grins ran around the circle. This was going to be good.

Nora stole a glance at Ennis, who looked as though he were about to choke on his cold marshmallow. 'Would you like to say more about your, ah, predilection, Mackenzie, and its regrettable effect on your life?'

'Only thing I regret is that now I have to give myself all those multiple orgasms instead of lying back and letting someone else do all the work.' She made a circling motion with her hand. 'Swear I've got a repetitive stress injury from running in place.'

The girls snickered audibly. 'No shit,' one whispered. Nora concealed a smile. Mackenzie had a point.

'Next girl,' Ennis snapped.

The circle turned toward Ashleigh, leaning close to catch her words.

She spoke in a breathy, wobbling rush. 'I'm here because I sent naked selfies to my dad's friend and my dad read my texts and found out that I blew him, too.'

Holy hell. That went beyond petty teenage troublemaking.

'Has he been charged? Because at the very least that's child abuse, and more likely it's rape.' Nora was on her feet, her stick abandoned on the ground.

Heads swiveled toward her.

'Mr Rivera.' Ennis' soothing voice stood in contrast to the snapping fire. 'Can you please help Ms Best understand?'

'At Serendipity Ranch, we focus on personal responsibility.' Luke scraped at the ground with the toe of his boot, addressing his words to it. 'For instance, when Sophie speaks of viciously disparaging her stepmother, is that the stepmother's fault?'

Yes, Sophie's defiant pout said. But she shook her head.

'Girls?' Ennis prompted.

'It's her responsibility to speak respectfully to her step-mother no matter what,' someone said in a singsong that fell a shade short of mockery.

'Quite right.' He looked again to Luke, who continued in a monotone.

'And when Mackenzie proclaims her fondness for sexual intercourse, whose responsibility is it to respect her body and not offer it up as a plaything?'

'Hers,' they droned.

Was Nora the only one who saw Mackenzie's middle finger twitch?

'As for Ashleigh' – the girl's head snapped up, the firelight highlighting the misery mapping her face – 'did anyone force her to send that man photos of herself?'

Nora could all too easily imagine it: the decades-older man aiming months of flattery at the vulnerable girl. And the sex – had she willingly approached him, maybe in a hallway while the rest of the family gathered at a barbecue outside, unzipped his pants, and . . . Or had he grabbed her, forced her head down, the girl too scared of *making a scene* – the thing girls and women were never supposed to do – to pull away?

The girls exchanged glances, some sort of current running through them. They'd enjoyed Mackenzie's brazen defiance, but Ashleigh's helpless quivering anguish fueled a different emotion. Once Nora had watched a pack of off-leash dogs dart across the road in front of an oncoming car, whose bumper

caught the last dog and flung him skyward,
loped back after the car sped past, circling l
helplessly in the road. Then they set upon l

The nausea that had attacked Nora then w:
now at the hard light glinting in the girls'
weakness galvanizing a feral, predatory respu..se as u.u as ..e
ages.

Sophie led off. 'No one forced you. You didn't have to
do it.'

They leaned forward, eager, mouths open, rows of perfect
teeth shining menace as each girl took a turn.

'All you had to do was say no. But sending him selfies?
That's a big, fat yes.'

'You wanted it, didn't you? Just like Mackenzie. But at least
she owns it. Admit it.'

'Admit it! Admit it! Admit it!'

The girls stomped their feet and jabbed at the air with their
sticks.

'Admit it!'

Nora's hand went to her mouth, pressing back bile. She
looked from Ennis to Luke, waiting for one or maybe both to
put a stop to the chant. Luke half-rose, but Ennis shook his
head. Luke sat back and stared at the ground, arms folded
across his chest.

'She probably liked it,' Sofia hissed. 'Glad for the attention.
Because just look at her. Only a geezer who probably wasn't
getting any from his wife would whip it out for her.'

'Shut up, you . . . you . . . carp face!' Ashleigh jumped
up and whipped her stick toward Sofia, whose permanent pout
and flat silvery eyes indeed had a fishy aspect. A melting
marshmallow spun off the stick and smacked into Sofia's face.

Sofia screamed, scraping the burning goo from her cheek.
'You fucking bitch! I'll kill you!' She charged Ashleigh, hefting
her stick like a spear.

Ashleigh fell and curled whimpering into a ball. Sofia's
sneakered feet thudded into her ribs once, twice, three times
before Mackenzie jumped on her back, wrapping her hands in
Sofia's curls and jerking her head back so forcefully Nora
feared her neck would snap. Luke shoved his way into the

pushing them apart, but not before Sofia plowed red rows down his face with her nails.

Ennis bounced on the balls of his feet, breathing hard, though he'd not left his place in the circle.

'Bonfire is over. Bonfire is over,' he squeaked, even as the fire blazed merrily, casting the girls alternately in light and shadow as they milled about, practically throwing off sparks of their own in their electric excitement.

Nora sat frozen in her seat. Luke took control.

'Girls, grab that water and douse the fire.'

The flames writhed, leaping away from the streams of water. The girls fell silent during the long moments it took for the water to subdue the blaze into hissing, glowing coals.

Ennis sank into his seat. 'Mackenzie, Sofia and Ashleigh – all of you back to First Rung. Ashleigh, starting tomorrow, you're on isolation for a week. Ms Best, please escort all three of them to the bunkhouse along with the other girls.'

It wasn't a request.

'Of course.' Even though she had no idea how to corral this restive, surging group.

'Single file.' Luke spoke so quietly that the girls fell silent, a technique Nora vowed to remember. 'Ms Best in front, followed by Mackenzie. Let's go.'

Nora moved off, holding her breath until she heard the soft footfalls behind her. Dear God, it was working.

Nora stood aside as they reached the bunkhouse, counting the girls as they filed in, Sofia with a hand to her burned cheek, Ashleigh's shoulders heaving in sobs.

Nora caught a whiff of tobacco and turned to see Luke beside her.

'Are you all right?'

She recoiled.

'You call that therapy? Victim-blaming a bunch of kids, setting them against each other? What the hell?'

He looked everywhere but at her. 'If it makes you feel any better, this sort of therapy wasn't part of my training. It's unique to Serendipity Ranch – well, years ago, it was unique. But apparently it works so well that other programs like this have adopted it.'

Nora was very, very tired of the excuses lobbed by the men around her, the alacrity with which they opted for the easy way out. Her husband and his fling with Charlotte in their own home, during their own farewell party. Her high school flame and his casual racism. Even her lawyer, urging her to settle with his ex-wife.

'Just because it works,' she snapped, 'doesn't make it right.'

Luke raised his eyes to her at last. 'There's a lot you have to learn.'

He disappeared into the darkness.

EIGHTEEN

Inside the bunkhouse, all was bedlam.

Ashleigh collapsed sobbing on her bunk, menaced by members of Sofia's posse. Other girls crammed into Nora's bathroom – an impermissible offense – where Sofia wailed into the mirror at the sight of her burned cheek.

Nora hesitated in the doorway, wondering just how quickly she could hitch up Electra and drive very fast and very far away from all of it.

She gave herself a swift mental kick in the psyche and bellowed, 'Everybody quiet or every last one of you is on isolation,' though she wasn't quite sure what offenses warranted isolation, or even exactly what it entailed.

It must have been bad, because the girls fell silent. 'And get out of my bathroom this instant.'

They got, in a great elbow-throwing, teeth-gritted scramble through her door all at once.

She put out a hand to detain Sofia. 'Let me see that. The rest of you, in your beds and lights out in five minutes flat.'

She led Sofia back into her bathroom, where the light was brighter. The girl, so defiant earlier, obligingly tilted her face.

'Will there be a scar? Will I need plastic surgery? When my mom sees this, she's going to sue the shit out of this place.'

'Language,' Nora said automatically, even as she remembered her own inner disparagement of Ennis' concerns about suit-happy parents.

She examined the girl's enviably smooth skin, suppressing an urge to harangue her to use sunscreen lest she end up with the roughened landscape that confronted Nora whenever she looked in the mirror. Then she laughed inwardly at the notion. Girls like Sofia grew up to be women who made full use of chemical peels and tiny vials of serum with prices that seemed to be calculated in terms of dollars per drop. Sofia's skin would never look like hers and – Nora examined the faint welt – today's mark would be gone within the week.

'Cold water,' she said decisively. Sophia bent obediently over the sink, rinsing again and again while Nora retrieved antibiotic cream from her Dopp kit.

'You must have ducked really fast. It barely grazed you. You'll be fine.'

Sofia stomped off to her bunk, muttering vengeance beneath her breath.

Nora took a long look around the room, doing a quick count to make sure everyone was where they were supposed to be, and switched off the light, pretending not to notice Mackenzie creeping from her bed to sit beside the last bunk until Ashleigh's tears finally subsided.

Nora fumed through much of the night, waking after a mere hour's sleep. Despite the room's chill, sweat soaked her sheets. They wrapped her legs and arms like manacles. Doubt crept in with the light leaking through the curtains.

Through her half-open door, she heard the girls moving about. She untangled herself from the sheets and peered into the bunkhouse, which looked much as it did on every other morning, girls getting dressed, brushing sleep-snarled hair with long strokes, gathering towels and toothbrushes for a trip to the bathhouse, everything in drowsy slow motion, the night's murky agitation seemingly smoothed away by the rising sun.

Maybe she'd been too hard on Luke. For sure, she had more questions for him.

But Ennis imposed silence during breakfast for staff as well as students, no matter what their rung. She trailed Luke from the dining hall, hoping to pull him aside after the meal, but he rounded the corner of the lodge, deep in conversation with Ashleigh, each of them casting quick glances over their shoulder as though hoping to avoid detection. She followed, daring a quick glance around the corner just in time to see him wrap the girl in a long hug. Nora jerked back, pressing herself against the lodge's rough log wall, breathing hard. Surely that violated every rule in the book. But what did it mean? Mere comfort? Or more?

She tried to distract herself by taking photos for the ranch's monthly newsletter. She'd turned in her first effort and decided she might as well get a jump on the second, roaming the various cabins and the lodge, clicking away as the girls worked on their art projects, sliced fruit in the kitchen, pretzeled themselves into yoga poses under the guidance of one of the instructors, and chose books from the insipid collection in the library – all designed to reassure anxious parents of their daughters' ongoing transformation into happy, healthy, *normal* girls. Even though, as far as Nora was concerned, most of the behaviors detailed at the previous night's campfire fell within the range of normal, albeit pushing the margins.

But when she turned her lens on Ashleigh, Mackenzie and Sofia silently at work on the recently delivered pile of rocks, loading them into a wheelbarrow and then taking turns trundling their ungainly burden across the clearing to the lodge, Ennis appeared in the doorway and shook his head.

'Not that,' he said.

'What are they doing?'

'Building a wall. It's part of earning their way back out of First Rung.'

'Couldn't the truck just have put the rocks over by the lodge?'

Ennis didn't bother to respond.

'Pick up the pace, girls,' he advised as he turned away. 'Ashleigh, we've set up the isolation room for you. As soon as you're done here, please report to it.'

Ashleigh and Sofia's enmity would have been obvious even

to a casual onlooker, but the girls were united in the gaze of pure loathing they directed at Ennis' retreating back.

They paused, sweat sliding down faces gone scarlet, blowing on palms scraped raw by the rocks.

'Come see me when you're done,' Nora murmured. 'I've got plenty of antibiotic ointment left. Look at Sofia's face. You can barely see a mark.'

Sofia hoisted a rock with two hands and hurled it into the wheelbarrow. It struck the others with a loud crack. Ennis turned. The girls' faces went blank.

'We wouldn't be stuck doing this if she hadn't thrown that fucking marshmallow,' Sofia whispered after the lodge door had closed behind him.

'She wouldn't have thrown the marshmallow if you'd kept your damn mouth shut in the first place,' Mackenzie reminded her.

'Both of you shut up. For all we know, he's got microphones buried out here somewhere.'

Mackenzie, Sofia and Nora all whirled in surprise at Ashleigh's suddenly assertive tone. Nora took advantage of their distraction, as well as Ennis' departure, to snap a quick, surreptitious photo, spurred by the same rebellious impulse that led to drinks with Luke and the gallons of coffee she'd consumed since being confronted with the ranch's tea.

Maybe, thought Nora as she left, the girl had hit some sort of rock bottom of despair, much as Irene Bell must have done. But if that split-second glimpse was any indication, Nora wasn't worried that Ashleigh would fling herself from some fatal height. The intensity burning in the girl's eyes was not the kind that flamed internally.

If Nora had concerns for anyone's safety at the moment, it wasn't Ashleigh's or even her own. Charlie Ennis, she thought, would do well to watch his back whenever Ashleigh was around.

But Luke had also sat silent during the Twelve Step-style confessionals at the bonfire, failing to quench the flames of the girls' accusations. What had he said to Ashleigh that morning within the confines of their surreptitious embrace that fixed the quivering point of her resentment so firmly on Ennis?

NINETEEN

Nora lurked in Electra until she saw Luke strolling from the lodge toward his cabin. She used a walk with Murph, that reliable alibi, as a pretext for interrupting him.

'Oh, hey,' she said airily, as though she hadn't been waiting for the last half-hour, Murph leashed and impatient, by the trailer door. 'We're trying to get our walk in before the storm hits.'

The wind was up, the pines bending before it, creaking and groaning in an eerie, almost-human chorus of protest. Dark clouds sped overhead, knitting together and then unraveling into wisps before regrouping. Nora zipped her jacket to her chin.

Luke fell into step beside her, but not before she caught the look he cast back over his shoulder, as though checking to see who in the lodge might be watching. 'Crazy weather,' he said. 'Typical for this time of year, though. Couple of days from now, it's supposed to feel like summer again.'

Nora didn't have time for chitchat.

She was back on duty in the bunkhouse for a second night running, and while this hour was listed as free time for both her and the girls, she knew better than to leave them to their own devices for too long.

The idea was that they were supposed to be outdoors and in view during free time, but they tended to scatter in ways that made it impossible to watch them all, a couple of groups pacing circles around the clearing, arms wrapped around themselves against the wind, others hunched on the picturesque split-rail fences that flanked the grand gate, some even balancing on the few feet of stone wall that Sofia, Ashleigh and Mackenzie were building. A few had found sheltered spots in the lee of a classroom cabin, and sat with book in hand, or simply leaned against a tree, eyes closed, faces slack, free for the moment of their characteristic wary expressions. Nora would bet their thoughts were on lives pre- or post-Serendipity Ranch.

'What's isolation?' she said without preamble.

A gust knocked him sideways and he stumbled against her. The wind snatched his apology away.

'Just what it sounds like,' he said when the trees took advantage of a lull to straighten, their branches swaying to a halt. 'Time alone – from a day to several in the worst cases – living and studying apart, no conversation with anyone, certainly no contact from home if we're talking about an upper rung girl – to give them time to settle down, to realize that whatever behavior triggered the consequence isn't worth it.'

'If Ashleigh's in isolation, why was she working on that wall with the other two?'

She watched his face carefully, alert to any change at the mention of Ashleigh's name, but saw none.

'She can do the punishment with them, but she's not allowed to talk with them, or with anyone.' Like her, he kept his voice low. 'She'll attend her classes so as not to fall behind, but she'll sit apart from the others. And she'll take her meals and sleep in a separate space.'

Nora had envisioned some sort of prison-type solitary confinement, the girl in a narrow dark room, scratching off the days with hashmarks on the wall. The scenario Luke sketched out sounded unpleasant but no worse. She decided not to mention Ashleigh's impermissible comment at the rock-pile that morning.

'About the bonfire . . .'

'What about it?'

The wind emitted a renewed shriek, sending the girls running for cover in the lee of the bunkhouse. Nora shouted above it.

'That sort of thing, the fight – does it happen often?'

He shook his head. 'There's tension, sure. But Irene's death has everyone on edge. Let's face it – every single one of these girls fantasizes about getting out of here, and not by ascending the rungs. But most don't think of taking Irene's way out. I hate the idea that they might see it as a possibility now.'

She tried to think of a tactful way to formulate her next

question. He was a psychologist after all and she, the rankest of amateurs. Still . . . 'The, uh, therapy session at the bonfire. It seemed . . .'

He moved toward the art cabin and she followed, huddling with him in the doorway. He turned to her and cocked an eyebrow. 'How did it seem?'

'I just don't get it. So what if Mackenzie likes sex? Most people do. As long as she's taking appropriate precautions against pregnancy and disease, and isn't in abusive relationships, who cares? I thought we were long past treating sexually active girls as sluts.'

She fell silent as two of the girls ran past, the wind grabbing at their hair, streaming like banners behind them.

'Another thing,' she said with renewed heat when the girls were beyond earshot. 'That business about Ashleigh choosing to send that guy photos of herself. Who knows how he talked her into it? Or even coerced her? Putting it all on her is just bullshit!'

She spoke with such vehemence that Murph, who'd been straining toward a pair of squirrels sheltering in the roof's overhang, chattering impertinently just out of reach, turned back to her. She stooped to stroke his head, still talking to Luke with her back toward him. 'You said this sort of therapy wasn't part of your training.'

'It wasn't.'

'Then why go along with it?'

'Because I'm told it works.'

She gaped at his wording. 'You're told? Don't you know?'

He rubbed a hand across his face. When he lowered it, his eyes flashed an expression so tortured it took her a moment to recall why it seemed so familiar. In Mackenzie's portrait, Irene had flashed that same look.

'And because . . . because . . . listen, Nora.'

He closed a hand around her wrist. 'There's something you need to know.'

'Ms Best! There you are!'

She turned to see Ennis hustling toward them, his white hair wafting like cornsilk over his forehead. 'Oh, hello, Mr Rivera.'

Luke dropped her wrist.

'Ms Best, I know it's your free time, but do you have just a few moments to look over our newsletter? I'd like to send it to the printer tomorrow. I think you'll be very happy to see how your design turned out.'

'Nice talking with you, Mr Rivera,' she said, deliberately formal in Ennis' presence.

She headed back toward the lodge, holding her arm – still burning from the intensity of Luke's grasp – into the suddenly welcome cool of the wind.

TWENTY

'I don't really need you to proof the newsletter tonight,' Ennis said. 'It's perfect. As I knew it would be.'

Nora had suspected his interruption was a pretext but was surprised to hear him so readily admit it.

Ennis awarded her his most cherubic smile, plump cheeks lifting so high they nearly obscured his eyes.

'A friendly reminder, Ms Best. We discourage relationships among staff, you know. It's—'

'Yes.' Nora preempted his use of the annoying phrase. 'It's in the manual. It's also been considered, at the very least, a reasonable guideline everywhere I've ever worked.'

'Of course. I wasn't assuming anything.'

Then why bring it up? 'We were having a follow-up discussion about the incident at the bonfire. I was curious about that form of therapy.' She hated calling it that. 'Along with the reasoning behind isolation. The more I learn, the more effective I can become,' she hurried to add.

A sparrow, riding the gale, thudded into the window, fluttering against it for a stunned second before tumbling from view. Nora jumped.

Ennis brushed past her to the window.

'It's all right. Addle-pated, is all. It just flew away. As to your question, isolation is something we've developed over the years. It may seem harsh at first, but trust me, isolation is effective. You see, as I may have mentioned before' – yes, ad nauseum – 'Serendipity Ranch is, for most of these children, the first time they've had to take responsibility for their actions. Faced consequences. Moved within the real world that most of us navigate every day.'

Nothing about this bears the least resemblance to the real world. Nora, mutinous, continued her mental footnoting of Ennis' lecture. She couldn't help herself. Her thoughts burst free.

'Carrying rocks? The silent treatment? And shaming a girl who quite possibly was abused by a man her father's age?'

'Consequences, Ms Best. Consequences that are lifted as soon as proper behavior returns. Believe me, no one wants them to last a moment longer than necessary. As for Ashleigh, we take her allegations very seriously. We've spoken with her privately and obtained the name of the man in question and reported him to authorities in her hometown.'

'You have?'

'Of course.' He tugged at the chain on his desk lamp, the sudden warm glow chasing away the storm's ominous darkness. 'Can you imagine a more disturbing situation? Ashleigh's outburst merits sanctions. Consistency is one of the most important precepts. But all of us – myself, Luke and Mother – are being especially watchful with her, now that we know of her possible trauma. I'm assuming I can count on you, also?'

Nora's tension fled in a gusting sigh. The bonfire had singed her growing enthusiasm for Serendipity Ranch's program. Ennis' words acted as a soothing balm. 'I hope that goes without saying. Anything I can do to help.'

He took both her hands in his, gazing at her with such warmth that tears threatened.

'Ms Best. You have no idea what a help you've already been. You can't see it yet, but the girls truly respect you. The day I stumbled across your resume was a lucky one for Serendipity Ranch.'

The dopamine rush of praise flooded Nora's synapses, washing away her curiosity about whatever Luke had been trying to tell her. She went to bed that night full of renewed determination to excel at her job.

Nora rolled over and reached for her phone.

The numbers glowing there confirmed what the utter blackness had already told her. Dawn was still hours away.

She lay a moment, wondering what had awakened her. The wind still moaned through the trees, low and intermittent now, as though exhausted by its own early fury.

That must have been it. That, or Murph. He was not a small dog, but snored like something larger still, in satisfied and stentorian blasts that more than once had roused her from a sound sleep. Or maybe it was the disorientation of being back in Electra after the previous night in the bunkhouse. Or even the constant unsettled emotional current sparking and crackling like a faulty electrical connection just below the surface of her awareness, even as she strove for the steadiness that this year was supposed to provide.

She placed the phone face-down on the nightstand, glad that it was only two in the morning, plenty of time to lull herself back to sleep and wake reasonably ready to face another day of challenges.

But no. There it was, an unmistakable tappity-tap-tap, too deliberate to be one of the errant pinecones that sometimes struck the trailer, cracking like gunshots against its aluminum surface. Murph awoke in mid-snore, snuffling into alertness, head up, body quivering. The cat stretched and yawned, and pressed a paw into Nora's side, claws extended in languid preparation for battle, if need be.

Nora sat up and felt for the tumbler of water she kept by the bed. She took a swallow, hoping to clear her head.

Had one of the girls slipped from the bunkhouse, holding her breath as she tiptoed past Mother Ennis' open door? It seemed unlikely. Nora imagined the woman, despite her age, spending a wakeful night propped against the pillow, knitting needles clicking a pointed warning at any would-be escapees.

A raccoon, scavenging for food or just as likely in this wild and isolated part of the world, a bear? No, Murph would have lost his mind by now, instead of crankily nudging the cat aside with his nose and settling into a more comfortable position, one that took up even more of the bed.

She hooked a finger in the shade, pulling it an inch away from the window. A dark form, features indistinguishable, leaned against her door.

She gasped and let the shade drop, memory of that first night assailing her, the men in the forest, the insolent hands roaming her body. What if Ennis had hired security again after the bonfire incident and neglected to tell her?

'Nora? Nora, are you awake?'

Oh, for Christ's sake.

She jumped from bed and stomped to the door, flinging it open, hissing into the darkness.

'Luke. What in the world?'

TWENTY-ONE

She reached for the light, but he beat her to it, snatching her hand and pulling it away. The wind grabbed the door and slammed it shut behind him.

'I'm sorry. I'm sorry. I just . . .' His voice cracked. 'Got any more of that whiskey?'

She hesitated, her internal warning system pulsing scarlet. Their earlier companionable drink in the soft darkness of early evening, resulting from an invitation issued and accepted, was one thing. But this?

'Let me check,' she said. She yanked open a drawer, feeling for a knife.

'You keep your whiskey in a drawer?' His voice leveled out, icy, clipped.

She laughed weakly, even as she palmed a paring knife and lay it silently on the counter behind her, within easy reach.

'Sorry. I'm only half-awake. Maybe coffee instead of whiskey?' Something that would require filling the pot, finding the filter, measuring out the coffee with its reassuring fragrance that recalled morning's brightness, preparation that would consume enough time for her to formulate an escape. Maybe throw the hot java in his face and make a run for it?

Murph, normally her first line of defense, had fallen traitor-ously back into cacophonous slumber as soon as he recognized Luke.

Nora banged cabinet doors open and shut, making a show of searching, hoping against hope that the racket would somehow carry to the bunkhouse, to an instructor's cabins, all the way to the lodge, a sound so strange and unexpected in the middle of the night that any reasonable person would come running.

If only any reasonable person could hear over the wind's keening.

'Here it is,' she said finally, when Luke failed to take the hint about coffee. She splashed a little whiskey into a mug, some sloshing onto her hand in the darkness.

'Here.'

He downed it in one gulp. 'More.'

Nora obliged, pouring more carefully this time. Would it be better to fill the mug in the hope that he'd drink it and pass out? Or would that make him more dangerous, loosen inhib-itions clearly on hiatus given this middle-of-the-night . . . what, exactly?

She bent her head to her hand and licked the whiskey from it, wanting badly to tilt the bottle directly into her mouth, knowing she didn't dare. Whatever was happening, she'd need her wits about her.

Luke drank more slowly this time. She still couldn't read his expression but as her eyes adjusted to the dark, she saw the defeated slump of his shoulders, his chin drooping nearly to his chest.

When he spoke again, he addressed the floor, his words barely audible. 'I have a favor to ask. Please don't think of me as some sort of perv.'

Too late for that, buddy.

'Barging into a woman's trailer at two in the morning and demanding alcohol makes you *not* a perv?'

'I know it looks bad.'

She cut him off. 'It doesn't just look bad. It *is* bad.'

'I know. I know. But I've had the worst day. Worse than anything in Iraq. Worse than when my wife told me she was leaving and taking our son with her.'

Nora's hand, still sticky with whiskey, went to her throat. 'Did something happen with one of the girls?'

'Yes – no. Not exactly. No.'

She sucked in air and reached behind her for the knife, gripping its slender handle as though somehow the very action would steady her next words.

'You should probably go now.'

He extended his hands in a plea, the gesture more felt than seen in the darkness.

'Nora. I'm not here to hurt you or to ask anything from you. No. That's wrong. I want to ask one thing. Please, please, let me stay here awhile. Just let me lie down until my head clears.' He pushed past her and collapsed onto the bed without waiting for permission. 'Just an hour or two. Look, we'll keep Murph between us. I just. I just . . .' His voice faded. Was that a sob?

She heard a soft lapping. Murph, licking at Luke's face. The dog had an unerring bullshit detector. If Luke so much as twitched the wrong way, Murph would tear his throat out.

Still clutching the knife, she lowered herself on the dog's other side, her body rigid, calves tensed, ready to leap from the bed.

Luke whispered something.

'What?'

'Your hand. Would you give me your hand?'

She closed her eyes and reached across Murph's body. He took her hand, pressing it briefly to his cheek before twining his shaking fingers in hers.

'Thanks,' he whispered. 'Don't let go of me. Please don't let go.'

When she next opened her eyes, Luke was gone and light leaked through the shades.

She reached for Murph and found only space. She lifted her head to see him sprawled at her feet and then she remembered.

At some point in Luke's brief time in her bed, Murph had eased away from them and Luke rolled toward her, spooning so naturally, the arm around her so gentle that she felt sheltered rather than threatened and so nestled against him and, improbably, fell asleep.

Now she lay wide-eyed, trying to process it.

Either something terrible had happened to Luke, or he'd heard some terrible news. Either way, he'd turned to her for succor. Which meant . . . what?

Still more confusing, despite her initial flash of fear, she'd liked it. She'd forgotten how deeply comforting it could be to simply sleep with someone – and she was going to have to spend every one of the next forty-eight hours with that someone.

With a forecast promising a brief return to mild weather before winter truly swept in, Ennis had scheduled an overnight hike as a way to defuse any lingering tensions from the campfire. She and Luke would be sleeping within feet of one another, their only barrier the thin polyester walls of their tents. They'd be surrounded by dozens of people. But a warm wave of reassurance, mixed with confusion, washed over her at the thought of such proximity.

Luke had been frightened into desperation because of something involving one of the girls. Maybe she could get him alone during the hike and persuade him to talk about it. She dressed in a hurry and headed for the lodge, where Ennis had called a pre-hike staff meeting. She grabbed a whole-grain muffin dense with wheat germ and took a seat across the semicircle from Luke. His hair was still wet from the shower and he'd shaved, the turmoil of the previous night seemingly erased. He held his face immobile, but his eyes flashed quick gratitude toward Nora and she crinkled the corners of her own in response.

'Most of you have participated in our hikes before,' Ennis said. He paused and sipped at a mug of the vile tea, glancing at Nora. 'For those who haven't, it's a way of putting the girls in situations where they have to cooperate – setting up camp, preparing meals, cleaning up afterward and the like. Hard physical activity in the out-of-doors is the best cure for nearly all ills. I assure you, they'll return a different group of girls.'

Nora averted her eyes from his plump form, wondering just how long it had been since he'd followed his own prescription.

Nora, while skeptical about the ability of anything at all to soften the willfulness of teenage girls, hoped the hike would work Ennis' promised magic on her as well. She'd always loved the solitude of the wilderness, the way that, but for her own footsteps, the sounds of humanity fell away, leaving only birdsong and the wind soughing through the pines.

But her most recent hike had been a march at knifepoint after being kidnapped from her trailer in the middle of the night, stabbed, pushed from a bluff, and left to die. She touched her hand to her side, rubbing the scar as though a talisman, reminding herself that she'd survived. Maybe this hike would cancel out the lingering bad karma from that ordeal.

Ennis did a quick head count, assigning the adults three girls each for whom they'd be responsible.

'If one girl acts out and all the adults respond, the others might take advantage of the distraction,' he explained.

And do what? Nora wondered. Scatter into the impenetrable wilderness? Her skepticism must have shown on her face.

'You'd be surprised,' Ennis said. 'Disagreements, jealousies – you got a taste of it at the bonfire – can bubble up during an extended time together without the diversion of classwork or art projects. Think of it as the hot compress that's applied to bring a boil to a head before lancing it – fresh air and exercise serving, in this case, as the scalpel. Whatever painful situations might erupt on the trail or in camp, everyone will come back refreshed and ready to start anew.'

Nora suspected they'd also come back tired and dirty but kept that thought to herself.

'There's always an inherent risk when you remove them from their daily environment. Don't worry. Just be watchful. You're free to go now. The girls are waiting.'

Nora wrapped the remnants of her muffin in a napkin and sneaked it into a trash can on her way from the room.

But Ennis beckoned her aside and, out of earshot of the others, said something that made the world go dark.

TWENTY-TWO

'What? *What?*'
'Lower your voice.'
Ennis spoke under his breath.

'I'm counting on you, Ms Best. This information just came to us last night, too late to call off the hike. Besides, Luke is our most experienced outdoorsman, and he also has the EMT experience from his time in the military. It's one of the reasons we hired him. He needs to be on the hike. But don't leave him alone with any of the girls, especially not one-on-one.'

Nora looked wildly around, trying to ground herself in the mundane everydayness of a morning that had turned out anything but.

The girls stooped over packs laid in a row on the ground, or tightened laces on clumsy hiking boots as the instructors stood by, giving advice that as far as Nora could tell was largely being ignored.

Luke stood off to one side. He hefted his pack, frowned, and dropped it to the ground, opening it and rearranging its contents.

'I thought he was involved with Carolee,' Nora protested. She suddenly, devoutly wanted that earlier possibility, seemingly so remote upon her rudimentary investigation, to be true.

'We thought he was, too. That may have been some sort of smokescreen. Legally, I'm not allowed to tell you anything. Let's just say we're looking into . . . reports.'

Reports, multiple. Jesus.

'But he meets with students. The counseling sessions!'

'Group, mostly, thank heavens. Going forward, if there's a need for one-on-one, we'll mandate that he leave his door open and either Mother or I will be nearby.'

Nora cast another glance at Luke. He strapped himself into his pack, took a couple of steps and gave a satisfied nod.

Revulsion iced her body, only moments before still languid with the contentment of their chaste embrace.

So that's why he'd banged at her door in the middle of the night demanding alcohol. He'd just been accused of molesting a child, a career-killer for just about anyone, but especially for a counselor working with teenage girls.

He'd seemed so nice. But wasn't that how predators worked, slithering into positions of trust, all those priests and coaches and Scout leaders, the ones about whom – when a child finally pointed a trembling finger – people said, 'Oh, no. He could never. He's *too nice.*'

Of course his embrace had been platonic. She was a few decades beyond being his type.

She thought back to her first day in the art room, the girls smashing Sofia's 'mushroom' sculpture, gleefully at first, then with increasingly grim determination. No wonder.

'How can you possibly keep him on in this situation?'

The lines in Ennis' face deepened. His lips tightened. 'Believe me, if it were up to me, he'd have been sent packing last night. Our lawyer was quite clear we're obligated to do a thorough investigation. Otherwise . . .' He rubbed his fingers together, signifying once again, his fear of a punitive lawsuit.

Nora thought that a lawsuit from the parents of an abused girl might be equally, if not more, ruinous, but figured that possibility had already been taken into consideration.

'I saw him with Ashleigh,' she blurted. 'Hugging.'

Just as he'd hugged her, only a few short hours earlier.

'Hug' sounded so innocuous now, given what Ennis had just told her. Had it been that sort of hug? A quick, familial clasp? Or something more, grinding his body into the girl's as she stood frozen within his filthy embrace? Another grown man, just like Ashleigh's father's friend, unerringly sniffing out the most vulnerable girl, the one who wouldn't tell?

'When did you see this? Where? We need to document everything.'

'Yesterday morning, right after breakfast. I didn't say anything because . . .'

Why?

Because her own nascent attraction to the man spurred an

unwillingness to believe what her eyes told her? The very sort of disbelief that led adults everywhere to let victims down?

Ennis patted her arm. 'The important thing is that you told me. The few of us who know about this – myself, Mother, and now you, and of course the girl involved – are all engaging in self-flagellation. We all think – thought – so highly of Mr Rivera. In our eyes, he was the father figure so many of these girls lacked. Safe to say that we're all in shock.'

Nora thought back to when she'd been hired, the way Ennis seemed ignorant of her recent troubles, and wondered if Luke's own employment process had been equally cursory. No, she told herself, a police check would be mandatory for a psychologist. Maybe this was Luke's first offense – or, as these things tended to be, the first *reported* offense.

Ennis' hand was still on her arm. He gave it a reassuring squeeze. 'I'd have canceled the hike if it weren't for your presence. Besides, canceling would have signaled to the girls that something is wrong.'

'But something *is* wrong.'

'So wrong.' His voice broke and he took a moment to compose himself. 'We're dealing with the lesser of two evils here by opting to act normally rather than impose a break in routine that might further upset the girls. I have complete faith in your ability to protect them for the next two days. We're moving as fast as we can with this. We hope to have it wrapped up shortly after you return.'

He nodded toward the group. The girls bent beneath their packs and fell into line behind two of the instructors, who wore their own bulky packs – their faded colors and duct-tape patches a testament to frequent use – with ease. 'You'd better get going. I hope I wasn't wrong to say anything. I'd been warned not to discuss it with anyone, but it seemed unfair to keep it from you.'

'I appreciate it,' Nora whispered. 'Thank you for confiding in me.'

She swung a day pack onto her back. The hike would be an overnight event, and the girls all carried true backpacks. But her belongings were divided among First Rungers Ashleigh, Mackenzie and Sofia.

At the sight of the girls bent under their unwieldy loads, Nora opened her mouth to protest. But Luke shook his head almost imperceptibly.

She drew back, not wanting to engage with him, given what she'd just heard. Her gut twisted. She scanned the girls ahead of her. Which one? Or ones, given Ennis' initial reference to more than one report? And what had happened? Insinuating comments? Fondling? Rape?

She tried to hurry ahead of the group as they set out, but Luke caught up with her, chatting easily, his middle-of-the-night torment seemingly forgotten, at least on the surface. Sidelong glances revealed the telltale signs – a grayish tinge to his skin, a muscle setting the flesh along his jawline aquiver, a blankness to his gaze.

Fury flashed through her at the memory of how easily he'd manipulated her, showing up at her door, hinting something had happened with one of the girls, where in reality he'd been the thing that had happened.

She set her own face, trying to keep her disgust from showing as he spoke.

'It's just a short hike. We'll only go five miles today.'

She thought back to their conversation that day in the woods, when he'd dodged her question about the boot camp aspect of Serendipity Ranch and had mentioned that western states were more lax when it came to regulating such programs. Now she wondered, Is that why you're here?

She bit her lip against the question.

They walked in silence for several yards. She sensed him glancing at her every few steps. She dredged up a less freighted question, even as she wondered how the hell she'd feign interest in a single thing he said for the length of the hike. The marks on his cheek from Sofia's fingernails were fading. Nora now wished Sofia had done far worse.

'What good does it do to add the extra weight to the First Rungers' packs?'

'It's just like the oatmeal at breakfast. Move up a rung, get a lighter pack. And so on.'

He walked staring at his feet, his steps deliberate, almost a stomp, each raising a puff of dust from the trail. He seemed not to think much of the rung system, but then, he wouldn't. That sort of discipline and near-constant surveillance must have made it more difficult for him to take advantage of the girls. She vowed not to let him out of her sight for the whole hike, even if it meant surreptitiously following him into the bushes on pee breaks. She sucked in a breath and reminded herself for the fiftieth time to act normal. Still, she couldn't keep a waspish sting from her voice.

'I still don't see how any of this jibes with the concept of positive reinforcement?'

'I suppose you could consider all of those rewards as positive.'

Not exactly a ringing endorsement. Nora looked at Ashleigh and Mackenzie and Sofia, struggling to keep up with the rest of the girls, and wondered if the positive really outweighed the negative. Luke's next words erased such theoretical concerns, and even – briefly – supplanted her queasiness at the length of their conversation.

His steps slowed, letting some distance open between them and the girls. She reluctantly slowed hers to match his, though keeping well to her side of the trail, to avoid even accidentally brushing against him.

'The extra weight will be the least of their worries today. This trip could be tough emotionally on some of the girls, especially Ashleigh. But some have asked about it, and we feel they need it for closure.'

'What do you mean?'

'We'll be visiting the spot where Irene Bell died.'

TWENTY-THREE

To Nora's relief, Luke didn't take many pee breaks. Which was good, because dealing with the girls required the full attention of all the adults.

The hike that was supposed to fill their lungs with fresh air and suffuse their spirits with the wonders of the great outdoors quickly devolved into a series of complaints and accusations.

'She's walking too close behind me.'

'Jenny keeps pulling on my pack. Make her quit.'

'I'm getting a blister. Can we stop?'

And the inevitable: 'Are we there yet?'

'You know we're not. And you know exactly how long we've got left. You've been here before.'

Luke dealt with the whining far more quickly and effectively than Nora, responding patiently to each new gripe, deflecting the girls' attention away from the misery of the moment and onto something positive.

She wanted to scream a warning as he engaged them, quizzing them on the fall wildflowers and the names of the various shrubs and trees, promising an extra serving of dinner to whomever got the most right. But unless the girls were far more skilled actors than she realized, none gave any indication of the loathing she felt.

When the grievances reached a crescendo, Loraine Whaley, the head instructor, called a break. Luke shrugged out of his pack and drew a store of power bars from it. From the girls' sudden enthusiasm – 'Chocolate? For real? Not that carob shit? Oops, sorry, I mean crap. Er, stuff.' – Nora gathered they were a forbidden treat. Was this how he lured them into his clutches, power bars the modern-day equivalent of nylon stockings and perfume?

But still she saw no wariness among the girls, who continued to lob questions his way after they arrived at their campsite.

'Mr Rivera, she's setting up the tent wrong. Can you help us?'

'Mr Rivera, could you show us how to do that tepee thing again to make a fire? Ours won't start.'

'Mr Rivera, would you like an apple or an orange after dinner?'

He wordlessly showed them how to fit the tent poles together and slide them through the tabs in the fabric; then collected dry twigs and built the miniature cone filled with duff that guaranteed a successful fire.

And he requested both an apple and an orange though Nora later saw him swiftly and surreptitiously toss one to Mackenzie and the other to Ashleigh. Because he felt sorry for them as First Rungers? Or because they were his intended prey? Nora moved closer to the girls as they ate.

They'd stopped for the night in a small clearing hemmed with leaning pines. A narrow stream chortled at its far side. The girls made several trips to it, always in pairs and always with one of the adults, pumping water in filter bottles.

Beyond the clearing, the forest stretched endlessly, north across the nearby Canadian border, west into Idaho. During their hike they'd followed a trail cut through stands of doghair pines, skinny young trees growing so close together as to form barriers impervious to anything but a chainsaw. Every few years, Ennis told her, a foolish girl took off into the forest, head full of romantic notions about surviving in the wilderness.

'We mount an immediate search, of course. Conditions are just too dangerous. The trail is only a few miles long, and if they leave it, they could find themselves hopelessly lost within minutes. But invariably, when we find them, they've already turned around, stumbling back to us, tired and dirty and hungry and cold. We've been very fortunate. Until Irene Bell's terrible choice, we'd not lost a single girl.'

Dinner was hot dogs – vegetarian, of course – and canned baked beans, not even brand-name but the generic store variety. Nora was surprised, given what she'd learned about Serendipity Ranch's jaw-dropping tuition fees. At the very least, she'd expected those fancy freeze-dried meals that cost an arm and a leg and frequently tasted of cardboard but had the advantage of being easy to prepare and even easier to clean up.

That said, the franks and beans were at least flavorful and nearly as easy when it came to preparation, and the girls worked swiftly and silently, with only the occasional elbow-jab and hissed imprecation, during dinner prep and serving. They ate from paper plates that later went into the fire, and plastic utensils, which would be packed back out in accord-ance with leave-no-trace practices. It seemed wasteful to Nora, but she supposed metal tableware was viewed with the same sort of suspicion at Serendipity Ranch as it was by airlines and prisons, given its potential nefarious uses.

After clean-up, the girls – still barely speaking – paired up to hoist their packs high into the trees, away from bears in the midst of their fall feeding frenzy, bulking up before the long months in hibernation. There was a strained quality to their quietude and when they'd finished with the packs, they stood in awkward groups, shuffling their feet and looking everywhere but at one another.

Luke and Loraine stood, exchanged glances, and nodded. Luke raised his voice.

'Everybody ready? Good. It's time to remember Irene. Let's douse the fire and get going. We don't want to be walking back in the dark.'

This time he led the group, moving quickly up the trail, which began a steep climb up a series of switchbacks that made Nora wish she hadn't eaten seconds at dinner. She estimated they'd gone about a half mile, when Luke held up his hand.

They'd reached a bluff with a steep drop-off. The stream that had burbled so prettily beside their campsite was a rushing torrent below. Nora shoved her shaking hands into her pockets. The site was entirely too similar to the one from which she'd been shoved after being stabbed.

Breathe in, she told herself. *Breathe out. It's daylight – albeit barely. You're with other people. No one here is going to hurt you.*

Thankfully, the girls were too intent upon their own mission to notice her agitation. They lined up near the edge of the bluff and pulled nubs of candles from their pockets, holding them mutely away from their bodies. Luke walked down the row, setting each wick aflame with a cigarette lighter. Nora fingered the water bottle dangling from her belt, wondering if it would be enough to quench a fire, should anyone drop a candle. Ashleigh was already sniffling, doing her best to hold in full-blown sobs.

'We gather tonight in memory of our beloved Irene,' Luke said, his voice cracking.

Suspicion raised the hairs on Nora's arms. *Beloved.* She made a mental note to tell Ennis about Luke's terminology.

Was Irene the girl he'd harassed? Is that why none of the other girls seemed particularly bothered by speaking with him? And more to the point, and worse still, was Irene's death indeed a suicide, as Ennis had characterized it?

She directed a death stare at Luke, who stood before them intoning sanctimonious shit like someone who gave a good goddamn.

'I invite anyone who'd like to say a few words to step forward,' he said.

'But not too close,' Loraine added.

The girls offered the sort of bland, monotone praise that might be expected for someone with whom they'd had such a brief acquaintance. Their candles flickered against the fast-advancing darkness, illuminating their soft young faces.

'She helped me with my math homework.'

'She was kind.'

'She was funny.'

A voice rose above the rest. 'She didn't deserve to be here! And she should never have died this way! She was terrified of this place!'

The other girls clustered around Ashleigh, shushing her. 'You're still on isolation,' Mackenzie reminded her. 'You can't be talking.'

'I won't shut up! You all know it's true. Why won't you admit it? Look how far down that is! Can you imagine her jumping?'

Nora forced herself to walk to the edge and look into the gorge. The drop was high – easily high enough to kill someone – although several outcroppings offered a possible way down for a cautious climber.

She looked again. Saw color, a patch of electric blue at odds with the green of forest, the slate gray of the rushing stream. Was that . . .?

'Hey!' she called to the group. 'Hey!'

They turned as one to look. But forgetting her vow to keep Luke in sight at all times, she was already scrambling down, holding onto branches, feeling with her feet for the next ledge.

Ashleigh screamed, short and sharp.

'Nora!' She glanced up to see Luke leaning over the edge,

watching her, along with several of the girls. 'Nora, what are you doing? Come back!'

Nora kept going, sliding the last few yards, leaving long strips of skin on the rocks, somersaulting and landing face-first next to what had looked from the bluff like the body of a woman bobbing half-in, half-out of the water, and upon her tumbling arrival turned out to be exactly that.

TWENTY-FOUR

S hrieks sounded above.
Nora, barely able to breathe, scrambled backward away from the body and tripped, toppling into the creek's frigid rush.

She crawled out, gasping and shaking, just as Luke landed beside the body. He pushed himself to his feet, then held out a hand. She took it, forgetting he was the enemy, and together they stared at the woman lying face down before them, her broken body contorted, her neck at an impossible angle. Her curly chestnut hair lay in tangled strings across her face, obscuring her features.

'It looks like . . .'

Luke released Nora's hand and approached the body carefully. He knelt beside it and pressed two fingers, first to her neck, then her wrist.

'Don't touch her! This might be a crime scene.' Nora's experiences in Wyoming, unwelcome though they were, had taught her a thing or two.

'Sorry. Habit. Even though it's obvious she's . . . Anyway, I'm a medic. Or was, in Iraq.'

He retrieved a stick from the litter of detritus tossed up by the stream. 'I have to be sure of something.' He touched the stick to the woman's forehead and swept her hair back from her face, revealing empty eye sockets and a partially chewed-away nose within the ghastly pallor of what was left of her face.

'God. I was afraid of that.' He dropped the stick and turned away, retching.

Nora looked up and saw a line of faces peering over the rim. 'Ms Best! Mr Rivera! What's happening?'

They'd left the girls alone with just the young instructors.

'We've got to get back up there.' Nora eyed her haphazard route down, considerably more intimidating as a climb.

'You go first. That way, if you start to fall, I can catch you.'

'I won't fall.' Despite their recent hand-clasp, Nora shuddered at the thought of his hands on her body, something she took as a sign she was getting past the initial shock.

'Just give me a minute.' He bent, hands on his knees, and gagged again. When he straightened, his eyes were wet. 'It's Carolee.'

The trip back up the bluff felt interminable. Despite her silent vow to avoid his help, a thin branch Nora grasped gave way and only Luke's swift grab, hooking his fingers in one of her belt loops as she started to slide past him, saved her from a second plunge to the streambank.

Above them, the girls wailed.

When Luke boosted her over the lip of the bluff – at this point, she'd ceased to care whether he touched her – they clustered close, clinging to her.

'It's Ms Hanford, isn't it?' Mackenzie demanded. 'That's her favorite shirt. We all made them one day in art workshop.'

Nora pulled away briefly and glanced over the edge, the bright tie-dyed pattern of the woman's shirt barely visible in the gloaming.

'I never met her,' she hedged.

'Mr Rivera?' The girls turned as one, reading their answer in his gray face. 'Oh, Mr Rivera.' They abandoned Nora and hurried to him, in those few steps casting aside the need for their own reassurance and instead showering him with sympathy.

'We're so sorry. Are you all right? Of course you're not. How can we help?' The spirit of cooperation and empathy that had eluded them so far was suddenly on full display –

ironically bestowed, Nora thought, upon the person least deserving of it.

'Thanks. I appreciate that. But we'd better take care of her.'

Ashleigh curled on the ground, clutching her arms to her chest, rocking and moaning.

Nora hadn't even noticed her absence. She rushed to the girl, berating herself for her inattention, and squatted beside her, lifting her a little and cradling her.

'Shhhh. Shhhh.'

She couldn't think of a single thing to say that wouldn't offend.

It'll be all right.

How could it? A woman was dead.

You're safe.

Was she? Were any of them? They were five miles from the ranch, full dark now, with a corpse nearby and a mass of girls, already deeply troubled, spinning fast toward frenzy.

Luke's voice, deep and authoritative, interrupted her skittering thoughts.

'Let's head back to camp. Get your packs down from the trees. Break down your tents and pack them up. We're hiking out.'

A predictable hubbub of panicked objections arose.

'But it's dark. It's so far.'

Loraine backed him up. 'We're lucky that it's a clear night. We can see well enough to get back to camp. Each of you has a headlamp in your pack. As soon as you get your packs down, get your lights out, turn them on, then break down your tents and let's get going. The quicker we get on the trail, the better.' She clapped her hands, the abrupt noise seeming to startle them into order.

Luke sidled close to Nora. 'I've got an emergency beacon. I've already activated it. But if we move quickly, we'll be home by the time the sheriff can scramble a search crew. The quicker we can get these girls home, the better. I'll help them pack up the tents. You stay with Ashleigh. And for God's sake, don't let on that you're scared.'

'Aren't you?'

He drew a quick, sharp breath. 'Yesterday, I was as scared

as I've ever been in my life. Now that looks like nothing by comparison.'

The girls moved like automatons as Luke took charge.

'Single file, and even though we've got headlamps, I want each of you holding onto the pack of the person in front of you. I don't care if it takes us until morning, we're going to get home safely. Loraine, you take the lead. Carmen, in the middle,' he said to another instructor. 'Ms Best and I will take up the rear.'

He turned to Nora and whispered, 'I want Ashleigh between us. I'll go in front of her, you behind her.'

It made sense, Nora thought, even as she mentally probed Luke's eminently practical plan for some heinous purpose. He shouldered Ashleigh's heavy pack as the girls fell into line. Ashleigh sobbed so hard she could barely stand. Nora took the girl's hand and folded it around one of the straps of the big pack Luke now carried. She moved behind her and grabbed a handful of Ashleigh's sweatshirt.

'Let's go,' she said softly. 'I've got hold of you. We'll do this together.'

The line began its halting progress, headlamps bobbing like a string of pearls against the velvety blackness of the forest all around them.

TWENTY-FIVE

The sheriff's team and the EMTs milled outside the lodge as the girls straggled into the clearing.

A rosy haze suffused the sky, its loveliness incongruous given the inevitable grimness of the coming day.

The instructors headed off en masse to Loraine's cabin. The girls stopped in front of the bunkhouse. They stared silent and hollow-eyed at Nora. They were on an emotional knife-edge, in danger of tipping into hysteria with the slightest remark.

Nora took a breath and stepped into her still unfamiliar role.

Give them things to do, she reminded herself. Keep them busy with manageable tasks. Help them return to normalcy – as much as possible under the circumstances – by degrees.

'Pick those packs up and dust them off. Bring them inside but put them on the floor beside your bunks when you unpack them. Don't get dirt all over your bunks.' Tiny, meaningless details, but better to focus on keeping their bunks clean than flashing back to the horror they'd so recently witnessed.

She'd noted the stretcher poles, the folded body bag, to the side of the sheriff's group. The fewer girls who saw those, the better.

She talked on, hoping to keep them distracted with orders upon orders. 'They weren't planning on us being here for breakfast. Mackenzie, you and' – she fished for a name and made a wild guess – 'Jen, please go to the lodge and ask them to put together brown bags of fruit and cheese and bread, and to send along some juice and cups. Tell them I sent you. We'll eat picnic-style in the clearing. The rest of you, after you're finished unpacking, please go wash up while we're waiting for food.'

Ashleigh had finally stopped crying, but her zombie-like state was no improvement. At some point on the endless walk back, Mackenzie had broken ranks to walk beside her, speaking soothingly all the while, nonsense phrases mostly, but just enough to distract the girl from the despair sucking her into a mental void.

Nora called to the group of instructors, crooking a finger to summon one of them back. 'Stay with Ashleigh,' she whispered when the young woman came over. 'I'm going outside to talk with the director.'

The search group had coalesced around Luke and Ennis.

'I take it there's no need for Life Flight?' one of the deputies asked Luke.

'Afraid not, Jim.'

So they knew each other. Nora wondered if Jim would be so friendly when he found out about Luke.

Luke turned to Ennis and said something under his breath. Nora strained to make sense of it.

The deputy sheriff called to him. 'Be better if you could come with us.'

Luke's shoulders sagged and pity briefly gnawed at Nora's heart. He'd been up for twenty-four hours already and was looking at at least another half-day on the trail and back.

Ennis answered for him. 'That's a good idea. Ms Best, I'll need you in the office.'

She followed him, but craned her neck for a backward glance at Luke, whose muttered comment to Ennis had finally sunk in.

'It's Carolee,' he'd said, before lowering his voice. 'Are you surprised?'

Nora stood before Ennis like a recalcitrant pupil in the principal's office, albeit one who was dog-tired, grubby from the trail, and desperately in need of a shower, food and the oblivion of sleep that would erase, at least for a few hours, the grotesquerie of the previous night.

She thought of the coffee waiting in her trailer, not to mention Mooch and Murph. Before the hike, she'd entrusted one of the young instructors with her key and a note on when and how much they needed to be fed, and Murph's schedule of potty breaks and walks. She couldn't wait to stretch out on her own bed, Murph snoring heavily beside her and Mooch purring at her head.

Ennis informed her otherwise.

'We need to get ahead of this. Write a new letter to parents. Figure out how to keep the press at bay.'

Nora stopped mid-sniff of her clothing – was that really her own funk? – and gawked.

'Keep them at bay?' In her unfortunate experience, nothing kept reporters at bay; in fact, any hint of avoidance usually brought them sniffing around like scavengers on the scent of roadkill.

'We can't have any publicity about this. It's not newsworthy. Another suicide is clearly a private matter. Especially since Ms Hanford was no longer our employee.'

'But how do you know it's suicide?'

'Ms Best.' He spoke slowly and carefully, as though to a none-too-bright student. 'You found her in the exact spot where a student had taken her own life. Ms Hanford and Irene Bell were very close. Irene trusted her, looked up to her. It had to be a terrible blow to lose the girl. And then, the more I think about it, the more I believe Carolee must have found out that her own supposed relationship with Luke was a sham. She may have had an inkling of his alleged abuse of the girls. You saw that email. "I can't anymore." Clearly she was in despair.'

Nora folded her arms. 'Respectfully, I have to disagree with this plan. Why put a letter out now before the news even becomes public? What if it never does? Why don't we just wait and see?'

He favored her with a pitying look. 'Some of the higher-rung girls are allowed contact with their families. We monitor all their communications carefully, but they could – and probably will – blurt out something before we can end a phone call. The minute one parent finds out, he or she will immediately contact all the other parents. After, of course, contacting an attorney.'

Nora would have sold her soul, would have handed over Murph and Mooch and maybe even Electra to the devil, for a cup of coffee at that moment. Anything to help her negotiate the minefield Ennis had laid at her feet.

But she'd learned something, after all, from that first letter-writing experience.

'I've been awake for more than twenty-four hours. I'm going to go back to my trailer, shower and change and walk the dog. And, because I'll need to be at the top of my game for this, I'm going to sleep for at least one hour, maybe two, and have a quick bite to eat. Then I'll come back refreshed and ready to give this my full attention.'

She stood within Electra's tiny shower long enough to drain half the trailer's freshwater tank, her skin turning pink then bright-red as she tried to scrub away the greasy feeling coating her as she contemplated penning Serendipity Ranch's latest excuse.

TWENTY-SIX

Nora never got that much-needed nap. After her shower, she lay rigid, afraid to close her eyes, fearing the vision of Carolee's ruined face would rise up behind the lids, staring at her with those vacant eye sockets, bone showing white around them; her rictus grin, lips stripped away from teeth.

Mooch and Murph, sensing her agitation, kept close, the cat pacing the bed, the dog lying his muzzle across her thigh. She finally got up, gave each of them a treat, and walked over to the lodge, dread dragging at each step, reminding herself of the lessons she'd learned in the decades at her old job.

'Never lie,' she'd told the college administrators when one crisis or another arose. 'The press – and these days, people on social media, too – will catch you out, and things will spiral out of control before you take your next breath.'

'That said,' she would add, 'you don't have to elaborate. Keep it short and sweet. Yes, the honors college dean has been accused – and it's important to say *accused* – of accepting bribes to admit students to our very prestigious program. Then in your very next breath pivot to something positive; say, the immediate and thorough steps the university is taking to address the issue.'

Except, how could she possibly find anything positive to say in the aftermath of Carolee's death?

And her mind kept circling back to that first and most important rule: never lie. She tried to put it more tactfully to Charlie Ennis. Maybe this time, unlike with Irene's death, he'd listen.

'We don't know for sure that it was suicide. Maybe she just wanted to see the place where Irene died. The sheriff told me people sometimes slip near the falls. Maybe the same thing happened at the bluff. Anyway, they haven't even recovered the body yet. There hasn't been an official ruling.'

Ennis surprised her by agreeing with her. 'Of course, of course. But we can certainly say that all signs point to another tragic instance of suicide.'

'Certainly?' She thought she'd said it under her breath, but the room was small and deathly quiet. He'd heard.

'Certainly. Because what else could it be, Ms Best? Maybe an accident, although it seems unlikely, given the email she sent. So what else does that leave? Murder?'

The word hung between them, a nearly visible, vibrating presence.

'N-no, of course not,' Nora stammered. 'That's crazy.'

'Someone stalking our girls, our female employees, and killing them?' he continued, implacable. 'For what possible reason, Ms Best?'

For the same goddamn reason girls and women the world over are killed, she thought.

He gave a small, mirthless chuckle, saving her from a response. 'The kind of person who perpetrates that sort of crime would have a far easier job of finding victims in just about any other location than this one. Don't you agree?'

He had a point. Of course.

Nora began to type, fingers jerking as though burned with each keystroke, employing the backspace key more than all the others put together as she tried to reduce the horror she'd seen just hours earlier to bloodless prose.

'It is with great regret that we've learned of the death of our former colleague . . . many of you knew her . . . the Serendipity Ranch Foundation will be funding a state-of-the art computer lab in her name . . . see information below on how to donate.'

She hit 'print' and closed her eyes, awaiting his verdict, her guts twisting like snakes on a scalding surface.

Charlie Ennis' voice sounded very far away. 'Yes, yes. This will do nicely. You've got a real knack for this, Ms Best.'

'Thank you,' she said. 'Excuse me.'

She rushed from the room, making it to the bathroom just in time, albeit not to the toilet. She threw up into the sink instead.

* * *

'Animals,' the sheriff said.

'Excuse me?'

The retrieval party returned with their grim burden just as Nora emerged from the bathroom, having failed despite repeated efforts to rinse the sour taste from her mouth.

Now she sat facing the sheriff, each of them in folding chairs, his creaking a little beneath his weight. Mud streaked his khaki shirt, probably from the same long slide down the bluff she'd endured.

She'd already told him the basics – that she'd looked over the edge, spied a spot of color that resolved itself into a tie-dyed shirt. She didn't tell him about the flashback that had propelled her over the edge, the memory of her own fall acting like a hard shove to the back, the prayer she'd breathed during those long seconds on the way down: 'Don't be dead. Don't be dead. Don't be dead.' Even though she and God had been on the outs for a long time, and apparently still were.

'Luke was the one who knew it was Carolee,' she told him. 'I'd never met her. Wouldn't have recognized her even if I had. Her face . . .' She turned her head away. Bile burned anew in her throat.

'Animals can do a number on a body. Birds, more likely, in this case. Ravens, going after the soft spots. Being partway in the water the way she was, she'd have cooled down fast. Less of a scent to draw predators.'

'Please.' Nora scrubbed the heels of her hands against her eyes as though to erase the image.

'I'm sorry. I wish, when people took a notion to kill themselves, they gave a thought to the ones they'd leave behind. Not to mention whoever's unlucky enough to find them. Be glad it was just a fall.'

'Just,' Nora echoed faintly.

Condescension tinged his words. 'It could have been a gun.'

Which brought her to what she really wanted to know.

'Are you sure it was suicide?'

He removed his Stetson and turned it in his hands. 'Ms Best. It appears you have a mind that takes a dark turn.'

Too late, she remembered she'd posed the same question about Irene Bell.

'I'm even more certain of it than I was with that child's death, and I was ninety-nine percent certain in that case. In this case, there was a note. Charlie Ennis told me he showed it to you.'

'It was an email. Do people usually email suicide notes? Especially a couple of weeks in advance?'

The hat, black felt with a cattleman crease and a small silver buckle on the narrow leather band, rotated again in his hands.

'These are modern times. I guess that's what people do now. And we don't know how far in advance it was. My guess is she'd been there at least a few days. As you, unfortunately, could tell.'

'But when did she come back here? She'd taken some time off after Irene Bell's death. She wasn't even here when she sent that note. How'd she get here and hike up that trail with none of us seeing her?'

'Those are all things we'll be looking into, Ms Best. I'm sure if you have any thoughts about them, you'll let us know.' A none-too-subtle way of letting her know he thought her a pain in the ass.

She might as well prove it. 'Sheriff Foley. A few days ago, a van came here in the middle of the night. June Ennis said it was delivering flour. But what if Carolee was in that van?'

'Why would she come here in the middle of the night? Anyway, I'd seen Miss Hanford around town over the years. She drove a Subaru, not a van.'

A perfectly logical question, one Nora couldn't answer. 'Maybe she flagged it down . . .?' Her voice trailed off.

'I'll be sure to check with the Ennises. Heck, I'll even look in the kitchen myself. If I don't see a bunch of fifty-pound sacks of fancy flour, you can believe I'll have some questions for them.'

He was mocking her now and, Nora had to admit, not without reason.

He parked the hat back on his head, adjusted it and stood, looking down at her from beneath its brim.

'Fact is, Ms Best, it makes a sad sort of sense that Miss Hanford chose to die in the same place as her student. Everything about this is sad. Including you.'

'Excuse me?' The second time she'd had to ask his meaning.

'You look all done in. That was a helluva night you had. My advice? Get a good meal, a night's sleep. You'll feel better. Maybe some details will come back to you, something you forgot when you were down there at the bottom of that bluff, or maybe something you heard about Carolee Hanford that might help us in our investigation. If that happens, give me a call. Here's my card with my cell number.'

He'd done everything but pat her on the head and said, 'Run along, little lady.' She snatched the card from his hand, royally pissed but too tired to do anything about it.

'Investigation, my ass,' she muttered at his departing back. He'd already made up his mind.

Just because Sheriff Foley wasn't inclined to seek out answers didn't mean she couldn't.

TWENTY-SEVEN

Ideally, she'd have waited until her next day off and headed for the library and its lovely, large computers and their full-size keyboards.

Nora didn't have time to wait for ideal. She huddled behind the lodge in the darkness, poking at her phone's keyboard with her index finger, backspacing over typos in every other word.

But at least there was one thing she didn't have to worry about.

'Are you bringing the security guards back?' she'd whispered to Ennis at dinner, granting those two bullies a modicum of dignity they didn't deserve.

The tender flesh beneath Ennis' eyes looked as though someone had scribbled at it with one of the fat charcoal pencils from the art room. His voice rasped. 'Not this time. Given what those girls experienced out there, I don't think anyone will be running off into the woods. That said, I've taken the precaution of doubling up on adults in the bunkhouse. One of the instructors will join you tonight.'

He held up a hand before Nora could ask. 'Not to worry. She'll sleep in Irene's bunk.'

'Thank you. I'll take all the help I can get.'

Thus reassured, she crept behind the lodge, Murph close at her heels, to do as much research as possible on the frustrating limits of her cellphone.

As she suspected, there was nothing online yet about Carolee's death. It was too soon for an obituary.

Carolee's LinkedIn profile showed a woman with a tangle of dark, curly hair and a crooked front tooth that lent an impish quality to her smile. She'd held a number of teaching positions, including a decade at a juvenile correctional facility, making Serendipity Ranch a natural transition. Otherwise, her name popped up mostly in the results from a handful of marathons. Nora, the slowest of runners, looked at Carolee's times, blinked, and thought it a shame that Carolee simply hadn't tried to outrun whatever demons were pursuing her – she'd surely have escaped with room to spare.

But she'd spent all those years dealing with juvies, kids with worse problems and with far fewer resources than those in Serendipity Ranch, without succumbing to despair. It didn't make sense, at least not to Nora, that whatever Carolee encountered in the ranch's luxe-rustic environment would have pushed her, literally, over the edge.

Next, she searched Luke's name, reasoning that people didn't just start molesting children in midlife. Maybe he'd been arrested before. The fact that she had his birth date, thanks to the celebration two days after her arrival, helped pinpoint her search.

Sure enough, his name popped right up, but not as part of an arrest record.

'Local Marine termed hero in firefight.'

A photo of a younger but still easily identifiable Luke, striking a reluctant pose in full combat gear, accompanied a years'-old story on a New Mexico news site about how the twenty-six-year-old medic had singlehandedly cleared a way for the men in his unit to escape after being surrounded in a house in Fallujah. He'd lobbed grenade after grenade, somehow ducking incoming fire, until every other Marine had fled, barely managing to escape behind them with his own life. A later story noted he'd been awarded a Silver Star.

Which didn't mean anything. War heroes could be creeps, too. In fact, maybe the stress of combat had snapped some final restraint within him, the thing that kept him from acting on his darkest impulses. Nora had her own recent experience to thank for the knowledge that people were all too often not what they seemed.

She returned Murph to Electra and herself to the bunkhouse, where she spent a largely sleepless night going over plans to mine a resource she expected to be far more fruitful than the internet: the girls.

Generally, Nora discouraged chatter in the art room on the pretext that it kept the girls from focusing on their work, but mainly because of its tendency to quickly devolve into sniping and backbiting.

On this day, though, she nudged it along.

'I wish I'd known Miss Hanford,' she sighed to the Sophies, as she'd come to collectively think of them.

'You'd have really liked her,' said Sophie. She wrapped her auburn curls in one hand, twisted them into a knot atop her head, and jammed a slender paintbrush handle-first into the mass to fasten it.

'Why?' Nora prodded.

'She was nice.' That least informative of words.

The others chimed in. 'So sweet. And funny.'

The same sort of generalities they'd mouthed about Irene.

Nora tried again. 'What made her so nice?'

Sofia fingered the mark on her cheek, barely discernable now, left by Ashleigh's marshmallow, and murmured a response so heartfelt Nora's breath caught.

'She believed in us.'

Then, before Nora could ask, Sofia added, 'No way she killed herself.' She looked to the others for confirmation. 'Remember that time Skye went missing and Miss Hanford found her with one end of a torn T-shirt around her neck and trying to tie the other to a doorknob?'

'That's why all the doors have latches now instead of knobs,' Sophia interjected.

'Miss Hanford untied everything and called all of us in and had us all hug Skye and tell her one after another why she needed to stay with us. Said that no matter what, it was never, ever the answer – that if we ever thought of it, we had to talk to her immediately, no judgment.'

'And that she'd never tell Director Ennis.' Sophia again. 'Otherwise, it's First Rung for sure and probably isolation besides.'

'No,' Nora interjected. 'That can't be right.' She reminded herself that the girls, for all their useful information, thrived on drama.

But all three nodded now, identical bobbleheads, arms folded across chests, expressions grim.

Punishment, even isolation, for someone so severely depressed she'd attempted suicide? How could that possibly help? Normally she'd have taken her question to Luke, the resident treatment expert. Now she wondered if he'd impose isolation on a girl as a way of getting her alone; whether Carolee had suspected his proclivities and so was keen to avoid telling any of the other adults about Skye's attempt.

Nora clasped her hands behind her back, squeezing tight, then spreading her fingers wide, trying to release tension. Forget about Luke for now, she reminded herself. The idea was to get the girls to answer the questions the sheriff hadn't given her a chance to ask.

'Maybe, given how strongly she felt about that other girl's – Skye, right? – attempt, she took it personally when Irene succeeded,' she suggested.

They were doing everything in unison now, identical snorts and eye-rolls.

'*If* Irene killed herself. Can't imagine her having the guts to jump off that cliff. You think Ashleigh's wimpy? Irene was ten times worse, a total crybaby about every little thing.' Sofia, in her role as leader of the pack. A sneer curled her lip.

She leaned in close and spoke beneath her breath, as though expecting Ennis to walk in at any minute. 'She'd had some big crisis, some kind of breakdown, crying and screaming and throwing shit around. It happened right in this room. You should have seen it. She trashed this place.'

Other girls drifted toward them, slowly at first, materials in hand, making a brief pretense of not listening, then abandoning it in the thrill of revelation, vying to be first with the most shocking details.

'Paint was everywhere!' Sierra said. She pointed to a yellow splotch on the wall that Nora had attributed to a carelessly wielded brush.

'She grabbed a hammer from the sculpture table and threatened to bash her own head in!'

'Or drink the turpentine, which is stupid because that would take forever. Well, it would,' Jen said as heads swiveled her way.

Sofia raised her voice, reclaiming leadership before it slipped away. 'They brought in the whole team – Miss Hanford and Mr Rivera and Director Ennis – to take her back to the lodge and talk with her. And it looked like they'd gotten her settled down.'

'They had.' Sierra elbowed her way to Sofia's side, usurping one of the other Sophies, a move that Nora suspected she'd pay for later. 'She seemed fine when she came back to the bunkhouse that night. Even joked about it a little. Wanted to know if we'd enjoyed the show. But then she slipped out in the middle of the night. They found her the next morning.'

Sofia stepped in front of her. 'Stupid to run into the woods. Nobody ever makes it out of there.'

Sierra peered around her. 'Nobody who runs away from here ever makes it anywhere. Everybody who lives around here knows to call the sheriff when they see a girl hitchhiking. And all the girls know what'll happen if the sheriff picks them up.'

'What are you saying?'

The eye-roll was collective.

But before she could ask details, Sofia brought the conversation back to Carolee.

'Miss Hanford never came back after Irene left,' she intoned dolefully.

'Yes, she did.' Sierra deftly claimed the last word. 'And

somehow waltzed right through here and over that cliff without any of us seeing or hearing a thing.'

The girls looked at each other and then at Nora. They hadn't told her anything new. But at least they'd let her know she wasn't the only one posing the question so quickly dismissed by the sheriff.

He'd questioned her at her lowest point, just a few hours after finding Carolee's body, when she was physically exhausted and emotionally wrung out. She'd let him dismiss her far too easily. It wouldn't happen again.

TWENTY-EIGHT

Nora sped toward town on her next day off as though the sheriff might escape before she arrived. With a few days' rest under her belt, she was ready to confront him with her questions.

Winter had delivered a preview, laying down a blanket of snow that softened hard edges and quieted the landscape so thoroughly that the rumble of Nora's truck seemed intrusive. She didn't care, wrestling the wheel as it slewed around curves and righting its path on the straightaway with a vicious stomp to the accelerator.

After days of guarding every word, every facial expression, even every gesture, it felt good to drive fast. She hit the radio and cranked the volume high, only to be rewarded with bursts of ear-splitting static until landing on a faint signal emitting a scratchy rendition of 'Don't Fence Me In'. Perfect. She shouted-sang along. No hobbles for her, at least not on this day. A high, bright sun emitted just enough warmth to melt the snow on the road, leaving the shoulders and meadows beyond glittering beneath it.

Nora skidded around another curve and came up behind a car with its flashers on, moving so slowly that she nearly clipped it as she whipped the truck past it.

'Get off the road,' she hollered, savoring the sheer

satisfaction of the sort of rudeness that would never be toler-
ated at Serendipity Ranch. She glanced in the rear-view mirror
at the fast-dwindling vision behind her.

Looked again.

Hit the brakes.

Jerked the truck around so hard she left rubber on the road.

A girl was stumbling through the snow along the side of
the road, the car trailing behind her.

As Nora bore down on the unsettling scenario, she thought
back to that weeks-ago morning in Indiana, the two men dragging the girl from the house. Her first instinct had been wrong
then.

Maybe this would be, too.

And it was, sort of.

Even as she reached for her phone to dial 911, she registered
the person behind the wheel of the car: June Ennis, for once
free of her knitting needles. Although, as Nora pulled along-
side, she saw a mass of yarn in the passenger seat.

She lowered her window but June shook her head, waving
her off as the car rolled past.

'What the . . .?' Nora parked the truck by the side of the
road, activated her own flashers, hopped out and snapped a
quick photo before sprinting after June's car, which moved so
slowly she easily caught it. She didn't yet know who the girl
was, swaddled as she was in one of those anonymous parkas.
But for all the warmth of the coat, she was shod in sneakers,
the shoes and her thin khaki pants wet to the knees.

Nora jogged beside the car. June flashed her a smile as
though they'd encountered one another on an innocuous errand,
and then looked straight ahead, down the empty expanse of
road.

Nora banged on the window.

'June! Open up. What's going on?'

The girl stopped running – trudging, really – and turned to
Nora, swaying as she stood.

It took Nora a moment to recognize Sophie, her auburn
curls so dark with sweat they looked almost black against her
ashen face.

June finally lowered the windows but spoke first to Sophie. 'Keep moving.' She touched the accelerator and the car inched forward.

'June!'

'Sophie cursed Director Ennis this morning. Now she's dealing with consequences.'

Nora punched a button on her watch and blinked at the number there. 'It's twenty degrees. Her feet are soaked and she's sweating in the cold. She could end up with frostbite. A fever. Maybe both.'

Nora might as well have pointed out a hangnail. 'That's why I'm here, dear. To supervise. Keep moving,' June said to Sophie. 'That will keep you from getting sick and should alleviate Ms Best's concerns.'

'Like hell it does! What are we, three miles from the ranch? How much farther are you going to make her go?'

June tossed a smile toward Sophie. Head down, deep within her hooded parka, she didn't see it. 'That's up to Sophie. We're awaiting an apology.'

Nora sprinted around the front of the car. The passenger side bumper nudged her as she dodged past. June must have given it a little gas. She grabbed Sophie by the shoulders, forcing her to stop.

'Sophie, no matter who was in the wrong, just apologize. You're going to get sick, really sick, if you aren't already.'

'Like I give a shit.' The girl's eyes glittered in her flushed face. Nora shoved up the sleeves of her coat and shirt and lay her wrist against Sophie's forehead. It was clammy with sweat, but not hot.

Nora turned her back, shielding the girl from June's view. 'What happened?' she whispered.

'Director Ennis came back in the kitchen when we were cleaning up after breakfast and started giving Ashleigh shit. The usual petty stuff. She was leaving streaks when she dried the dishes, putting things away in the wrong place, that sort of thing. She's a whiney little bitch and I can't stand her, but she doesn't deserve what they're putting her through. So I told him to ease up.'

'That's it?' Defiance, yes; a mortal sin in the Serendipity

Ranch lexicon, usually resulting in a reassignment to First Rung. But this?

'I may have called him a fucking asshole.'

Nora grimaced.

'And thrown a bowl of that disgusting three-day-old oatmeal in his face. And—'

But June leaned on the horn, drowning out whatever the girl had been about to say next. 'Move!'

Nora leaned through the open car window and was relieved when June braked. She hadn't been sure she actually would.

'I'm taking Sophie back with me and putting her straight into bed after she gets a hot shower and changes into warm clothes, and I'm going to order whoever's working in the dining hall today to bring her all the hot soup and tea she can handle. And if you try to stop me, I'm going to drive to the nearest place where I can get a cell signal and report this whole operation to Child Protective Services. In fact, I'm going to do that anyway. You people are so worried about lawsuits—'

The car jerked forward. Nora lurched away just in time, ending up on her ass in the snow, watching as June's car sped back toward Serendipity Ranch, June driving with the same sort of single-minded speed she herself had employed on her aborted trip to town.

TWENTY-NINE

She'd expected to see Ennis waiting upon their return, or maybe even the united front of both Ennises, but the sight that greeted her was nearly as unwelcome.

Luke shot from the door of his cabin as she pulled up in front of the bunkhouse, evidently having lain in wait.

She waved him off as she hustled Sophie toward the bathhouse. 'Later,' she commanded.

'Not now,' she said as she jogged back toward the bunk-house, emerging with towels and sweats for Sophie.

'Don't even think about it,' she said when he tried again as she led Sophie, her body still wafting the heat from the shower, back to the bunkhouse.

She put Sophie in her own bed, added an extra quilt, then headed for the dining hall – 'Dammit, Luke. Back off' – for a thermos of soup and another of tea, along with a couple of cookies filched from the top rung supplies and sat with Sophie to make sure she ate it all.

When Sophie halfheartedly pushed the cookies away, Nora reminded her of her miles-long slog through the snow. 'You earned those extra calories.' At which point, the girl wolfed them down with an alacrity that made Nora wonder just how many meals she routinely skipped.

'This sort of thing,' she ventured, as Sophie licked the last of the crumbs from her lips, 'does it happen often?'

Sophie slid down and pulled the covers up to her chin. 'Sometimes. To Irene, once, after the first time she ran away.'

The first time? 'How many times did she try?'

Sophie yawned. 'Two, three? The first time she went in the woods but got scared and came back. She got isolation for that. The second time, she headed to town. Her bad luck that the first car that passed was somebody from Ponderosa. Everybody in town knows about us girls. The sheriff brought her back. Helped himself to a feel while he was fastening her seatbelt. Director Ennis said if she wanted to run to town so badly, she could run as punishment. She got off easy in one way – it was summer – but she had to run farther than I did. Her feet blistered so bad she limped for a week.'

Nora suppressed an urge to yank a blanket from the bed and wrap herself in it, so badly had Sophie's words chilled her.

'That's awful,' she managed. Awful being wholly inadequate to express her horror.

Sophie's eyes closed. She turned on her side and pulled the covers closer around her.

'They try to break you here,' she mumbled. 'C'mon, Ms Best. Haven't you figured that out yet?'

Nora couldn't put it off any longer.

The only way to deal with Luke, she figured, was to go on the offensive.

Sure enough, he was hovering by the door, stomping his feet and swinging his arms as an antidote against his chilly vigil.

She brushed past him, heading for the lodge and its cell signal. 'I'm calling Protective Services.'

He ran after her and caught at her arm.

She spun and jerked away. 'Don't touch me!'

He held up his hands. 'OK, OK. But do not make that call.'

'Why not? What do you have to fear from Child Protective Services, hmmm?' Letting him know, despite Ennis' admonition of secrecy, that *she knew*.

He didn't even blink. 'Not a goddamn thing. But believe me when I tell you that yours won't be the first such call they've gotten about this place. And it won't do any good.'

Despite her resolve, he'd caught her off guard.

'What do you mean?'

He glanced toward the lodge. 'I'm supposed to explain to you the value of today's exercise.'

'Exercise? Try child abuse.'

He shook his head at her. 'Walk with me. I'm going to freeze if I stand still one minute longer.'

Nora wanted to tell him she didn't care if his dick froze off – that for the girls' sake, she wished it would – but the cold was seeping through the soles of her boots, and she'd jammed her hands deep into her coat pockets, where they were only slightly frozen.

She stalked the perimeter of the clearing as he kept pace beside her. 'How is this not child abuse?'

'It might look it to you and me – and, for that matter even to CPS. Problem is, they can't do anything about it.'

'I don't understand.'

'They don't have any control over these programs. Remember how I told you western states went easier on these places when it came to regulations? It's that whole libertarian thing.'

Nora picked up the pace until she was nearly jogging. 'I suspect even libertarians object to child abuse. I'm calling CPS. You can't stop me.'

'And I won't try. I just want to save you the trouble. Any

complaints about programs like this go to a whole separate agency, one that regulates businesses, not schools.'

That stopped Nora in her tracks. She tried to puzzle it out. 'But surely businesses have regulations against mistreating children.'

Luke's half-smile was the sort bestowed upon a very young and not terribly bright child.

'There are rules against mistreating *employees*. A complaint would have a better chance of success if you'd been the one running beside that car. Go ahead and make your call, Nora – either to CPS or the other agency. It won't be the first. And it will get the same result as all the others . . .'

Now he looked nearly as angry as she did. They squared off, facing one another, hands withdrawn from pockets, arms folded across chests.

'You'll get nothing. Nothing at all.'

THIRTY

Luke strode away, leaving her standing alone in the center of the silent, snowy clearing.

The girls were in the various classroom cabins, lunch still an hour away. The rest of her day stretched empty. She'd been on her way to town and could still go; still could make that call.

Luke had sounded almost triumphant when he'd told her it would do no good. How sweet it would be to prove him wrong.

But as she turned to head back to her truck, the lodge door opened. Ennis stood within, beckoning her close.

'I've just heard.' He ushered her inside and led the way to his office. 'What a terrible, terrible experience. Are you all right? Please, sit down. Have some tea.' He poured her a cup.

Nora sipped with her eyes closed, miming gratitude.

'I'm fine. But Sophie is not. You'd better hope she doesn't get sick. I hope you understand that I have to report this.'

Words that had come easier when she'd thrown them at
Luke. It was more difficult to be angry with Ennis, his cherubic
features soft with concern. She closed her eyes and sipped
again. Maybe if she didn't look at what was in her cup, she
could pretend it was whiskey.

'If she doesn't, it's due to your quick action. Thank heavens
you got to her when you did.'

Nora's eyes flew open. 'What do you mean?'

'I assume you heard about the, ah, incident that precipitated
this.'

She dipped her chin.

'Because of my own involvement, I felt it best to recuse
myself from determining the consequences. I assumed a
demotion to First Rung, some extra chores, naturally.'

'Naturally,' Nora echoed faintly.

'And when I heard exercise . . . well, you've seen our gym.
I made another assumption.' He shook his head. 'You'd think,
with all of my experience in this field, I'd have learned never
to assume.'

'I've seen Mrs Ennis supervising outdoor exercise before.'
Nora was disinclined to let him off the hook.

'Yes. But even she was concerned about this particular
assignment, given the weather. She was assured, though,
that it was appropriate. I wish she'd come to me with her
concerns. She wanted to respect my wish to distance myself
from the proceedings, so there'd be no whiff of retaliation
about the consequences. And now we have this terribly,
terribly unfortunate situation.'

Unfortunate seemed too tactful. Criminal would be the better
word, Nora thought. But . . .

'If Mrs Ennis didn't impose the consequences, who did?'

She hadn't needed to ask. Really, if neither Ennis had sent
Sophie stumbling through the snow beside the road, there was
only one other possibility. Ennis confirmed it.

'Luke.'

Nora gulped the rest of her tea.

'All the more reason, then, for me to contact whatever state
agency is responsible. May I use your phone? That would save

me the drive to town, or at least to wherever along the road cell service kicks in.'

She reached for it but he covered it with his hand.

'I have a better idea.'

She waited.

'We're just finishing up the review of the allegations concerning Luke's improprieties. Ah, *reported* improprieties. Why don't we fold this incident in with it? That way, everything will go directly to the police.'

'When will that be? Because he's already been able to hurt another girl. Not in the same way, of course, but real harm was inflicted today.' Her voice rose. 'We need to get rid of him. Yesterday, if possible.'

Ennis rose. 'I couldn't agree more. And I admire your passion in protecting Sophie. Some people would be reluctant to stand up for her, given that the consequence was imposed by our so-called expert. Even my dear June was too cowed to object. She's so ashamed. She's in our living quarters, crying her eyes out. In fact, I need to go to her now. I hope the effect on you hasn't been quite so traumatic. Promise me you're all right.'

'I'm fine.' A fib that fooled neither of them.

She gave up the idea of going to town. She doubted Luke's contention that Child Protective Services had no control over practices at Serendipity Ranch, but if Charlie Ennis was going to inform police, it didn't matter.

She went back to her trailer and, much like Sophie, crawled into bed and burrowed beneath the blankets, shivering as though she'd been the one slogging through the snow, wet and chilled to her core. Sophie's distress had been physical, though. The warm, dry clothes and bedding, the hot tea and soup, the day's rest, combined with the restorative powers of youth, would probably return her to something like fine in short order.

Nora, whose distress was merely mental, wasn't sure she'd recover so quickly.

Each of the thousand times she relived the incident, her mind snagged on one fact. June Ennis hadn't seemed ashamed at all as she'd forced Sophie to keep pace with her car. Nora turned it over in her mind.

The Ennises seemed the most loving of couples. But Charlie

Ennis was surrounded daily by lissome girls on the cusp of adulthood – a temptation that already seemed to have proved irresistible to Luke.

Nora mentally imposed a leering satyr's mask over Charlie's round face. The image blurred and dissolved; impossible to make it stick. But maybe June, teetering at the edge of the cliff that would plunge her from middle into old age, her face ravaged by time, her body long ago having betrayed its youthful form, was one of those women who suspected the worst of every other woman with proximity to her husband. Maybe she actually enjoyed Sophie's degradation; sent Mackenzie back to First Rung more often than strictly warranted; suppressed the occasional urge to stab a girl with one of those knitting needles.

It was a queasy-making thought, one that Nora shied away from, given that she herself frequently met alone with Ennis. But June Ennis might consider Nora a near-contemporary, well past the age of sparking temptation. Nora wondered anew about Carolee, who if the photos were an indication was probably in her mid-thirties.

The sheriff had dismissed her theory that Carolee might have been in that van. Charlie Ennis hadn't known about it at all. And June had been quick to supply the flour-delivery explanation that, the more Nora thought about it, made no sense at all. Had June summoned Carolee back to Serendipity Ranch for some sort of heart-to-heart, and then . . .?

If the last few months had taught Nora anything, it was that men didn't have a lock on murderous impulses.

Worn out by her fruitless speculating, she finally fell asleep, her last thought the fear that getting rid of Luke might not end the problems at Serendipity Ranch.

THIRTY-ONE

On Monday, Nora braced herself for a tough week, expecting the girls might act out in response to Carolee's death and Sophie's outburst. But they fitted themselves smoothly into the daily routine, although with a simmering energy that kept her on edge, alert to mischief or worse.

The Ennises likewise wore their usual serene expressions, though Charlie Ennis' eyes were watery with exhaustion and June's knitting needles clicked double-time, her most recent scarf unfurling over her knees and down her calves.

Only Luke seemed outwardly troubled, his face set and eyes downcast, his distress so obvious that Mackenzie approached him after breakfast. 'Mr Rivera, are you all right? We're all worried about you.' She hesitated. 'You're not going to do anything, too, are you?'

'You mean, kill myself? Some days, I get why Irene and Carolee . . .' Bitterness drenched his words. Nora, eavesdropping, flinched.

'Mr Rivera, don't talk like that!'

He pressed his fingertips to his temples. 'You're right. I'm sorry. I didn't mean it. And forget what I said about Irene and Ms Hanford. We don't know for sure what happened with either of them.'

Nora, walking with studied casualness behind them, barely within earshot, stifled a gasp. She'd figured Luke to be in lockstep with the official line about their deaths. In other circumstances, she'd have asked him about his suspicions. Now, she wouldn't trust a thing he said. And the fact that he was sowing doubt among the girls – even now, he was whispering something to Mackenzie, the girl leaning close, whispering back, grabbing his arm in agitation.

'Mackenzie!' She ran to catch up with them. 'Can you help me with Murph?' she called, counting on the sure-fire distraction of the dog.

She caught Luke's look of hurt as she pulled the girl away. Too bad. Mackenzie probably attributed his despondency to Carolee's death, rather than the fact – so far unknown to Mackenzie – that he was just days, maybe even hours, away from being exposed as a child molester.

Which reminded her. She escorted Mackenzie to her trailer, handed over Murph and his leash, and went to the lodge in search of Ennis. She found him in his office, reviewing copies of her newsletter with its sun-drenched photographs of smiling girls in groups of two and three around the clearing. But for the log buildings in the background, it could have been a come-on for an ivied prep school.

He held one out to her. 'They just arrived from the printer. You did a wonderful job.'

'You paid for a wonderful job. And I don't just mean my salary.' She ran a finger over the newsletter's glossy surface, noting the weight of the paper. 'These must have cost a fortune. Wouldn't it be cheaper just to email it to the parents?'

'Email is so ephemeral. This gives parents something to hold, to take out again and again during the long, hard months their girls are with us, tactile reassurance that the worst is nearly behind them, with better days ahead. Not to mention the fact that a quality product underscores the quality of our program.'

That made sense. 'But speaking of the worst being behind us: How much longer before Luke is arrested? I just had to peel him away from Mackenzie. Most of the girls still seem to trust him. It's exhausting, having to watch out for every interaction.'

She handed the newsletter back and he squared it atop the pile on his desk, fingers trembling. 'It's good you stopped by. I was going to tell you later.'

'Not another delay. This is ridiculous.' Nora abandoned her brief effort to keep the outrage from her voice. After all, Ennis probably shared it. 'Is it the sheriff? Is he dragging his feet? Is there someone else, someone above him, we can report to?' Given her impression of the sheriff – and what the girls had said about him – she'd have preferred to report it to anyone else.

Ennis shook his head sorrowfully. 'It doesn't matter.'

Nora's frustration morphed into something darker. 'Why not?'

'The girls.' Ennis fell into his chair and dropped his head into his hands. 'They've changed their minds.'

'What do you mean?' Her voice rose higher still.

'Close the door, Nora.'

She closed it, took a chair, and pulled it up to his desk. 'Are you saying they recanted?'

'Such an ugly word. But I'm afraid that's what we're dealing with.'

She thought about Luke's long and impermissible hug with Ashleigh, his furtive conversation with Mackenzie moments earlier.

'I think he's been working on them,' she blurted. 'I've seen him talking with them, one on one.'

Ennis started up from his chair. 'But he's never supposed to be alone with them! He knows that! Why didn't you tell me?'

Indeed, why hadn't she? A lingering shred of attraction, the memory of her easy, companiable moments with Luke leading to a persistent wriggle of doubt?

'I was going to, but it seemed so trivial, just a couple of quick conversations with the girls on the way to or from class or the dining hall, or during free time.'

Ennis' hands muffled his voice. 'It doesn't really matter. Without a formal complaint from the girls, we can't do anything without risking a lawsuit from Luke for breaking his contract for no reason. Can you believe it?'

The only thing Nora believed at the moment was that Charlie Ennis had hired the wimpiest attorney on the face of the earth. 'But what if he assaults another girl? And her parents find out there was a prior complaint? Has your lawyer considered the size of the suit this place would face if that happened?'

Ennis raised his head. His eyes were haunted. 'That's the sort of thing that keeps me up at night. Not so much the chance of a suit, but the damage possibly being done to our girls. Ms Best, it's up to us to make sure nothing happens to them at the hands of Luke Rivera. All of us – you, Mother and myself – are going to watch him every minute of every day. If there's the least little infraction, I've got the separation papers drawn up and ready to go. In my line of work, unfortunately, you hear about cases like this. People like this, they always slip up. Always. It's a terrible compulsion, one they're nearly powerless over. Under other circumstances, I'd feel compassion. Now, though, I confess that my only emotion is a deep and abiding anger.'

Something crashed outside.

Nora followed Ennis to the office door.

'My God,' he breathed at the sight beyond. 'The man has no shame.'

Luke stood on tiptoe beneath one of the smoke detectors, Sofia at his side holding a large cardboard box. 'Sorry,' Luke called without turning around. 'I dropped one of the batteries.'

Nora wanted to rush to Sofia, grab her and pull her to safety – and maybe kick Luke's legs from beneath him as she passed. Instead, the casualness with which she spoke was so obviously forced that even Luke turned to stare, brows knitting.

'Sofia, could you please help me with something in the art room? I'm sure Mr Rivera can manage on his own.'

Sofia set the box of batteries on the floor.

'I'll keep my eye on him,' Nora mouthed to Ennis. 'Nothing will happen to the girls. I promise.'

THIRTY-TWO

Maybe because she herself was so on edge, but Nora felt it the minute she walked into the art room, a hum of nervous, upbeat energy.

She moved warily among the groups of girls, trying to divine the darkness underlying their burbling enthusiasm. Because it had to be there, right? Normally, she'd have asked Luke about the psychology of it, about the best way to handle it – if, indeed, there were an *it* to handle. What had the sheriff said? 'It appears you have a mind that takes a dark turn.'

'Of course I do,' she'd wanted to retort. 'Do you have any idea what I went through this past summer?' But he didn't, and nor did anyone else here, and she very much wanted to keep it that way. It was logical to think it had left her with some sort of PTSD, probably – she told herself – accounting for her present jitters.

So she merely smiled and nodded as she moved through the room, hoping to conceal her unease at the breezy cooperation that supplanted the normal simmering enmity among the girls in the art room.

Mackenzie and Sofia enthused about their near-completion of the hated rock wall. 'We should be done tonight,' Sofia said. 'And then we're going to add fall flowers and plant bulbs at its base so they'll come up in the spring. Look.'

She pointed to Mackenzie, working on a watercolor instead of another of her tortured oil portraits. The pastel landscape, suffused with the mellow glow of late summer, featured a flower-strewn rock wall like the one she'd just described.

'This is a study for the mural I'm doing in the dining hall,' McKenzie explained.

The mural was her reward for coming off First Rung. The idea was that she'd cover an entire wall of the dining hall with an image of the ranch and its grounds. Privately, Nora thought the idea was stupid – why paint something students saw every day? – but Mackenzie seemed excited about it. Now a table full of brushes and cans of paint and turpentine, along with folded stacks of rags and tarps, sat in one corner of the dining hall, and a blue sky streaked with wispy white clouds had begun to creep across the top third of the wall.

Maybe, thought Nora as she smiled warily at the girls, such things were their way of coping with trauma, papering it over with pleasantries, a suspicion that grew stronger when Gabriela organized a lengthy clean-up that put the room in better order than it had been during Nora's entire tenure.

Two of the girls lugged in the large, bear-proof trash can that sat behind the cabin and they set to work collecting the stacks of discarded drawings, dried and misshapen lumps of clay, near-empty tubes of paint, the empty gallon milk jugs they'd been collecting for some unnamed project they'd apparently decided against, until the can was filled nearly to the brim and they had to summon a third girl, busy in the supply closet, to help them drag it outside again.

'That's not all,' Gabriela said. 'We made something for you. To help you feel better after what happened with Ms Hanford. And to thank you for, you know, putting up with all of our shit. I mean, our nonsense.'

The girls moved aside and Sofia stepped forward with a woodsy centerpiece of feathery pine fronds in a clay vase

Gabriela had thrown on the wheel, and that Mackenzie had painted with forest scenes. It sat on a wooden tray sanded and varnished by Sierra and surrounded by the pinecones Nora and Luke had collected in the woods, a fall piece elegant enough to fit in with the offerings at any high-end florist shop.

'It's for your trailer,' Mackenzie said. 'Please, can we see how it looks? Please, please, please? Look at me. I'm Murph.'

She made mock-puppy eyes, so akin to the face Murph turned on Nora whenever she sat down to dinner that Nora laughed along with the other girls and finally relented – a little.

'You can't come in. It's my personal space and I hope you'll respect it just as I respect yours.' She paused, waiting for the girls to remind her they had no personal space to speak of. But they kept silent until she added, 'But I'll open the door and you can look in from here.'

The ensuing hubbub carried enough high-spirited urgency that she put aside her daily inventory of the art room and its potentially problematic contents, locking the door behind her and hurrying to catch up with the girls as they ran toward her trailer, the centerpiece bobbing madly between Sofia and Mackenzie.

No doubt, Nora thought, the trauma of Carolee's death would hit them hard at some point. She'd need to be prepared. But for this moment, she decided to accept the girls' generosity. After all, she too responded well to positive reinforcement.

She unlocked the trailer, rescued the centerpiece and positioned it on the dinette, then stood aside as they took turns in twos and threes peering inside, craning to see the bed covered with the quilt that was one of the few things she'd taken from her childhood home, exclaiming at the sterling silver coffeepot that sat beside the tiny stove.

'Oooh, Gorham Chantilly,' Gabriela said. 'It's my mom's pattern.'

Mackenzie lingered longer than the others, closing the door reluctantly, dragging her feet as she walked with Nora to the lodge, where lunch awaited. Mac and cheese, a reluctant favorite, its creamy goodness offsetting their wariness of fat and carbs.

'I wish I had a trailer like yours. What's it like to be able to go anywhere you want whenever you want?'

'I don't know yet,' Nora said honestly. 'It's something I'd planned and looked forward to for years.'

Those long-ago daydreams still teased her, visions of exploring the redrock canyons of the Southwest, the mysterious, fog-shrouded Cascades; of the long drive south and east to discover the secrets hidden within the Everglades' tangled waterways.

'It hasn't exactly worked out as planned. And I'll be here for the next year, so I won't know until after that.'

'But you're still going to do it, right?'

Nora wondered what it was like for Mackenzie, a girl who'd probably always been given whatever she wanted until she took too much and ended up at Serendipity Ranch, facing limitations for the first time in her life.

'Of course,' she said. 'Tell you what,' she said. 'I'm rotating into the English class next week. Maybe I can talk your instructor into reading *A Dream Deferred*. It's probably a good lesson for all of us.'

A suggestion for which she kicked herself later that night, when she'd sneaked behind the lodge to poach its Wi-Fi signal again and refresh her memory of Langston Hughes' poem.

She was no better than Ennis, thinking *The Scarlet Letter* a perfect lesson on consequences. Far from touting the rewards of deferring a dream, Hughes rued the way the dream might fester over the long bitter year it went unrealized, and wondered, 'does it explode?'

A line that came back to Nora when she awoke that night to the acrid taste of smoke, a writhing molten-copper glow and the shouts of 'Fire, fire!' that told her this was no dream.

THIRTY-THREE

'**M**s Best! Ms Best!'
Mackenzie pounded at Electra's door.
'Get out!'
Nora grabbed her coat, stuck her feet into shoes and fled into the night, registering only as she ran that the bunkhouse itself was safe. The girls huddled before it in a fluttery white mass, blankets thrown over their nightgowns, feet jammed into sneakers, watching the lodge burn. Nora did a quick headcount before turning her attention to the spectacle before them. Flames leapt from the dining hall's shattered clerestory windows. The front door gaped open, belching black smoke. The girls turned toward her, letting their blankets slide from their shoulders as heat blasted across the clearing.

'Look!'

The girls swung back in a mass at Mackenzie's shout.

Ennis staggered around the side of the building, his arm around his wife, dragging her away from the flaming wreckage of their life's work. Nora ran to them and took June's other arm, pulling the trembling woman close.

'The smoke detectors,' June gasped. 'We never heard them. Nothing.'

'I heard a window shatter. That's what woke me,' Ennis added. 'Otherwise.' His voice cracked as he stopped.

'Nora!'

She turned to see Luke dragging a garden hose across the clearing. 'Help me out.'

'Are you crazy? A garden hose? We might as well spit on it.'

'No shit.' His face, backlit by flame, was a mass of shadow. 'It's for the other cabins. It's calm now but the slightest breeze could carry embers to them. We called nine-one-one but you know how far away town is. There might be some buckets in the supply shed. If you find some – or any sort of container – pass them out to the girls. We need all the help we can get.'

She ran back to Electra for her master key, pushing through the group of girls, shouting to them on her way back to get ready for a bucket brigade.

Her hands shook as she tried to fit her master key into the supply shed lock, its metal housing hot to the touch. She put her shoulder to the door and shoved her way into the darkness, feeling for a switch, instead encountering the cold and clammy grasp of a human hand.

Later, Nora wasn't sure who had screamed louder, her or Ashleigh.

The girl's shriek subsided into a wail of relief upon recognizing Nora in the wavering light that barely illuminated the cabin's interior.

'I . . . thought . . .' she gasped between sobs. 'No one would find me. That I'd burn to death.'

Nora's fingers, still searching, finally found the switch. She flipped it. Nothing happened. The fire must have shorted out the ranch's electrical system.

'Only the lodge is burning.' She stopped herself from adding, 'for now'. 'Ashleigh, what are you doing in here?'

Sirens howled in the distance as the flames leapt higher, finding their way through the lodge's roof, burning triumphant against the night sky. Flashes of firelight intermittently illuminated the cabin's interior, bare of the supplies that were its stated purpose, furnished only with a pallet on the wooden floor, a gallon bottle of water, and a bucket. Nora sniffed the air. Even the choking scent of smoke failed to disguise the bucket's purpose as a toilet.

Her hands shook as she lifted her phone and shot a photo, the flash rendered moot by the leaping light of the flames across the clearing.

Ashleigh offered a hiccup and a sad smile.

'Welcome to isolation.'

Nora and Ashleigh emerged from the shed just in time to duck a blast of water from one of two fire trucks in the clearing.

Fat drops pelted them in cruel mimicry of the drenching rain that would be the fire's only true antidote.

'Ashleigh, dear child.' June Ennis approached, arms open wide, her motherly face streaked with soot. 'Thank God you're safe. We were just coming for you.'

'Sure you were,' Ashleigh muttered.

Nora dashed the water from her eyes and moved in front of Ashleigh, shielding the girl from June's embrace. 'She was in a shed! Locked in! She could have burned to death!'

'She was in isolation,' June corrected. 'And we never would have let anything happen to her – that's why I was coming for her.'

A booming crash cut her off. The clearing lit up like daylight as the flames licked still higher against the sky. They all turned to see the dining hall roof collapsing, freeing the conflagration within. A roar arose from the watching girls, half-cheer, half-growl, its animal undertone raising the hairs on Nora's arms despite the heat from the blaze.

Ashleigh stood so close she could feel the girl shaking.

'That shed. Is that your idea of isolation? Sleeping on the floor, a bucket for a toilet? What the hell is this, some sort of Soviet-style prison camp?'

A tear cut a track through the layer of soot on June's cheek. For Ashleigh? Or for herself?

'Oh, my goodness, I can see why you might think that. This isn't our normal isolation practice. Far from it, in fact. We have a comfortable room in the main lodge set up for any girl who might be in isolation. Unfortunately, we discovered a plumbing issue at bedtime last night so we moved Ashleigh into the shed just for a single night and thank heaven we did. Otherwise, she might still be –' June swung her arm in the direction of the smoking disaster of the lodge – 'in *that*. Those conditions that so upset you? They might very well have saved her life.'

She turned to Ashleigh and her voice sharpened. 'You do realize that, don't you dear?'

Ashleigh wrapped her arms around herself, rocked on her feet and stared at the ground. 'Thank you, Mother June.'

Nora wanted to shake her. 'That's crap. You could have put her in Carolee's cabin. It's empty.'

'Oh, my dear.' June actually chuckled. 'The luxury of a

whole cabin to herself? Isolation is, after all, supposed to be a punishment. The room in the lodge is quite spartan. I wish I could show you.'

She moved past Nora and guided the girl away. 'Let's get you back to the bunkhouse, get you cleaned up and warm. This isn't the way any of us would have chosen, but your isolation is over. Luke, do you have any tea in your cabin? Father, please go with him and rustle up a pot of tea for our girl here.'

Nora found herself alone in the middle of the clearing. She glanced over her shoulder. The instructors had surrounded the rest of the girls, who stood in a gaping group outside the bunkhouse. Luke and Ennis headed off toward his cabin.

The fire's consumption of the roof was its last hurrah. Now, under the hissing stream from the pumper truck, it subsided bit by bit, showing only as a warm, almost homey, glow through the shattered windows.

A firefighter approached her, his face, helmet and yellow Nomex shirt streaked black. Only when he stood before her did she recognize Paul, one of the two firefighters she'd met during that first visit to town.

'Nora, right? Has anyone done a head count? Are they all OK?'

She thought of Ashleigh, the pallet on the floor, the bucket. 'They all got out safe, if that's what you mean. Do you know what started it? Some sort of electrical issue? Mr Ennis said there was a plumbing problem last night – could they be related?'

He took off his helmet and rubbed a glove hand across his sweat-damp forehead. 'I don't know anything about it. And sure, an electrical problem would be the obvious thing to look for. But you gotta wonder about all the rocks on the floor.'

'Rocks?'

'Under the windows,' he said. 'Which were broken when we got here.'

She remembered her first view of the fire, the flame writhing from the windows, snaking up the exterior walls of the lodge. 'I just assumed the fire blew them out.'

'Which happens. But when it does, the glass ends up on

the outside, not the inside. Which is where the rocks were, too.'

Nora's gaze slid toward the stone wall so laboriously constructed by Mackenzie and Sofia. Its once-smooth top was as jagged as a skeletal jaw missing half its teeth.

'What do rocks have to do with a fire?'

'Nothing with starting it. But all that air coming in through the windows would make sure it burned like hell. Whatever got this thing going, even if it was an accident, somebody wanted to make sure it didn't go out.'

THIRTY-FOUR

Ennis called an emergency meeting with the senior staff – that being his wife, Nora and Luke – in the cabin that had formerly housed Carolee Hanford.

Nora scanned the interior but anything that might have given her a clue to the woman's personality had been removed. The cabin had the canned warmth of a high-end guest ranch, with its rustic log furniture, stone fireplace and idealized Western scenes on the walls, all golden aspens, bugling elk and snow-spangled pines.

None of the images suggested what the area surrounding Serendipity Ranch must have looked like when the lumber mill that supported Ponderosa and other nearby towns was going strong, the forest quaking with the crash of toppling trees, the grinding roar of skidders and feller bunchers, and the gnashing of the loaders' gigantic steel claws.

Through an open door she glimpsed a bed covered with a homey quilt and strewn with the armful of clothing the Ennises had swept from their closet before fleeing the blaze.

Nora tried to make conversation. 'A good thing this cabin was unoccupied.'

The air between June and Nora fairly hummed with the intensity of June's glare. Ennis glanced at his wife and hastened to speak, cutting off whatever she'd been about to say.

'Look around you.' He twisted in his chair, gesturing toward the windows. 'So many ways for an already emotionally disturbed girl to escape. The only way we could keep someone safe in a cabin like this would be to put bars on the windows, and that wouldn't send the right message, would it?'

June held her knitting needles upright, small pointed spears quivering in her hands as though poised to launch. Nora nearly pointed out the obvious – that nothing resembled a prison cell more than the interior of that shed – but thought better of it just in time and swallowed her words. The acrid smell of wet charcoal hung in the air, coating the back of her mouth, stinging her eyes.

June Ennis coughed wetly into a Kleenex. She crumpled it into a ball, tossed it listlessly toward a trash can, and resumed knitting, stopping every few moments to fiddle with the yarn. 'I keep dropping stitches.' Her voice caught.

Luke murmured sympathy. Scarlet threads laced the whites of his eyes. Black lines of soot arced beneath his nails. Only Charlie Ennis looked as though he'd showered and shaved, his skin pink and smooth and smelling faintly of a floral soap that Nora guessed Carolee had left behind.

'The most important thing is that we maintain routine. These girls have already been through so much in the last couple of weeks, losing Irene and then the discovery of Carolee's body. Now this fire, upending their whole world. We need to show them that's not the case.

'Luke, I've already scheduled counseling sessions. They'll be mandatory for everyone.'

Nora started.

Ennis' glance caught hers before fastening back on Luke. 'We'll do joint sessions, you and I. Two heads always better than one in such a dire situation.'

Luke knotted his hands together. 'That's not necessary. We could split them into groups, get everyone done faster.'

'Mmm.' Ennis appeared to consider it. 'You make a good point. But I think it's really best we do it together.'

Luke grimaced. 'Fine,' he said, and Nora let the breath she'd been holding escape.

'Now, as for food, Mother's already called the café in town.

They're putting together some casseroles for dinners for the next few nights. We'll reheat them in the cabins' ovens. Nora, I don't suppose your trailer has an oven that can accommodate a casserole?'

'Afraid not. But the fridge is pretty good-sized. We can use it for storage. And may I make a suggestion?'

Ennis nodded permission.

'I'd propose getting something completely unhealthy for the girls. Something sweet – a cake, doughnuts, some sort of treat to boost their spirits. At a time like this, the smallest thing can soothe.'

June lofted a knitting needle. The scarf waved like a flag. Nora flinched. 'Lovely idea, Nora. How very thoughtful.'

Nora wondered if anyone else caught the sarcasm in June's tone. She hurried on. 'If you like, I can run into town and pick up the casseroles, and maybe stop at the store for some greens for salads. Everything will fit easily in my truck.'

She slid her hands beneath her thighs, crossed her fingers, and bit her lip hard. Please, she prayed.

'Wonderful. Much appreciated.' Ennis beamed. 'And some cereal and milk and fruit for breakfast. Bread and tuna for lunch. We'll keep things simple until they determine the extent of the damage and how long it will take us to get a working kitchen back in order. Until then, think picnic. Nora, I'll give you some cash.'

Nora ran her tongue over the sore spot on her lip. It had worked.

'I'll go right now,' she said, wanting to head for town before they changed their minds.

Nora did due diligence, whipping double-time through the small grocery store, throwing heads of lettuce, green peppers and carrots into the cart, then hotfooting it to the cereal aisle for boxes of Cheerios and Lucky Charms, designed to evoke childish pleasures.

She'd brought the ranch's biggest cooler for the gallons of milk and grabbed a couple of pounds of coffee for herself, guiltily adding her own money to the envelope Ennis had handed her to cover the cost.

At the café, she gnawed at the inside of her cheek, trying to hide her impatience as Marian the waitress clucked endlessly about the fire as she fetched tray after tray of lasagna, shepherd's pie and meatloaf, along with a half-dozen pies. Nora mentally checked sweet treats off her list.

'When you start to run low' – Nora couldn't imagine when that might be – 'just give me a heads up,' Marian said, her cheeks pink with exertion and excitement. 'Charlie Ennis doubled our entire week's business with one phone call.'

Would the woman never stop talking? 'I'd better get this back to the girls while it's still hot. You're an angel.'

She drove around the corner and tapped the brakes in front of the fire department, the real goal underlying her offer to pick up the food. She breathed another prayer. 'Please be there.'

Silly to even worry. Ponderosa's fire department was so small that of course Paul was there – as was his curmudgeonly partner Fritz, who aimed a high-powered jet of water at one of the trucks as Paul moved in with a rag to polish it clean.

She leaned out of the truck and hailed them. 'I just wanted to thank you for your fast work last night.'

Fritz raised a skeptical eyebrow. 'It's our job.' He shut off the hose and turned his back to her as he coiled it.

'And to bring you a pie,' she called. The hose fell from his hands.

Nora climbed down from the truck, holding the pie before her like a trophy.

Fritz snatched it from her hands, his dour expression softening. 'Is that pecan?'

It was, and apparently pecan was Fritz's favorite. 'I'll just cut us a couple of slices.' He disappeared with the pie.

Nora estimated the time it might take for a hungry man to cut two slices of pie, and dispensed with pleasantries. 'Hey, Paul. Any determination yet on what started that fire?'

He rubbed at a bit of mud above one of the truck's wheels. 'I can tell you what it wasn't: the wiring. It all seemed fine. Funny thing, though.'

He moved to the front of the truck, attending to the bright

work around the headlights, casting quick glances toward the door through which Fritz had disappeared.

'What's that?'

'Every last one of the smoke detectors, the ones that hadn't melted, anyway, had dead batteries in them. That's why the Ennises didn't hear anything. They were lucky to get out with their lives.'

'But they were changed just recently. I saw Luke doing it.'

The rag stopped its slow circles around the headlight. '*Luke?* I know the guy. Are you sure?'

Nora folded her arms across her chest. 'He's the only other man there. It's not as though I might confuse him with Charlie Ennis.' Tread carefully, she told herself. She opted for playing dumb.

'Dead smoke detectors wouldn't start a fire, would they?'

He resumed polishing. 'Of course not.'

Nora took a steadying breath. 'If it wasn't an electrical problem, what was it?'

'Still checking. Listen . . .' He glanced back toward the door and turned to face her. 'There was an accelerant. The place reeked of it.'

Nora dropped her voice, even though the door remained firmly closed. Gooseflesh raced up her arms. 'Are you saying it was set?'

'Any reason there'd be turpentine in the dining hall?'

Nora's shoulders slumped. 'Actually, there was. Mackenzie was doing a mural. Her easel, all her equipment – her paints and brushes and yes, turpentine – were set up in the dining hall. So maybe it was just an accident after all.'

The rag slid from his hand. 'How much turpentine does it take to clean a few brushes?'

The door opened. Fritz bumped it wider with his hip, emerging with a paper plate in each hand, a wedge of pie and a plastic fork balanced on each. 'Break time!'

Paul's eyes bored into Nora's. 'Think about it,' he muttered.

He took one of the plates and pasted a smile on his face as fake as her own. 'Thanks for the pie. We'll keep you posted.'

THIRTY-FIVE

Paul's words banged around inside Nora's head on the too-long drive back to Serendipity Ranch.

He clearly thought someone had set the fire. And just as clearly, despite what she'd told him about seeing Luke changing batteries on the smoke detectors, he didn't think it was Luke. But he didn't know the things about Luke that Nora did. She wondered if Luke, maybe still believing himself on the verge of losing his job, had set the fire to turn Ennis' attention elsewhere, maybe even give himself a chance to play the hero.

She recalled the way he'd rushed toward the fire with a skinny garden hose, the girls gasping appreciation. 'Bastard,' she said aloud.

For once, she was glad when Ennis summoned her to the makeshift office he'd set up at the two-person table in Carolee's cabin. A fire sparked and flickered in the grate, normally a cheerful sight, unnerving under the circumstances.

'The girls can take care of unloading. You've done more than enough,' he said.

He'd asked her to again bring her laptop. 'Here.' He pulled out a chair. 'Take a seat.'

Nora's initial enthusiasm dissolved. She regarded the setup as she might a nest of rattlesnakes, coiled around one another, tails a vibrating, clattering blur.

'Another letter?'

'It *is* your job, after all.'

She nudged the chair away with her foot. 'There's something I need to talk over with you first. Something important.'

'Of course, Ms Best. Here. Sit down. You've already had a long day.' He moved the chair away from the table and pulled up another facing her, so close their knees nearly touched. 'What's troubling you?'

'Two things, actually. Although, they're related.' She took a deep breath.

'I think the fire was set. And I think Luke may have set it.'

He drew back. 'Ms Best! Those are extremely serious allegations.'

No more serious than child molestation, she wanted to say.

'One of the firefighters said the batteries in the smoke detectors were dead. I saw Luke changing them. You saw it, too.'

'I asked him to change them.' He frowned. 'He's so much taller than I, and at my age, Mother tends to worry when she sees me climbing so much as a stepstool.'

'Understandable. But that doesn't take away from the fact that Luke might not have changed them after all.'

The smile vanished. 'Nor is there any proof of that. And dead batteries – if they were, indeed, dead – don't tend to start fires. Ms Best, I hope that's not the sum total of your so-called proof.'

Was she imagining a mocking tone? A hard glint in his usual twinkle?

Her voice faltered. 'One of the firefighters said they detected an, uh, accelerant.'

'Accelerant? A three-dollar word meaning fuel, I believe. What sort of accelerant, Ms Best?'

No. She wasn't imagining the tone.

She looked away. 'Turpentine.'

'Ah.' He sat back. 'The turpentine that Mackenzie Masterson was using to clean her brushes in our mural project – which, sadly, will never come to be.'

He closed his eyes and bowed his head as though in memoriam of the stillborn mural and Nora, after a moment's hesitation, followed suit.

Ennis cleared his throat and Nora opened her eyes. 'Now,' he said, 'which firefighter passed along this damning information?'

'His name is Paul. I don't know his last name.'

'I don't know this Paul. But I spoke to the chief just moments ago. It appears our misfortune was a terrible accident. Spontaneous combustion, most likely, caused by the sunshine on a turpentine-soaked rag on the table next to Mackenzie's work. It likely smoldered unnoticed by all of us throughout the evening and burst into flame long after we'd left the dining hall.'

'That could be how it started, but we still don't know why Luke would salt the smoke detectors with dead batteries,' she persisted.

Ennis shook his head sorrowfully. 'You have quite a vivid imagination, Ms Best.'

There it was again, an echo of the sheriff's assessment of her 'dark turn' of mind, though more tactfully worded. She started to say something about the rocks Paul had found in the lodge – rocks evidently pried from the stone wall and hurled through the windows – but decided not to open herself up to further skepticism. Why wouldn't these men take her concerns seriously?

Ennis, at least, told her why.

'Vivid,' he repeated. 'And one might even say overactive, if you're citing that as some sort of proof of arson against one of our most valued employees.'

Nora gaped. 'Valued? You've been telling me to watch him twenty-four/seven to make sure he doesn't assault any of the other girls!'

'The girls, the girls. Such extremely troubled young ladies, with a history of lying. Might I remind you that those allegations have since been withdrawn.'

Nora rose so quickly her chair overturned. 'You're defending him now?'

Ennis remained seated. But when he spoke again, it somehow seemed as though he were looking down on her.

'The more I learn about you, Ms Best,' he said, 'the more it seems that Luke Rivera is not the employee I should be concerned about.'

Time froze, thawing so incrementally that Nora almost expected her voice to come out deep and distorted, as when news shows purposely slowed the recording of an interview to protect the anonymity of a source.

'What are you talking about?'

Ennis returned to the table now serving as a desk and sifted through the litter of files. 'Fortunately, the fire largely spared my office. There's quite a bit of water damage, but the files were largely protected. Here it is.'

He extracted one and thumbed through the papers within.

'It seems you forgot to mention a few details during your job interviews. That's interviews, plural, so you had several chances to include them. Yet you chose not to.'

She felt her lips move, heard the words from an even greater distance than before. 'What details?'

Maybe he didn't know all of them.

Ennis tilted his head back and stared at the ceiling's shellacked pine beams.

'Nora Best. Nora Best,' he mused. 'Arrested on suspicion of kidnapping her own husband, who was later found dead. Others eventually charged in the case, but one wonders. Oh, yes, one does,' he said musingly, as though he were wondering still.

'And then there's the matter of a decades-old murder case, concealed all those years. One can only imagine what secrets lay hidden still. So many questions.' His chin dropped to his chest, the weight of those problematic queries nearly visible.

'One might want to know, when hiring for a position involving children, especially such troubled children, that a potential employee's background is so deeply concerning. One might expect an ethical job candidate to come clean on her background. One might wonder about the legal liability stemming from the failure to disclose such crucial information.'

Nora, so exhausted moments earlier, was wide awake now, nerve endings tingling as though she'd grasped a live electrical wire, shock shooting through her system.

She slammed her laptop shut. 'You could have found all of that out with a single click of a mouse before you hired me. Or done a background check.'

'Oh, we did that.' He pushed the file across the table toward her.

'Open it,' he said.

She read through the compilation of the worst moments of her life: her mother's death, and the posthumous public recognition of the unforgiveable sin that led to it; her own detention as a suspected kidnapper and possible killer. A screenshot from the Wayback Machine of the now-deleted Facebook page – 'Joe's Johnson' – set up by generations of aggrieved female law office subordinates to complain about her husband's harassment. Her own discovery of Joe with her best friend, and the way she'd snapped a photo, then shared it with partygoers – those last details gleaned from Charlotte's recently filed lawsuit.

If nothing else, Ennis – or, more likely, whomever he'd hired to dig up dirt on her, because what she'd just reviewed had the marks of a pro – was thorough.

She dropped the file back onto the table.

'You knew this and yet you hired me, anyway.'

He offered a bland smile. 'At Serendipity Ranch, we believe in second chances. After all, it's our raison d'etre.'

Now he was just toying with her. She wanted to take that little French flourish and throw it back in his face, but the only word she could think of was 'merde' and that seemed too ridiculously juvenile, something one of the girls would say.

'Besides,' he added, 'who says we knew about it?'

'Uh, this?' She hefted the file again, waving it at him.

'Never seen it before.'

'But *I've* seen it.'

'So you say. And who would believe the word of someone with your problematic history?'

He reached across the table, plucked the file from her hands, and fed it into a soot-streaked shredder beside him, slivers of paper curling into the waiting trash can. The machine's whirring stopped.

Ennis detached the trash can, rose and carried it to the fireplace. The bits of paper shriveled blackly as they hit the waiting flames, flaring with false cheer.

Nora said the only thing possible under the circumstances.

'Fuck this. I quit.'

Ennis retrieved a document that had escaped the shredder.

'I think not. You might want to refresh your memory.'

Nora skimmed the contract she'd signed laying out the terms of her employment at Serendipity Ranch, her gaze landing on a paragraph that Ennis had thoughtfully highlighted, the one that said if she left early, she was obligated to repay the salary she'd received until that date.

The contract fell to the table.

'This is blackmail!'

The word hung in the air between them. Ennis folded his hands together.

'Your term, not mine.'

They stared at each other a long moment. Ennis leaned forward and placed a stubby forefinger on the contract's highlighted paragraph. 'Now, Ms Best. Let's send that letter.'

She swiveled back to her laptop and tapped at the keys with fingers gone frozen.

Ennis watched, the clicking of the keys and the occasional crackle from the fire the only sounds in the room.

Nora stopped typing.

He rose to stand behind her, bending to read her screen. She forced herself not to flinch away.

'Perfect.'

'I'll email it to you.' She pulled the laptop toward her, preparing to shut it down. She was nearly free of him.

'No. Send it as before. You've already got the list.'

The last time he'd asked her to send something from her laptop, he'd also said the ranch's computer system was undergoing maintenance. And the time before that, too. How did the saying go? It came back to her as she pasted in the email list and hit 'send': 'The third time is never a coincidence.'

Exhaustion tinged with shock was quickly overtaking her. She wanted nothing more than to go back to her trailer, stretch out on her bed with a cold washcloth over her eyes to quiet the tiny sledgehammers pounding away within her skull, and process what she'd just learned.

But there was more.

'Satisfied?' she asked.

'Yes, very. Now, if anyone objects to the wording of these letters, I can say that you took it upon yourself to write them on your own, without supervision. Given your track record, it's just the sort of thing you would do. Isn't it, Ms Best?'

He gestured to the door, inviting her to show herself out.

THIRTY-SIX

Nora paced Electra's ten-step length, readjusting everything she knew about Serendipity Ranch.

Despite his misgivings about her background, Ennis seemed determined to keep her. Otherwise, why remind her of the thousands of dollars she'd owe the ranch if she left now?

Much as she hated to admit it, Ennis' discoveries about her background, no matter how belatedly revealed, were accurate. Which meant that the accusations against Luke, even if the girls had recanted, might be grounded in fact. Yet, Ennis had also kept Luke on. Were employees that hard to find, and retain, at Serendipity Ranch?

At least he wasn't accusing her of something sexual, the third rail of dealing with children. Not yet, anyway.

Her previous suspicion about Irene and Carolee's deaths flared anew. More than ever, she doubted that they'd killed themselves. But if they hadn't, who would have pushed them?

Nora had seen enough of the girls' behavior not to rule out an impulsive, pissed-off shove from a fellow student in Irene's case. But it seemed improbable. The site was five miles from the ranch, and the only way two girls could have ended up there would have been on a hike, in which case the other girls would have talked endlessly about it. Nor could she imagine either of the Ennises struggling up the trail toward the bluff. Luke? His name whined in her brain, insistent and annoying – and far more troubling than a bloodthirsty night-time mosquito.

The question pummeled her, coming so fast and hard she felt almost physically bruised, especially given the discovery she'd made just before returning to her trailer.

Everyone – Ennis, the firefighter Paul and his chief, Fritz – attributed the fire to the turpentine at Mackenzie's workstand. But Paul had shaded his assessment with a question: 'How much turpentine does it take to clean a few brushes?'

And he'd added, 'Think about it.'

She had. She remembered the woodsy centerpiece the girls had presented her on the afternoon before the fire; their high spirits that day. The way they'd cleaned the studio so thoroughly and had been so eager to see the arrangement installed in her trailer, that she'd left the art room without doing the usual inventory.

With that in mind, she'd detoured toward the art cabin on her way back to her trailer. She looked over her shoulder, ensuring the clearing was empty, unlocked the door with her master key, and ducked into the cabin. She hadn't switched on the lights, not wanting to alert anyone to her presence. By this time, she knew the room well enough that she walked directly to the rear storage closet without bumping into any of the tables and easels along the way. The closet was even darker than the main studio, where the outsize windows at least admitted the gray early-winter light.

She ran her fingers across a tabletop, counting the hammers and chisels and files for the sculpture projects; dipped her hand into the canisters that held paintbrushes of varying sizes, so tightly packed as to reassure her nothing was missing. The tools and brushes, usually ranked highest in terms of concern, all seemed to be there and anyhow weren't her focus on this day. There. At the far end of the table, large tinplate canisters of turpentine stood in rows. She counted them, placing a hand atop each one to be sure. All there.

She chided herself for paranoia and turned to go.

Paul's words nudged her again. *Think about it.* She turned back. Hoisted one of the cans. Empty.

As was the next.

And the next.

How had they done it?

There'd been such a bustle of activity in the art room that day. Easy enough for a couple of girls to slip into the supply closet and pour the turpentine into . . . what?

Back in her trailer now, she smacked her forehead so hard that Mooch and Murph started up from their enviable slumber. All those empty gallon milk jugs. The girls had said they were going to make birdfeeders, but that they'd changed their minds when the cold weather swept in. So easy to fill the jugs with turpentine, conceal them in the trashcan, and drag it back around to the rear of the building.

She fell back onto the bed, the scenario flitting like the herky-jerky films of old behind her closed eyelids.

The girls, waltzing back into the art room and making a big, distracting fuss over presenting her with the centerpiece. Dragging her to her trailer before she could remember that she hadn't done the inventory.

Biding their time through the interminable afternoon and into the dinner hour and the free time that followed it, through the face-washing and teeth-brushing and changing into night-gowns and the forever it took to ensure that the instructor who had night duty was well and truly asleep.

Creeping ghostly in their white gowns from the bunkhouse – how many of them? Surely no more than two or three – and tiptoeing through the cold, retrieving the jugs of turpentine, maybe wrapping a rock in a blanket to silently smash the first window.

Holding the milk jugs high, their pungent contents glugging through the jagged opening.

Tossing the match.

Jumping back.

Flinging the other rocks – no need for silence – and sprinting back to the bunkhouse so as to be safely in their beds when the outcry began.

But why?

For weeks, Ennis had warned her about the girls' darker impulses, warnings she'd brushed aside as exaggerated. And now, of course, Ennis' own actions had proven as disturbing as anything he'd attributed to the girls or Luke.

She wasn't sure of anything anymore – except that she had to leave.

She could hit up the few friends she had left for money. Or take out a bank loan, putting Electra up as collateral if need be. Whatever it took, she'd send Ennis the money she owed and escape this supremely fucked up situation.

'*Now,*' she said aloud.

The clock on Electra's microwave showed midnight. If she left now, she could be in a city by morning. Not one in Montana

– she thought about what Luke had said about buying off the legislature so that places like Serendipity Ranch could avoid regulation – but the Idaho border was not far away. Though, her hazy knowledge of Idaho was that its northern reaches were just as rural as the area where she now found herself. Best to head for Seattle, only a day's drive away, with big-city police and sophisticated social services.

No. Not Seattle, which once she hit the highway was pretty much a straight shot from her present location and where they might suspect she'd go. Portland, maybe. It was only another hour farther away and a less obvious destination.

She opened Electra's door and gazed into the darkness, thinking through her next moves.

To hitch up the trailer, she'd have to start the truck, and back it up. Raise the trailer's stabilizers with a whining electric drill. Hook up the clanking safety chains, then haul truck and trailer across the clearing and through the gate, by which time, she'd have made enough noise to wake half the people there.

If Ennis was so conniving as to dangle the possibility of blackmail if she openly quit her job, what might he do if she tried to sneak away in the middle of the night?

She'd have to find a legitimate excuse to leave with Electra, something that would let him think she was returning, then drive hell for leather to a place that offered safety, a situation entirely too reminiscent of the way she'd left her marriage. She pushed away the memory of how safety had been the farthest thing from what she'd found then.

Saturday was her weekly day off. By then, she'd have a plan.

THIRTY-SEVEN

On Saturday morning, she stood beside Electra, staring at the trailer with what she hoped was a mixture of concentration and concern, waiting for someone to walk past.

'Oh, no!'

Mackenzie and Ashleigh, the last to leave breakfast thanks to their clean-up duties, stopped at her outburst.

'What's wrong, Ms Best?'

She held a bit of frayed wire in her hands. 'Something chewed through my breakaway cable. Maybe a squirrel.'

They regarded her with blank looks.

'Can you please find Director Ennis? I need to ask if there's a good garage in town.'

She could have found him on her own but didn't trust herself not to go all wobbly in his lair. She preferred the open air, where the world could hear his manipulative comments.

The girls returned shortly, Ennis in tow.

Nora thrust the wire toward him, the severed wire convincingly frayed after an hour's work with a file to make it resemble something a rodent might have done.

'It's my breakaway cord.'

He looked no more enlightened than the girls.

'It's a safety mechanism. I wouldn't want to tow the trailer more than a few miles without it. I think maybe a squirrel or a pack rat got it. It's usually covered in a kind of oil that tastes good to animals.' Complete fiction. She hoped Ennis had never hitched up a trailer. 'I have to keep the dog away from it.'

He eyed her warily. 'A good thing you're not driving anywhere anytime soon.'

'Yes, exactly.' She took care to be her most agreeable. 'But since today's my day off, I wonder if you could recommend a garage. That way, I could drive it into town and leave it there.'

He eyeballed the slender cord in her hands. 'It doesn't seem as though that tiny little thing could do much good.'

'It's hugely important. It plugs into an electrical system that triggers a brake if the trailer somehow comes unhitched and the cord detaches. Ideally, the brake keeps the trailer from rolling down the road and smashing into other cars.'

'Yes. Well. I doubt the garage in Ponderosa would have such a thing.'

'I do, too. But I don't want to take a chance on driving it

any farther. And it doesn't matter how long it takes to order it. As you said, it's not as though I'm going anywhere.'

She'd drawn up a list of talking points designed to reassure Ennis and memorized them the night before. She mentally checked one off and launched another.

'One more thing. I want to apologize for some of the things I said the other night. Finding Carolee's body shook me up more than I realized. Once I settled down, I realized that you were right. I should have told you about my background. This job means a lot to me. I really want to do well at it.'

She took a breath and rushed on through her last point. 'I've even thought about going back to school when my contract here is up, getting a master's in education or social work. Maybe, if I do well here, you could write a recommendation?'

In her previous life, she'd always instructed clients to throw as many facts as possible into their talking points. Now she was taking her own advice, including to make her point and then pivot, pivot, pivot.

'But what I want to know from you is, do you have any experience with the man who runs the garage in Ponderosa? Do you trust him? Installing a new cord, once it comes in, should be fairly straightforward. But Electra – my trailer – is my baby.'

Was she imagining it, or had his expression softened somewhat?

'Tell you what. I'll call Walt and let him know you'll be bringing your Airstream in. I'll let you know what he says.'

'That would be wonderful. Thanks so much.' Her face ached from smiling. She unclenched her jaw as he walked away and called to Mackenzie, who'd waited a discreet distance away, to direct her as she backed the truck into position to hitch up the trailer.

'Are you leaving?'

Mackenzie hurried to help her fasten the safety chains.

'Thanks, Mackenzie. No, I'm just taking it into town. I need to replace the breakaway cord. The garage can order it for me.'

The well-rehearsed lie came easier still the second time around. But maybe there was something in her tone.

'You're coming back, aren't you?' The girl's voice wavered. Nora straightened in surprise.

'Of course I am.' She stooped to raise the stabilizers, avoiding Mackenzie's gaze, hoping the shriek of the drill covered any strain in her own voice.

But when she stood to continue the conversation, her smile pasted firmly in place, Mackenzie was gone.

Ennis returned with the unwelcome news that the garage owner was picking up parts for someone else and wouldn't return until late afternoon.

'I'll just drop it off.' Nora hoped her impatience didn't show. The quicker she got away from Serendipity Ranch, the better.

'No.' Ennis was firm. 'Best he's there when you come by. I didn't even talk with him directly. When he didn't answer the phone, I called Sheriff Foley. He's the one who told me that Walt's out of town for most of the day. He suggested you bring it by around five.'

Five! That was hours away, hours that felt like years. Even allowing for the slower speed hauling a trailer, she'd hoped to be nearly to Portland by then.

She tried to keep herself occupied as the hours ground past. Walked Murph. Read a book. Played Solitaire on her laptop. Made a sandwich but ended up feeding most of it to Murph and Mooch when her stomach, churning with nerves, rebelled.

Jumped about a foot when a knock rattled her door at four.

THIRTY-EIGHT

Mackenzie stood on the bottom step, looking everywhere but at Nora.

'I'm supposed to take Murph.'

Hearing his name, Murph climbed down from the bed and trotted to the door, tail lashing the air.

Mackenzie reached for him, but without her usual cooing enthusiasm.

'What do you mean, "take him"?' Nora grabbed his collar and dragged him away from Mackenzie.

'Director Ennis says for me to take him. To watch him while you're in town.' Mackenzie rubbed one sneakered foot up and down her other calf.

'Why?'

The girl shrugged miserably and mumbled what Nora was thinking.

'I think it's to be sure that you come back.'

Check and mate. Nora was outfoxed. She could shove Mackenzie off her doorstep, run to the truck, and haul ass out of the ranch. But Ennis had said he'd talked to the sheriff about her plan to leave the trailer in town.

No doubt he'd call Sheriff Foley even as her truck departed, foiling the head start she'd planned. She'd hoped to be across the state line, out of Foley's jurisdiction, before the garage owner reported she hadn't shown up. She couldn't think of a pretext for Foley to stop her, but that didn't mean he wouldn't try, given what appeared to be his cozy relationship with Ennis.

But to leave without Murph!

'We'll take really good care of him for you.' Mackenzie's eyes pleaded cooperation.

To show the least bit of reluctance would tip off Mackenzie, who possessed the skill of all teenage girls at divining weak spots.

Nora knelt and wrapped Murph in a hug, rubbing her cheeks dry against his kinked brown coat. She'd only had him a little while. Her family had always had Chesapeakes but Murph had been her mother's dog, acquired long after Nora left home. Still, he'd offered unstinting comfort in the agonizing days following her mother's death.

Ennis had well and truly called her bluff. If she changed her plans and stayed, he'd know her story about the breakaway cord for a ruse, and almost certainly continue to demand more and more onerous tasks from her, maybe even ones that would put her in legal jeopardy. Would she be the next Serendipity

Ranch staffer to face an accusation of some sort of sexual misdeeds?

She didn't have much time to make a decision. If she was going to go, it had to be now, to guarantee she'd be across the state line by the time the garage noticed she hadn't shown up.

'Murph. You're the best boy. The very best.'

She turned her head away, handed Mackenzie his leash and hurried into the truck.

Ashleigh, her face a study in curiosity and concern, had joined Mackenzie and Nora briefly composed herself enough to ask the girls to check her turn signals and brake lights. They gave her a thumbs up. She spent a few minutes checking things in the truck's cab – the dashboard light that told her the trailer brakes were engaged. Her phone charger. The cash she'd stashed in the glove box. She threw the truck into gear and pulled away from the ranch.

When she next looked into the rear-view mirror, the girls – and Murph – had vanished from sight.

By the time she hit the main road, she was crying so hard she could barely see. She pulled onto the first side road she saw.

Still sobbing, she pulled her backup breakaway cord from beneath the driver's seat, reciting the prepper redundancy mantra – 'Two is one, and one is none' – to calm herself.

She'd just finished screwing it into place when the trailer door opened and a voice sounded behind her.

'Ms Best? Are you all right?'

A collarless Murph bounded down the trailer steps and knocked Nora off her feet.

The sight of Mackenzie and Ashleigh emerging behind him flattened her anew.

'What the . . .?'

The girls stood shaking, arms entwined, talking over one another,

'Don't be mad.'

'You're not going back there, are you?'

'We couldn't stay any longer.'

'We promise we won't be any trouble.'

'You can drop us off anywhere.'

'But not here. It's too close.'

'Speaking of too close – can we get going again?'

'Pleasepleaseplease don't be mad.'

Nora was too shocked to be mad, though something surging within her told her anger – or some other strong emotion – would soon follow.

'How . . .?'

Full sentences eluded her.

'We jumped into the trailer as you were backing out.'

'But the door was locked.' Her words were coming back.

'Please.' Mackenzie rolled her eyes. She, too, appeared to be recovering her equilibrium. 'My parents would change the combo on our front door keypad when I sneaked out. I picked every other door and window lock in the house.'

Ashleigh nudged her and whispered something. Mackenzie nodded and spoke again.

'But Ms Best, we've got to hurry.'

Nora raised an eyebrow. The girls were thinking far faster than she was. They'd already summoned Murph and coaxed him back into the trailer.

'Bye, Ms Best. Sorry to do this to you, but . . .'

A thin shoulder lifted in a shrug, and the door closed behind them.

Nora pushed against the latch until she heard the second click ensuring the door was sealed, then turned the useless key in the useless deadbolt. At some point, too far in the future to think about now, she'd see about getting a better lock.

She'd fled once before with Electra. But she'd been alone then and fueled by the righteous fury of her husband's just-discovered in-flagrante infidelity.

Now she was hauling four lives – two human, one canine and one feline – with her and, oh, what she wouldn't have given for a little of that fury. Instead, all she felt was fear.

THIRTY-NINE

N ora swung wide around Ponderosa's business district, taking side streets to avoid passing either the garage or the sheriff's office.

She hoped it would buy her a little time, at least until some of the good citizens of Ponderosa mentioned an airplane-bedecked Airstream lumbering past their homes.

Once out of town, she drove as fast as was practical on the serpentine, two-lane road, holding her breath every time a vehicle approached, checking the rear-view mirror constantly for any that might be following.

At some point, her roiling thoughts settled into a mere simmer, enough to allow her to focus on practicalities. The vaguest of plans began to coalesce.

Once across the border, she could drop down from far northern Idaho onto Interstate 90 and drive like hell into Washington state and then Oregon. She'd never make it before dark, but another partial day's drive would bring her to Portland, which would have the kinds of nonprofit groups designed to help runaway girls while keeping them out of legal trouble.

With the girls safely deposited, she could call her lawyer and ask how best to proceed in terms of legally getting out of her contract with Serendipity Ranch. She'd research state agencies in Montana to find out which one regulated programs like Serendipity Ranch. Luke had told her regulation was slim to nonexistent but there had to be at least a pretense of oversight. Despite Ennis' warning, she'd taken photos of the girls hauling rocks and eating only water and oatmeal for breakfast, not to mention Sophie's forced run through the snow. There was also the business of the free labor they provided in Ponderosa – that couldn't possibly be legal.

But first she had to get to Portland. The interstate would be the fastest way, but any campgrounds along the interstate where she might stop for the night would be in the treeless expanse of eastern Washington and Oregon, where Electra with her splashy decal would be hard to miss.

With darkness coming on soon, she made a snap decision.

She pulled into the next campground she saw, breathing audible thanks for the fact that it was lightly occupied with widely spaced sites carved deep into the pine forest. She found a pull-through site farthest from the campground host and parked without unhitching.

She rapped on one of Electra's windows, warning the girls to stay put, and jogged to the registration board. She filled out the registration, altering the final digits of her license number, trusting the host not to give either the form or the license plate more than a cursory glance. She studied the line for her name, bit down on the provided pencil, dangling from a bit of string nailed to the board, and finally wrote 'Mary Amelia', flipping Earhart's first and middle names.

She quickly filled out the rest of the form, specifying that she was a single camper with no pets. She put the fee in the envelope, thankful that she had enough cash, and dropped it through the slot.

Thus barely disguised, she hurried back to the trailer to deal with the unexpected complication of her two stowaways.

Over dinner, she explained her hastily revised rules of the road.

'Under no circumstances are either of you two to leave this trailer. We're going to get up and out of here first thing in the morning. With both of you missing from Serendipity Ranch, they'll be looking everywhere for you, which means they'll be looking for me.'

Something for which she cheerfully could have killed them. Happy as she was to have Murph back, the presence of the girls added layers of complexity to her dilemma.

'No, they won't.' Mackenzie, assertive as always. 'They'll search the forest first.'

Ashleigh, her loyal lieutenant, hastened to explain. 'We planned everything as soon as we heard you were taking the trailer to town. We figured we'd get at least that far, then try to hitch a ride with someone.'

'No way we believed that bullshit story of yours about the cord,' Mackenzie added, smugly superior.

Nora thought that was quite possibly the stupidest plan she'd ever heard. Two teenage girls in identical red polo shirts with Serendipity Ranch logos on a lightly traveled road? The only motorists were likely to be locals, who'd almost certainly call the sheriff to return them to the ranch, or – worse yet – an opportunistic traveler to whom the sight of two girls on their own might awaken predatory instincts.

'We told the Sophies we were heading up the trail to try and cross into Canada. Mackenzie even sneaked into the woods after lunch and dropped a hairband and some Kleenex off the side of the trail.'

Mackenzie took up the tale.

'And then, when Director Ennis told us to keep Murph for you, Ashleigh slipped off his collar and threw it into the woods and ran back, which in my opinion was a genius move.'

Ashleigh preened under the praise. In just a few hours away, she seemed to have grown taller, straighter, more confident.

'Did the Sophies believe you?'

'We think so. They said we sounded just stupid enough to try. They said we'd end up like Irene and Carolee, that we'd fall off the trail in the dark and bash our fucking heads in.'

Which sounded exactly like something the Sophies would say. But . . .

'Did you say *fall* off like Irene and Carolee? Not jump?'

Mackenzie stroked Mooch, who sat purring in her lap, waiting for her to sneak him another tidbit of her grilled cheese sandwich. Mackenzie had appointed herself as chef, making sandwiches so loaded with cheese it dripped from the bread.

'Nobody with half a brain thinks either of them jumped.'

'But to have two people fall accidentally from exactly the same spot . . .' Nora began. She took another bite of sandwich and chewed slowly. It tasted odd, likely a result of the anxiety flooding her system.

The girls looked at each other.

'She catches on quick.' Mackenzie spread sarcasm like butter over her words.

Ashleigh said what Nora didn't want to think.

'Of course they were pushed.'

Nora's hand shook so violently she spilled the wine she'd emphatically told the girls she wasn't sharing.

Mackenzie retrieved a towel, mopped it up, and refilled her glass.

'Thanks.' Nora slid her hands, those turncoats, under her thighs. She wanted the girls to think she was in charge. 'Do you know that for a fact? And who do you think did it?'

The girls exchanged a much longer look, some sort of silent conversation taking place between them, so tense that Mooch stiffened in Ashleigh's lap and flexed his claws. She yelped and tugged at him. His claws came free from her khakis with a tearing sound, leaving two lines of tiny holes in the fabric.

'I mean, *everybody* thinks it.' Mackenzie dipped her head for emphasis.

Nora clung to the vagueness for reassurance. 'Just because everybody thinks something doesn't make it so. Remember when everybody thought big hair and shoulder pads were a good look? Never mind, of course you don't.'

The girls were on their feet, clearing the table around her.

'You should get some sleep, Ms Best. You've had a tough day. And drink your wine. It's good for you. It'll help you sleep. You need it.'

She took another sip. 'I'm not sure. I think it's gone off. It tastes a little vinegary.'

Nonetheless, she downed the rest of the glass. The girls were probably right. She needed sleep. She was, suddenly, unaccountably tired, too exhausted to put much effort into wondering what was behind this new, solicitous Mackenzie. The girl probably felt guilty, and well she should, given the burden she'd added to Nora's half-baked escape plan.

Electra, seemingly so spacious for one person, felt cramped with the three of them, plus the dog and cat – the only two obviously enjoying the situation, given the extra attention lavished on them by the girls.

Nora tried to imagine a sleeping arrangement that would

leave the bed to her but couldn't. 'You two take the bed. The dinette benches convert into a bed – I'll take that.'

She dismantled the dinette as they did the dishes, grabbed a pillow and pitched onto the cushions face-first, too tired to even put on sheets.

Despite her exhaustion, she lay awake for a few moments, trying to come up with talking points for her lawyer. She'd call Artie in the morning and do her best to shower him with logic before he blew a gasket.

'The longer I was there, the shadier things seemed.' To wit: the deaths of Irene and Carolee; the way Ennis had her send the letters to parents from her own laptop, and then threatened to use those actions against her. The fact that he hadn't fired a likely sex offender as soon he'd received the first complaint. The fire, almost certainly arson.

Far more concerning was the fact that she was taking two minors farther from Serendipity Ranch every moment. She could only imagine what Artie might say to that.

She heard the girls moving about silently, getting ready for bed, a ritual made familiar in the bunkhouse, although there she'd had the luxury of her own space. Pain pulsed red at her temples. The last thing she thought before she fell asleep was that she should have trusted her instincts about the wine.

FORTY

Nora awoke to bright sunshine and the come-hither scent of coffee.

She turned her head and saw the refrigerator a few feet away. She shifted and felt the slick leatherette surface beneath her. She was on the dinette.

She craned her neck and peered down Electra's short, narrow hallway. Mackenzie, Ashleigh, Mooch and Murph slumbered tangled together like some sort of hybrid litter.

The previous day's events came back to her in an unwelcome rush. She'd planned to leave before dawn, but the sun's glare made her think it was considerably later. Not twelve hours into her escape from Serendipity Ranch, and things were going wrong at a discouraging clip.

At least there was coffee. The girls must have gotten up early to make it, then gone back to bed.

Nora hauled herself upright, poured a mug of coffee, and wandered outside, waiting for the coffee to clear the fog in her brain.

The sunlight had found its way into Electra through a single gap in the trees. The site was otherwise in deep shade, making for a see-your-breath morning. Nora wrapped her hands around her mug, grateful for its warmth.

Footsteps crunched on the far side of the trailer.

'Morning,' someone called.

Panic fluttered in her chest.

The man walking up to the campsite entrance stopped a few feet away. He looked to be in his sixties, outfitted in forest-green pants and shirt and a tan pullover fleece. Nora guessed him for one of the army of retirees who took on campground jobs as a way of minimizing housing expenses.

'I'm Clint, the campground host. You must be Mary Amelia.'

Who? Oh, the name she'd written on the registration card.

'Just coming by to make sure you had a comfortable night. You got in too late for me to do my usual check-in.'

'Oh, yes. Very comfortable. Slept like a baby. You keep a very lovely campground.' At least that last part was true. Had she offered enough reassurance to make him go away?

'The wife tends to the bathrooms. Everybody comments on how clean they are.' Of course he'd sloughed the campground's most onerous job off onto his wife, Nora thought uncharitably.

Every fiber within her strained toward the trailer, fearful of detecting the slightest sound: Murph, belatedly rousing to his role as watchdog, barking and drawing attention to the trailer that supposedly contained no pets. The girls, waking, chattering with one another, not realizing someone lurked outside. Mooch, yowling at some imagined slight.

''Course,' he nattered on, 'guess you don't need to use our

bathrooms with that fancy rig of yours. That's some decoration you've got.'

Goddammit to hell. He'd seen the airplane decal, the thing that distinguished her Airstream from any other on the road.

'And on the truck, too. Must've cost you a pretty penny. Worth it, though. It sure is nice.'

The truck? What the hell was he talking about?

'Um. Thanks. I'll be sure to check out those bathrooms before I leave.'

'You're just here for the one night, then?'

Would the man never leave?

'Just the one. Heading down to Arizona. I spend winters there. Meant to get an early start, but I overslept. Nice meeting you, Clint.'

He finally took the hint and wandered off. As soon as he'd rounded the bend, Nora tossed the rest of her coffee onto the ground and scurried around to the other side of the trailer where she beheld . . .

Not an airplane.

A wildly colorful jungle had grown up across Electra's flank in the night, all tall waving grasses and trees hung with vines. If she squinted, she could detect a curve of tire in a python wrapped around a tree, a sharp propeller disguised as a brittle blade of grass. The theme continued on the side of the truck, where a tiger, who looked suspiciously like a more brightly colored Mooch, peered from a thicket.

She touched a tentative finger to the image. It came away damp, with the slightest smear of green.

She banged back into the trailer. 'Girls!'

They lunged up, rubbing sleep from their eyes with paint-splashed hands, and she got another shock.

Sometime in the night, those long gleaming tresses, that hallmark of suburban teenage girls, had vanished, replaced with choppy, bristling cuts worthy of Annie Lennox, if only they'd known who she was.

'Who the hell *are* you?' was all Nora could manage.

Without all that hair half-hiding their faces, the girls' eyes seemed bigger, their cheekbones sharper.

'We disguised your trailer.' Mackenzie jerked her head, approximating the hair toss of her old boldness, except there was no hair to toss.

'And the truck, too,' Ashleigh added unnecessarily. 'Mackenzie did most of it. I just held your phone for a flashlight.'

Nora put a hand to her head. 'I can't believe I slept through all of that.'

'I ground up some Benadryl and put it in your sandwich last night. The same as we—'

'Shut *up,* Mackenzie.'

'The same as what?'

'Never mind,' Mackenzie mumbled.

'The same as we, uh, the same as we put in your wine, too.'

That explained the wine's sour taste and her subsequent sleep of death. But . . . 'You're not allowed to have drugs at Serendipity Ranch.'

Another defiant head-jerk. 'I have allergies. I can have over-the-counter meds. Mother Ennis gives them out, just a dose a day. I've been hiding them under my tongue instead of swallowing them, saving them up for an emergency. This seems like an emergency.'

Nora supposed she should be grateful they hadn't poisoned her.

'But my trailer! My truck!'

'We'll show you how to strip it off without hurting your decal or your paint job. I took the paints from the studio. You don't want anyone to know where you are, right?'

Mackenzie was right, although Nora had thought the need for secrecy would last only until she could get out of the damn backwoods and formulate a subsequent plan, one that even more urgently than before involved calling her lawyer for advice.

'You said you used my phone for a flashlight. Where is it?' The quicker she could call Artie, the better. There was no cell service in the campground, but she'd probably be back in range after a half-hour on the road.

The girls looked at each other. They looked down at the bed. They looked out the windows.

'Mackenzie. Ashleigh. *Where is my phone?*'

Mackenzie, who'd been doing most of the talking, defaulted to Ashleigh, whose lip quivered like that of a rabbit facing a grinning fox.

'You know your phone is a tracker, right?'

'No. I mean, yes, I know that. But . . . no.'

Ashleigh couldn't be about to say what Nora thought she was.

'We smashed it for you. And Mackenzie ran out of the campground and up the road a ways and threw it into the borrow ditch, so it'll look like you just tossed it out your window on the way to somewhere else. We left your laptop alone' – Nora supposed she should be grateful – 'but whatever you do, don't turn it on.'

As she spoke, Mackenzie crept from the bed and poured the remainder of the coffee into a go-cup and handed it to Nora.

'Come on, Ms Best. All due respect, you need to haul ass.'

FORTY-ONE

Nora drove in a daze, following her original course to Oregon because she had no better idea.

At least, she thought, no one knew the girls were with her, although she wondered how long the girls' running-away-through-the-forest ruse would hold before suspicion swung her way.

She crossed the Idaho line into Washington state by ten a.m. A rolling landscape with freshly shorn fields of grain unspooled in every direction. Miles-apart exits pointed the way to postage-stamp towns.

She pondered the likelihood that any of those towns might have a police department, and the still unlikelier possibility that her plight might warrant serious consideration – especially by small, rural agencies disinclined to sympathize with wealthy wayward girls and a woman who'd just taken them across not one, but two, state lines.

No, her best bet was to continue to Portland, follow her own first impulse to find a nonprofit focusing on runaways, one that would persuade the girls to call their parents, and then get the hell out of there and deal with her own problems.

Such thoughts carried her into the afternoon, when stomach and gas gauges both signaled dangerously low levels.

She swung onto one of the lonely exits, giving thanks that the gas station just off the ramp adjoined a convenience store. She pulled up to the pump and started to insert her credit card, then thought about the girls smashing her phone and reconsidered.

She'd thought them paranoid in the extreme, especially given what it was going to cost to replace her iPhone. On the other hand, it wasn't a bad idea to leave as little trace as possible. She gave thanks for Artie's advice to withdraw cash, and tried not to think how quickly her stack of bills would dwindle, especially the way the truck guzzled gas on these long hauls and with two more mouths to feed, even if only for a day or so.

She climbed out of the truck, stretched her arms over her head, did a couple of knee bends, and slitted her eyes against a gusting wind that swept her hair across her face. She reached back into the truck's cab and retrieved a hair tie and a ball cap and tried to banish the repetitive loop of her thoughts. They'd reach Portland in a few hours, after most agencies had closed for the day. Groups for runaways probably had twenty-four-hour hotlines, but she had no way of finding the numbers without her phone or using her computer to look them up. She'd have to find a library and use the public computers, easy enough in a town the size of Ponderosa but a bewildering proposition in a big city.

Still, at most she'd probably be stuck with the girls for another twenty-four hours, after which she could turn her attention to her own woeful situation.

She walked back to the trailer door, cracked it, and called Murph. He arrived with the girls close behind.

'Get back,' Nora hissed. 'I'm going to take the dog out, pay for gas and get us all something to eat. Any requests?'

'Diet Coke,' said Mackenzie. 'And something healthy to eat.'

'Fat chance. You'll get what they've got.'

Murph did his business with admirable dispatch, and she returned him to the trailer.

'Fill-up on pump two,' she told the store attendant, a stringy fellow whose graying hair badly needed a trim. Nora thought back to the librarian and the sheriff in Ponderosa, likewise men of a certain age. Had these rural towns seen a wholesale departure of their young residents? The clerk punched the requisite buttons and Nora wandered the store as gasoline flowed into the truck.

She kept her chin tucked, the cap shielding her face, as she perused shelves sparsely stocked with chips and canned beans and emergency automotive supplies. The girls' diet drinks were easy enough, along with a water for herself. She finally settled for prepackaged bologna and cheese sandwiches, stiffening in anticipation of the disdain that would greet them.

She brought it all to the counter and waited for the gas ticker to quit spinning through her purchase. On a television turned low, a bored-looking announcer droned on about a proposed local tax increase.

'Hungry?'

Nora hadn't thought about the optics of buying three of everything.

'I don't want to have to stop later.' As excuses went, it was paltry, but it seemed to satisfy.

The gas ticker stilled. 'That'll be seventy-five ninety-eight for the gas and another eighteen-fifty for the drinks and sandwiches.'

Nora peeled off twenties from the diminishing roll in her pocket as the clerk fit her purchases into a flimsy plastic bag.

The TV announcer's voice edged into a sharper pitch.

Nora looked up into an image of her own face, flanked by photos of Mackenzie and Ashleigh.

MISSING, blared the crawl.

The clerk craned his neck to look. 'Huh,' he said.

Nora swept the bag from the counter, resisting an urge to

tug her cap still lower over her face. How long would it take his synapses to fire on the fact that she'd ordered three of everything?

The faces vanished from the screen, only to be replaced by an image of Electra, resplendent with her airplane decal. Where the hell had Ennis gotten that?

The words 'notorious history' followed her own name on the crawl. Then: REWARD.

The clerk turned and studied her newly decorated trailer. 'Huh,' he said again.

Nora's heart and stomach performed a sort of Russian dance, all stomp and spin, within the inadequate confines of her body. Her breath caught.

'You going to the rendezvous?' he asked.

'Excuse me?'

'The big Airstream deal over on the coast between here and Portland. Had somebody in about an hour ago headed that way. There's a poster about it outside. They've been coming through all week. Some with fancy decorations just like yours. None with an airplane, though.'

Rendezvous! Nora thought it the most beautiful word she'd ever heard.

'Yes,' she said. 'Yes, I am. About how much of a drive do I have left? Feels like I've been on the road forever.' *In other words, I'm not that person on the TV, nope, not me.*

He pinched his lips between thumb and forefinger. 'Four, five hours, considering you're hauling.'

'Good thing I stocked up on food. Thanks for your help.'

'Keep an eye out for that trailer with the airplane,' he called after her. 'Maybe it's headed that way, too. Collect that reward money.'

Nora checked over her shoulder to make sure he'd turned his attention back to the television, ripped the faded poster about the rendezvous from the store's bulletin board, then tossed the Cokes and two sandwiches into the trailer and slammed the door before the girls could protest or the clerk could refocus his attention.

She headed back down the highway, smiling for what felt like the first time in days at the gift handed to her by the unwitting clerk. Ever since Ennis had floated his blackmail threat all of her decisions had been hasty, forced choices between dreadful and even worse scenarios.

Now she could go to the rendezvous, conceal Electra among hundreds of other Airstreams and, in the luxury of time, put some measured thought into what to do next.

FORTY-TWO

At least Nora was well acquainted with fear; and not just the gasping, garden-variety 'there's a spider in my shower' or even the spine-crawling 'that same guy has been that same distance behind me for three blocks now and there's nobody else on this street'.

She'd been immersed in the life-and-death variety and had surfaced whole, if not entirely undamaged. She knew its characteristics, including the oddest one, which is that in the midst of a prolonged crisis – and this was a goddamned, full-blown crisis – fear morphed into something like boredom.

The bologna and cheese sandwich was long gone. At some point, her newly empty stomach, stiffening joints, and the full-body fatigue of so many hours of driving elbowed fear into a corner, told it to sit down and shut up, because food and rest and please God some coffee were all that counted now. Fear could wait.

By her calculations, the rendezvous lay just ahead. The needle on the gas gauge twitched toward 'Empty'. Any minute now, the red warning light would blink on, cautioning her that she had only enough for maybe twenty more miles, maybe thirty if she took it easy. Which she did, the endless trees – even thicker than the forest surrounding Serendipity Ranch, their branches trailing long strands of moss – sliding past in syrupy slow motion.

Nora had passed a gas station a few miles earlier but reasoned that the rendezvous would have a station nearby. At least, she hoped so. While Nora had belatedly acknowledged the girls' wisdom in destroying her phone, she fiercely missed its bossy directions and especially the calculation of the distance remaining.

She slowed through a hamlet, scanning the roadside. It reminded her of Ponderosa, with its elementary school and café and bar, as well as probably the only convenience store in a hundred-mile radius lacking a gas pump. It disappeared from her rear-view mirror in a few disappointed heartbeats. The road began to climb, so steeply that the truck growled into a lower gear and the gas gauge indicator light glowed scarlet. Nora gave the truck just enough gas to hoist Electra to the summit, where a sign at the entrance to a pullout advertised a scenic overlook.

A break, she told herself, as she tapped the brakes and steered into it. Just five minutes to collect herself, roll down the windows, gulp fresh air, revive herself for the final push. She set the emergency brake and left the truck. She needed to let Murph out and reassure the girls that they were almost at their destination.

But first, a moment to herself, free from the confines of the truck's cab. A path, barely a car's width, led through a grove of trees to the edge of the overlook. She took it, noting the rusting beer cans and blackened campfire sites that bespoke a teenage party spot. She stretched and yawned, emerging from the trees onto the lip of the bluff. Nora forgot about her hunger, her fatigue, her fugitive status.

Below, the lowering sun lit up a sea of silver, beyond which the real ocean looked flat and gray by comparison. She'd found the rendezvous.

The girls sat cross-legged on the bed, slurping bowls of linguine alle vongole Nora had thrown together.

She'd kept the blinds pulled tight so that no one could see Mackenzie and Ashleigh, but had opened the windows to let in fresh air. The sounds and scents of the rendezvous flowed in. Steaks popped and sizzled on propane grills. Cries of greeting arose. Little dogs, perfect for life on the road, yapped incessantly. Someone played a guitar, all of it so achingly Norman Rockwellian as to push Nora to the verge of tears, so badly did she, too, wish to be part of such easy camaraderie instead of a woman on the verge of arrest.

She blinked hard and focused on the food.

'It's better with fresh clams,' she said, deflecting the girls' extravagant praise. 'And of course, with some bread to sop up the sauce.'

Ashleigh tilted her bowl to drink the last of the sauce like soup. 'We don't need more starch. Especially not with pasta.'

Nora relapsed into housemother/instructor/mentor role. 'Beware the diet trap. Look at both of you. You're young and healthy and strong. That's the important thing. Not starving yourself into somebody else's idea of perfection.'

They looked at her as though she'd just landed from some remote planet.

'Easy for you to say.' Mackenzie spoke as she twirled the last strands of linguine around her fork. 'You don't have to worry about that stuff anymore.'

Ouch.

'We need to talk about calling your parents.' Nora's words landed like a slap, a none-too-subliminal response to Mackenzie's insult.

The girls' eyes widened in the kind of fear she herself had been feeling for much of the drive. Nora jumped up and took their bowls before remnants of pasta and bits of clam sloshed onto the comforter.

In an instant, the girls went from know-it-all teens to terrified little girls.

'You can't. Ms Best, you just can't.'

Nora hadn't told them about the television news alert. She hadn't even turned on the truck's radio, for fear of hearing an expanded version of the report. Her original plan seemed laughably naïve in retrospect.

But maybe, just maybe, if she could get the girls to connect with their parents, she could explain her fears directly to their families, counter whatever nonsense Ennis had told them – although even to herself that plan seemed more cockeyed than the first.

Because who would the parents believe? A novice house-mother with the shady past that Ennis had already leaked to the media? Or the authority figure to whom they were paying six figures a year to return their girls to smiling submission?

But the longer the girls stayed with her, the more danger she was in. As for the girls, contacting their parents likely meant at best a lecture, at worst a return to Serendipity Ranch. The girls clearly feared the worst.

'You can't. You can't. They'll send us back. They'll use the . . . the . . .' Ashleigh had gone pale, gasping, too frightened for tears.

'The . . . the . . .'

Mackenzie wrapped her in a death grip. Her eyes shot fury at Nora. 'Water,' she commanded.

Nora hurried to comply, handing Mackenzie half a glass, fearful any more would spill. Mackenzie cradled Ashleigh's head against her chest and held the glass to her lips.

Ashleigh managed a sip and pushed it away, still shuddering.

Nora had to know.

'They'll use what, Ashleigh? What are you talking about?'

She'd thought the bonfire was bad enough, the way it pitted the girls against one another with accusation and blame. The isolation cabin, its conditions unthinkable, even if for a single night. Did Serendipity Ranch put the girls in some sort of restraints?

She directed her question to Ashleigh, but Mackenzie answered, her voice so venomous that Nora recoiled.

'The transporters, you stupid bitch.'

FORTY-THREE

'Transporters?'

They sounded like something out of a science fiction movie, clanking vehicles striding on tall metal legs above the forest.

'Vance and Allen. They're the ones who brought us here. I mean, not here. To the ranch.'

It took a moment before the names registered, with the same flash of fear she'd felt then.

Her first night at Serendipity Ranch. The two men in the forest.

'Those guys? I've met them.' As if *met* were the way to describe being slammed to the ground, face shoved into the dirt, a knee in her back. 'Not the best welcoming committee.'

She nattered on, hoping to calm Ashleigh, whose agitation was becoming more worrisome by the moment. 'Transporters? How does that work, exactly?'

A bitter laugh bubbled from Ashleigh's lips, so unexpected that Nora jumped. 'You want to tell her Mackenzie? Give her the R-rated version? Because you got off easy, right?'

Mackenzie flinched as the words struck her.

'There are these companies,' she told Nora. 'They specialize in bringing kids like us to programs like Serendipity Ranch. Remember, we're from all over the goddamn place and none of us is here willingly. You hear stories about kids whose parents try to bring them, kids grabbing the wheel, jumping from the car at red lights or rest stops, or even while the car is moving. So they use the transporters instead.'

'Wait!' It was Nora's turn to nearly send her pasta sliding from her bowl. 'I saw something like that on my way out here. Two men grabbing a girl. I thought it was a kidnapping. I even called nine-one-one. But her parents came out of their house and said she was going to rehab, and the cop backed them up.'

'Where was that? When?' Ashleigh's head jerked up, her voice sharp.

'A couple of weeks before I came to the ranch. Somewhere in the Midwest. I wasn't really paying attention. If I had my phone' – she aimed The Look at both girls – 'I could search my campground receipt and see exactly where.'

'No need. Do you remember the house?'

'Of course I do.' Impossible to forget its combination of too much money and not enough taste. 'It sort of looked like a castle. It had a turret. One of those arched wooden doors. The kind of place that might have a suit of armor standing guard in the hallway.'

'Oh, it does. Right inside the front door.'

Nora stared at Ashleigh, seeing instead the girl dangling between the two men, her long dark hair curtaining her face.

'That was you?'

'I could ask you the same question. I was half out of it but I remember some sort of commotion when they were putting me into the van.'

'Yes. That was me. Oh, Ashleigh. I'm so sorry. You must have been terrified.'

She tried to imagine it, the girl asleep in her bed, strangers bursting in – not just strangers, but men – grabbing her, hauling her from the house toward an unknown but too-easily-imagined fate.

'Yeah.' Ashleigh's voice was dry. 'You could say that.'

Mackenzie broke in. 'You want to know the funny thing?'

Nora guessed the funny thing wouldn't be funny at all. 'What?'

'They tell us those stories, Director Ennis and Mother Ennis, about why it's such a bad idea for parents to bring us in. About all the bad things that can happen. But I've never heard those stories from any of the kids in the program. So who even knows if they're true? But our parents hear a single story like that and they're happy to add another few grand on top of the crazy money they're already paying to "fix" us.' She wiggled her fingers in air quotes.

'Except.' She looked to Ashleigh, who'd gone from shaking and sobbing, to the eerie laughter, to an even more disturbing icy stillness.

'Except if we weren't broken before, we sure as hell are by the time those guys get through with us.'

Nora felt again the man's rough hand on her breast, his knee parting her legs. What had he said, his disappointment obvious?

An old broad.

Had they been anticipating a young woman? A teenage girl? And for what purpose?

Stupid, stupid. She chided herself. As though there were more than one purpose.

'Did they . . .?' She fumbled for a word. Not rape. Because

what if Ashleigh nodded? Her mind cringed away from the thought of an already-vulnerable teen, one traumatized by whatever her father's friend had done to her, at the nonexistent mercy, of those two thugs.

'Did they hurt you?'

'Hurt.' Now Mackenzie joined in the macabre laughter.

'Hurt? Oh, yeah. You could say that. Only thing that hurt worse? What Director Ennis said when I told him.'

Again, Nora feared to pose a question. If anything, she dreaded the answer even more than discovering what the men had done to Ashleigh.

She didn't need to ask. The girls riffed off each other in a role-playing grotesquerie.

'Wait. Wait. I can just imagine what he said.' Mackenzie puffed her cheeks, hooked her fingers in the waist of her khakis and thrust her flat belly forward in the best approximation of Ennis she could manage.

'They did what? Now, now, Ashleigh. Rigorous honesty is one of our most important precepts at Serendipity Ranch.'

Ashleigh mimicked the sobs that had wracked her only moments before. 'But' – gasp, shudder – 'I *am* being honest.'

Mackenzie tucked in her chin and looked down her pert nose.

'Manipulation is an across-the-board characteristic among our students. Part of the reason all of you have ended up in this program of last resort is that you've all wound your parents around your pinkie fingers for years, convincing them that you're mere victims rather than the architects of your own destruction.'

Mackenzie raised her head and beamed beatifically, freeing her fingers from her waistband and stretching her hands toward Ashleigh as though bestowing a great gift.

'The good news is, such behavior stops now.'

'No!' Nora's protest broke up the charade. 'That can't be.'

Like all the best lies, Ennis' spiel was wrapped in fact. Nora mentally grasped at those facts, a fleeting final hope.

The teens at Serendipity Ranch, like all smart teenagers everywhere, were of course manipulative, testing their limits like the velociraptors probing the electric fences in *Jurassic Park*, finding ways to escape the limits placed on them while getting into the least amount of trouble possible.

But it was one thing to breeze out the door on your way to a kegger, calling over your shoulder that you were heading to a friend's house to study.

Ashleigh's terror was real. And Nora had heard enough of Ennis' pontificating to find Mackenzie's mimicry believable.

She pressed her fingertips to her temples, trying to make sense of yet another shift in reality.

Everything had seemed so simple when the girls were mere stowaways. Her plan to turn the girls over to the care of an agency experienced in dealing with runaways – seemingly such a complication at the time – felt blissfully straightforward in retrospect.

Finding out she'd been portrayed as abducting the girls had added layers of risk, yet she'd clung to the hope that returning the girls to their families would smooth things over. This new knowledge, though, meant she couldn't in good conscience send the girls back to that situation. But every minute they remained with her heightened her legal jeopardy.

She rocked back and forth, moaning. 'Oh, shit. Oh, shit. Oh, shit.'

Something cold and wet jammed beneath her elbow. Murph, his face wrinkled in canine concern.

Voices pierced her misery.

'Ms Best. Ms Best. Are you all right?'

Was *she* all right? With everything she'd been through in this dreadful summer, with everything she now faced, she still was in a better spot than these two girls, sent away from their families and molested – and probably worse – by two grown men, and in Ashleigh's case, after already being preyed upon by a third.

Far more to the point, she was the adult. It was time for her to start acting like it.

She raised her head.

'Yes. I'm all right. This situation is not. In fact, it is supremely fucked up. But I'm fine and you're going to be, too.'

FORTY-FOUR

But how?

'We have to notify the police.' The knee-jerk response, one with obvious problems. But how could they fault her for having the girls if she said she'd taken them for their own safety – conveniently ignoring the fact that she hadn't meant to take them at all?

The girls fell into one another, Mackenzie joining Ashleigh in that same maniacal laughter that iced Nora's veins.

'The police? You mean, like Sheriff Foley? Yeah, Irene tried that. Look where it got her.'

The biting chill reached her capillaries.

She didn't even ask, just waited for the girls to tell her.

Mackenzie regained control first. 'I went with her. She'd just gotten off First Rung and said she needed to talk to the police about something that had happened to her. She wouldn't even tell me what it was. She started crying and wouldn't say anything else.

'We waited for a day when both of us were doing volunteer work in town. We sneaked out of the café and ran to the sheriff's office.' She shook her head at the memory.

'There was a woman at the front desk. She hollered that two girls from the school were there to see him. He was on the phone when we walked into his office. "Got the two of them in here now," he was saying. "I'll hold them for you." Only reason he didn't get all handsy was because there were two of us. But even after that, Irene talked to him. That's how I finally found out what had happened to her.'

Ashleigh clambered down from the bed, retrieved the water glass, filled it and drank. 'Sounds like it was the same thing they did to me.'

A few minutes earlier, Nora hadn't asked. A coward's reticence. She hadn't wanted to know. But that wasn't fair. The girls had lived through it. The least she could do was listen to it. 'Which was?'

Mackenzie put a steadying arm around Ashleigh. 'I'll go first. Because I got off easy with those guys. I yelled and kicked and hollered. They just . . .' She rubbed a hand over her breasts and her bottom. 'But Irene lived a long way away. It took them two days to get her to the ranch. After me, I think they started sedating the girls. She didn't have a chance.'

She pulled Ashleigh closer. 'And you didn't, either.'

Ashleigh spoke into Mackenzie's shoulder, her voice muffled. 'I could have kicked, too. I should have. Maybe then . . .'

'No.' On this one point, Nora was on firm ground. 'Nothing you did or didn't do was your fault. The only fault lies with those two bastards. Mackenzie, what did the sheriff do after Irene told him?'

Mackenzie's flair for acting rivaled that of the portraits she painted.

She plopped herself down on the dinette bench, leaned back and put her feet up on the table and spoke in an exaggerated drawl, as cruelly on target as when she'd aped Ennis.

'You girls forget I've heard every story under the sun about all the terrible things you go through up there at the ranch. Mr and Mrs Ennis, with all of their talents, could have settled anywhere in the country and yet they've chosen our tiny corner of the world to try and help the likes of you. And you come down here to talk trash about them to try and get them in trouble so you can go back to your mansions and keep right on doing the things that got you sent here in the first place.'

Ashleigh shrank into herself as Mackenzie spoke, exactly as Nora imagined Irene must have done upon hearing the sheriff's spiel.

'What happened then?'

'Director Ennis came and got us and both of us were put in isolation for a week and knocked back to First Rung when we got out.'

Nora kept trying to find something positive to grasp. 'At least you didn't end up in isolation in that shed. Are there two isolation rooms in the lodge?'

This time, the girls laughed so hard and so long that they fell to the floor. Murph, thinking it a game, gave a couple of excited yips and leapt around them while Mooch, always smarter, fled to safety.

'You . . . You . . .' Mackenzie rubbed tears away with the back of her hand. 'You actually believed that bullshit story?'

'Mackenzie!' Ashleigh mimed shock. 'How dare you use such language about the isolation rooms? The big, comfortable isolation rooms?'

Mackenzie choked back a final giggle and played along. 'The ones with the eight-hundred-thread-count sheets on the king-size bed?'

'That must have been yours. My sheets were satin.'

'Big whoop. I got the room with the Jacuzzi tub.'

'Yeah? Well, mine had a sauna.'

'All right, all right. You've made your point.' Nora wanted to laugh along with them, but the implications of their sarcasm were too distressing. 'You can't possibly be telling me that shed is the *actual* isolation room.'

The girls looked at each other. 'She's a smart one,' Mackenzie said.

'Let's bump her up a rung,' said Ashleigh. 'You can have the bed tonight, Ms Best. We'll take the dinette.'

Nora forced herself to focus on practicalities as a way of keeping the horror at bay. 'Mackenzie, you said they put you and Irene on isolation at the same time. But there's only one shed.'

'She gets smarter by the minute,' Ashleigh said.

Mackenzie finally took pity on her. 'The shed where you found Ashleigh? That's the good isolation room.'

Nora thought back to the utter darkness, the pallet on the splintery wooden floor, the reeking bucket. 'How could anything possibly be worse?'

'There's a room off the garage. Believe me, it's worse. The whole building stinks of oil and gasoline. The floor is concrete. Somehow it always feels damp. A few years ago there was this girl named Dana. She was in there a week and came out with pneumonia. Miss Hanford got into a big fight with

Director Ennis over taking her to the hospital. At least, that's the way I heard it.'

The story was secondhand. Forty-eight hours earlier, Nora would have dismissed it as typical teenage exaggeration. Now, she believed; oh, yes, she did.

'Anyway, that's where they put Irene. Isolation was bad for me, but at least I was used to it. I've been on First Rung half the time I've been here because I can't keep my mouth shut. But it was worse for Irene. She was supposed to move up to Fourth Rung – that's the one where you finally get to talk to your family again. The day she got out of isolation, Irene disappeared.'

Mackenzie made a swooping motion with her hand, her paint-splashed fingers slashing down and down through the air as though tracing Irene's plunge from the bluff.

She slid a glance toward Ashleigh. 'Ashleigh didn't know about any of this. If I'd known she was going to tell Director Ennis about what had happened to her, I'd have stopped her. But she didn't tell me until afterward. And then you were leaving and we just . . . jumped.'

Except they hadn't *just* jumped. They'd laid a fake trail into the woods, gathered the materials to repaint the trailer, and smashed her phone so she couldn't be tracked beyond the first night's campsite.

In her brief acquaintance with the girls, she'd seen them as defiant, spoiled, whiney, mean, sneaky and, yes, manipulative.

The past day and a half had also shown them to be generous and caring. Sneaky – yes, that was one way of looking at their actions. *Resourceful*, in ways she couldn't have imagined, seemed more accurate.

Nora had been trying to figure things out by herself, without turning to the two obvious resources at her disposal.

'Mackenzie, Ashleigh,' she snapped. 'Enough sitting around feeling scared and sorry for ourselves. Let's get to work on a plan. Oh – and given that we're in this together, maybe you should start calling me Nora.'

Nora found a piece of paper and they started making a list of places they could turn.

'Police,' she said over their protests. 'We're two states away. We could go to Portland – my plan was to go there, anyway. The police there will be way more professional than Sheriff Bozo.'

Mackenzie plucked the pen from her hand and crossed out the word. 'No police. Last resort only.'

'Then I need to call my lawyer, something else I was going to do anyway. Except you two deep-sixed my phone.'

'Please,' Ashleigh said. 'Just get a TracFone. That's what Jonathan got me so that we could keep in touch without his wife or my dad finding out. What?'

Nora and Mackenzie stared at her.

Mackenzie put Nora's thoughts into words. 'Didn't you have any sense at all how fucked up that was?'

'He told me he loved me!'

Nora and Mackenzie spoke together. 'They all say that.'

Ashleigh managed a small laugh, a real one this time. 'Jinx.'

Nora wrote down 'TracFone.' Then: 'My first thought was to look in Portland for some sort of outfit that helps runaways. But what about calling a rape crisis center? They're all about confidentiality, too.'

She held her breath, praying the girls would object, which would mean – she hoped – that Ashleigh hadn't been raped. But both nodded grim assent and Nora added it to the list with a shaking hand.

'The thing is,' she said, 'it all comes back to the police at some point. A rape crisis center can help you with the trauma. A group for runaways can talk about how best to reconnect with your families, or at least to tell them you're all right. No matter how angry you are with them, it's important to do that. But we can't just hide out forever. Even in the midst of all these Airstreams, I figure it'll take them another day, maybe two at most – three if we get unbelievably lucky – before they track us down. If they find us before anyone else does, it's going to be ugly. At the very best, you two will end up back at Serendipity Ranch, maybe even taken there by the transporters, and put on isolation for God knows how long.

'As for me, I'll probably end up in jail. Who knows what will happen to Mooch and Murph?'

She tried to say it lightly, making a joke of it by referencing the animals, although the reality loomed large.

Mackenzie wrapped her arms around Murph's neck and Ashleigh scooped Mooch into her lap. 'Never!'

Good, thought Nora. At least she'd turned their focus away from their own likely fate. 'And I'll end on some front page again . . . Oh!'

She slapped her forehead so hard she feared a lingering mark.

'I'm an idiot!'

The girls, still holding firmly to their animal companions, edged toward the rear of the trailer.

Nora almost laughed in her relief. 'Relax. I mean, as much as possible under the circumstances. Mackenzie, Ashleigh, I spent my entire career in public relations. A lot of it involving planting puff pieces about my university – you know, professors getting prestigious research grants, that sort of thing.'

The girls' lips began to curl in identical so-what sneers.

'Hear me out. Every so often, though, we'd have to do damage control. Somebody would embezzle money from the university. A high-profile athlete would drink and drive, or get into a fight, or assault a woman – God, those cases were endless. Anyhow, when things like that happened, it was my job to get out in front of the story.'

Nora told herself their evident bafflement was at least an improvement over the sneers.

'We need to go to the press. The internet – social media, forums, whatever. I'll put together something for traditional media. You figure out the online stuff, and then tell me what to post and where. Once we've got all our stuff together, I'll go to the library in that little town we drove through. If we're lucky, it'll have public computers just like the one in Ponderosa. While I'm gone, you girls are not to leave this trailer, not even with those haircuts. Understood?'

Their expressions told her they didn't, not at all. But they nodded assent.

'Give me a few minutes to get my thoughts together. I'll write something up, show you what I've got in mind. But here's the idea, so you can start thinking about it, too. When they catch up with us – and they will – they're going to trash us. I'm going to be a kidnapper, you two are going to be lying little bitches. We need to put out information exposing Serendipity Ranch for the abusive nightmare we know it to be.'

The hell with the nondisclosure agreement she'd signed. She was already in so much trouble it was fast becoming the least of her worries.

She was doomed already. She might as well go down fighting.

FORTY-FIVE

Nora had never realized how much she counted on her phone until she couldn't use it to hail an Uber or Lyft or even a regular taxi.

The truck was so low on gas that she didn't want to drive it until they fled the rendezvous. The town she'd driven through just before arriving at the rendezvous was within walking distance, as long as you counted three miles as walking distance.

Before she set out, she fetched a bubba chair from the truck's back seat and set it up strategically to block an easy view of its license plate. Then she donned her running gear and set out at a slow jog through the orderly rows of trailers for town, just another rendezvous participant out for some exercise.

She noted with relief that hers was not the only trailer embellished with fanciful decals. She passed trailers whose exteriors sported seascapes, wildflower gardens, mountainous terrain, even a trompe l'oeil of a cozy cabin interior, fireplace blazing, complete with sleeping Labrador retriever before it.

Whether they'd given free rein to artistic expression or stuck with basic gleaming aluminum, most at the rendezvous had arranged elaborate outdoor spaces. Mats topped the grass, and lawn chairs and even the occasional picnic table topped the mats. Twinkle lights dangled from awnings. American flags snapped in the breeze, frequently paired with a flag from the owner's home state. Dogs yapped in portable kennels, while cats sat in windows, surveying all with feigned disinterest.

Nora's heart ached all out of proportion to the energy expended in the course of her jog.

What must it be like to be here for the sheer joy of it, to flop down in one of the lawn chairs, accept a beer dripping ice from a cooler, swap tales about life on the road? To turn in at night and actually sleep instead of lying awake wondering exactly what sort of prison sentence might be meted out for kidnapping two minors – information she could have discovered if only she'd had her phone or been foolish enough to fire up her laptop.

She left the rendezvous behind and headed up the steep hill toward the bluff overlooking the encampment. Halfway up the hill, she slowed to a brisk walk, which had turned to a trudge by the time she reached the pullout at the top. She followed the track back through the trees and took a breather at the overlook.

Sweat stung her eyes, blurring her view of the shimmering aluminum sea below, the pale strip of sand and the actual ocean beyond. A few neon-colored spots indicated swimmers and she indulged herself in a few tortuous moments imagining diving into a cool wave with no more care than the porpoises frisking in the distance.

She turned and backtracked to the road, thankful to be on the downslope, trying not to think about the climb she'd face on the return.

The bare-bones selection at the gas station at one end of town did not include TracFones. 'Try Ocean View,' suggested a clerk who barely looked old enough to hold a job. Curly red hair flopped over his eyes and freckles nearly merged in a solid brown blur across his face. 'About ten miles on the other side of the rendezvous.'

Even when she'd been running regularly, a ten-mile run pushed the outer limits of Nora's capabilities. The phone would have to wait. She squelched her disappointment, grabbed a bottle of water from the refrigerator case, and asked about a library.

'Two blocks up, hang a left, and it'll be on your right. You heading over there now? Mind returning a book for me?'

He reached beneath the counter and handed her a battered copy of *Lonesome Dove*.

'Had to renew it twice to get all the way through it. Worth it though.'

'The best,' she agreed. She held the water bottle against her neck and resisted the impulse to snatch the book from his hand and dash from the store. The fewer people who saw her for any amount of time, the better. But she'd made a tactical error in acknowledging her own affection for the book.

'That scene with the snakes.' He shivered as he rang up her water. 'Gonna have nightmares. What's your favorite part?'

That was an easy one. 'Call's horse.'

'The Hell Bitch?' He gave her a funny look.

Great. Now, when she most needed to remain anonymous, she'd said something memorable.

'One and the same.' She wished she could channel the ornery mare and kick the memory of this encounter right out of his carrot-top skull. 'Thanks for the directions.' It took everything she had not to sprint from the store.

She caught a break at the library, which was in the middle of a children's story hour. A harried staffer relieved her of *Lonesome Dove*, gave her an instruction sheet for signing onto the computer and returned to the gaggle of smeary-faced, fidgety youngsters. Some short-sighted soul apparently had supplied them with frosted doughnuts, if the remnants in a pink bakery box were any indication.

A woman with a vest identifying her as a volunteer held up a copy of *Charlotte's Web*, and began reading in a singsong voice, robbing all the menace from E.B. White's portrayal of Mr Arable and his ax. This time, Nora was smart enough to keep her fondness for the book to herself.

Her fingers itched to query her own name, to see the latest on the search for her and the girls. But she didn't dare. She wished she were tech-savvy enough to know whether law enforcement could set up some sort of internet alert for such activity.

Instead, she followed Mackenzie's advice. 'Look for alumni forums' – something Nora hadn't thought to do when she did her inadequate research on the ranch only a few weeks earlier. 'If my regular high school has one, you know this place does.'

It took a single query to land on 'Serendipity Ranch Survivors'.

At some point, Nora quit hitting the 'down' arrow.

She looked around the room, trying to re-anchor herself in normalcy. The Story Hour children sat silent, mouths agape, the magic of E.B. White's words somehow having managed to overcome the volunteer's uninspired delivery.

Nora listened for a few moments, hoping the sweetness of the tale would trump the litany of distress that washed over her with increasing force with each post on the message board.

'I was lucky. My parents pulled me out when I tried to kill myself. Another girl, she tried to hang herself with a bath towel. They caught her in time and put her in isolation for two whole weeks.'

'I ran away. That fucking sheriff caught me hitchhiking. Ennis told me that since I liked to run, I'd have to run five miles a day for a week. Did I mention I sprained my ankle trying to get away from the sheriff? You can imagine where his hands went when he helped me up. They gave me a crutch so I could hobble around the clearing.'

'Got caught in bed with another girl. Mother Ennis came to me in isolation and read Bible verses about immorality and women having relations contrary to nature. When I came back at her with "Judge not lest ye be judged", bitch slapped me.'

And, over and over again, some version of 'when I told my parents, Ennis the Menace said I was being manipulative'.

The volunteer tried to approximate the goose's honk from *Charlotte's Web* as she described the world as a wonderful place for the young.

Not for the students at Serendipity Ranch, it wasn't.

'How in the world?' she murmured. Over and over, Ennis had assured her of the program's fidelity to best practices. Of its stellar ranking by the organization that governed Serendipity Ranch and programs like it. He must have lied and she, who'd been so relieved in those initial interviews that he hadn't checked out her background, hadn't bothered to check out his.

No time like the present. She'd done a cursory skim of the school's website when she applied and hadn't looked at it since. She typed in the address and there it was on the home page: Top-ranked by the Organization for Adolescent Programs.

So he'd been telling the truth after all. Nora slumped in her chair. What if everything else he'd said had been true? That the girls seized every opportunity to twist the truth? What if they'd played her for exactly the fool she was starting to feel?

She stared at the screen, taking deep breaths. She clicked on the link for the Organization for Adolescent Programs. Might as well know the worst.

Its website featured the sort of photos she herself had taken at Serendipity Ranch showing teens engaged in all manner of wholesome outdoor activities – hiking, riding horses, paddling canoes – as well as bent over books and staring into computer screens in bright, well-appointed classrooms. She clicked through the site's pages until she landed on its board of directors. And there, twinkling at her from the screen, was Charlie Ennis.

Nora sat up. Ennis was on the board that set standards for such programs?

She opened a new screen and typed in the name of another board member, which popped up immediately. Director, New Beginnings Home. She tried another name. CEO, Journeys of Hope Academy. And another – Rocky Mountain School.

She went through the whole list, waiting for the anomaly. There was none. Every single member of the accreditation body that claimed to set standards for the programs was also a program director.

In his way, Charlie Ennis had been right, she thought.

Manipulation was indeed the problem.

But not by the kids.

Nora couldn't type fast enough.

She created a fake email account, then looked up contact information for every daily Montana newspaper – there were precious few – as well as the major television stations and the public radio outlets, and did the same for media outlets in Spokane, Portland and Seattle.

She extracted the pieces of paper, now damp and crumpled, from her waist pack upon which she'd drafted a letter outlining the issues at Serendipity Ranch. She typed it in, adding quotes from the alumni forum and the links to the information about the bullshit accrediting process, then sent the letter to all of them. 'Photos provided upon request,' she added.

The photos of Sophie stumbling through the snow beside June Ennis' car, of the girls building the stone wall, of the isolation shed's grim interior were safely downloaded onto her laptop. If a news organization expressed interest, she'd risk turning on her laptop to send them, assuming she hadn't been arrested by then. For good measure, she sent a copy to the Montana attorney general's office.

And, using the same fake email address, she sent an email to Artie, attaching the letter she'd just sent out. 'It's Nora,' she wrote. 'You probably already know I'm in a ton of trouble. Here's my side of the story. I'll be in direct touch as soon as it's safe.'

Then she returned to the alumni forum and typed a query.

'Has anyone sued?' Someone, maybe several someones, must have. It would explain Charlie Ennis' paranoia about lawsuits, his blackmailing the staff into submission, and also his constant touting of Serendipity Ranch's high standards, even if those standards were an utter fiction. 'And if so, can you put me in touch with a lawyer you're working with?'

She looked at the words, so stilted compared to the free-wheeling prose of the alumni, and went back to the beginning of her post, adding a single word:

URGENT.

FORTY-SIX

By the time Nora got back to the rendezvous, she no longer cared that sweat matted her hair and dust caked her legs.

The late fee she'd paid for the rendezvous registration no longer seemed so exorbitant, given that it included a water hook-up. Two teenage girls, even ones who weren't going anywhere, would give Electra's shower a workout. The same tableaux that had seemed so inviting when she'd set out – the barbecues and cocktail gatherings and games of horseshoes and Frisbee – no longer appealed. She wanted only to be within Electra's safe confines, standing beneath streaming water and forgetting for a few blessed moments the fix she was in.

She barely registered, beyond a flickering resentment of testosterone-fueled privilege, the two men who passed so close she had to step out of their way.

'. . . old broad,' she heard one of them say, and for a second, she thought it was directed at her. She chided herself for taking it personally and tried to refocus on the prospect of a shower, clean clothes, maybe something to eat, all of which would calm her nerves.

Then memory rushed in, the hand clamped over her mouth, the searing pain of her arm being wrenched behind her back. 'What the fuck? An old broad.'

And she knew it *was* about her.

Nora chanced a glance over her shoulder. The men were headed toward a picnic area, the tables and benches shaded by towering Sitka spruce, their scaly trunks coated with moss, heavy fringed branches draping nearly to the tabletops.

Cloths covered several of the tables, where people were setting out Tupperware containers of food and stacks of paper plates and napkins. A bluegrass band unpacked their instruments on a platform at one end of the picnic area. Nora remembered reading something about a rendezvous-wide potluck. People streamed into the picnic area, carrying coolers of beer and soft drinks, staking out tables. The two men took one near a large tree.

Nora darted behind it, feeling like a six-year-old in a game of hide-and-seek. Except the worst you could expect in a childhood game was a tap on the shoulder. Ashleigh and Mackenzie had accused these two of far, far worse.

Nora peeked around the tree and what she saw dispelled any doubts about the girls' accounts of their time with the transporters.

Bad enough that she recognized their voices from that second night at Serendipity Ranch. But she knew their faces, too. She hadn't even heard of Serendipity Ranch on what now felt like that years-ago morning in Indiana, when these same two men had turned toward her, the girl she now knew to be Ashleigh dangling in their grip.

She shrank behind the tree, pressing herself into the rough damp bark, too afraid even to move away.

'That guy at the store said this is where they'd be.'

'Yeah, but he didn't tell us there'd be about a million goddamn trailers here. How are we supposed to find them?'

'Should be easy. Just look for the painting. Trees, something like that. Easier than checking every license plate in this place.'

Oh, thank God. Half the decals she'd seen featured trees. That might buy her a little more time.

She sagged, the bark scraping her skin. If they ever made it out of this, and she ever found herself with some extra cash – two things she couldn't imagine at the moment – she'd commission a painting by Mackenzie, whose hasty trailer redecoration gave them a fighting chance at escape.

'Let's split up.' Thug One, the tall man she'd seen that first time, the one who'd summoned the girl's parents to set Nora straight, seemed to be in charge. 'You take rows one through twenty. I'll take the rest. Text me if you find 'em. I'll do the same. Don't make a move on them until we're both there.'

'Got it. But let's get some food first. Hell, it's free.'

Due to Nora's late arrival, Electra was parked in the last row. Nora waited until she saw the men scooping food from the containers onto their plates, and set off at a sprint, not caring how much attention that might draw, thankful that she'd left the trailer hitched. She could raise the stabilizers, fold up the steps and latch the door shut in a flash. With any luck she'd be long gone by the time one of the thugs reached the row where Electra was parked.

And where would she go?

She'd worry about that once they'd cleared the rendezvous site. She pressed a palm to the stitch knitting her side and ran on, nearly sobbing at the sight of Electra ahead.

She burst through the door, calling a warning.

'We're getting out of here. I just saw those guys, the transporters. They . . .'

But she spoke only to Murph and Mooch.

The girls were gone.

'No!'

In her head, she'd screamed.

Somehow instinct kicked in and kept the single word to a drawn-out moan.

Wherever the girls were, she couldn't leave without them. But every moment she stayed put, the thugs drew closer.

Think, Nora. Think fast.

But all that came to mind was an image of herself in a prison cell and the girls . . . She didn't want to think about what might happen to Mackenzie and Ashleigh should the two transporters get their hands on them again.

All of which wasted precious time.

She ran back outside and stared at the trailer. Electra was the only trailer in her row still hitched to a truck. She fumbled with the safety chains and breakaway cord, raised the hitch off the ball, then got into the truck and parked it at an angle in her space, as though she'd driven it somewhere and returned, much as several of the other campers appeared to have done. Better.

Her eyes fell on the damnable license tags.

She returned to the trailer and rooted through Mackenzie's

backpack for the paints she'd brought, emerging with a thin brush and the tube of black.

Outside again, she checked her row, which appeared deserted, her fellow campers likely at the potluck. The faint plinking of a banjo reached her ears.

She knelt before the truck, squeezed paint onto the brush, and with a few quick strokes transformed a 1 into a 4, a 3 into an 8, and worked similar deception on the trailer's tag. Close inspection would reveal the fakery, but she doubted that, after inspecting row after row of trailers, Thug Two would be inclined to scrutiny. She hurried back into the shelter of Electra, mentally adding tampering with license plates to her legally actionable list of sins.

Mooch and Murph, divining her anxiety, plastered themselves to her side as she crouched on the bed, peering through the narrowest opening possible in the curtain until she saw one of the transporters – Vance? Allen? She'd never known who was who – approach with a quick, disgruntled scan. He stopped before Electra. Cocked his head.

Nora held her breath. Trees, he'd said. Mackenzie's mural was more tall ferns and animals, the eye drawn more toward the cavorting monkey, a harlequin macaw than the vegetation surrounding them. He squinted at the license plate, then looked at a piece of paper in his hand. Shook his head. Moved on.

She fell back onto the bed, not bothering to push Murph away as he covered her face with quick reassuring swipes of his tongue. She was safe, at least for the next five minutes. But she couldn't relax. He'd rejoin his partner. They'd compare notes. Come back for a second look. She needed to be ready to take off the minute the girls got back. She fed the animals and took Murph out, hustling him back inside the second he stopped peeing. She closed the trailer's windows, stowed loose objects, and re-hitched the trailer.

More than ever, she wished she'd ignored the fatigue of her first night and taken the extra few minutes to gas up the truck before pulling into the rendezvous. Now they'd have to waste precious time filling the tank at the nearest station, probably at that town ten miles away, even as they made their belated escape.

She popped open the truck's glove box to retrieve her cash. She'd have it ready in her pocket when they pulled into the gas station, not wanting to waste even a few seconds fumbling for it.

She found herself staring at the truck owner's manual and registration and insurance cards, lying lonely within.

The cash was as gone as the girls, and only a fool would think the twin disappearances were unrelated.

FORTY-SEVEN

Mackenzie and Ashleigh turned up at four in the morning.

Somehow, Nora had fallen asleep, slumped over the dinette, and didn't hear them until they banged on Electra's door, calling for her with enough volume to broadcast her name through half the rendezvous.

She yanked open the door and they fell laughing through it, reeking of drink and weed and sex.

Nora had lived fifty years without experiencing the blend of fear and fury particular to parents. Now, she learned it in a flash.

'Where the hell have you been? Are you all right? What the . . . oh, Jesus Christ.'

She leapt aside just in time to avoid an impressive spray of vomit from Ashleigh.

'Amateur,' Mackenzie slurred.

'Hold her hair,' Nora commanded as Ashleigh heaved again. Mooch and Murph cowered beneath the dinette as Nora grabbed an entire roll of paper towels and tried to clean up.

''m sorry. So sorry.' Ashleigh bucked a final time but came up dry.

'Get her some water. And for God's sake, open a window.'

Nora finally got a good look at the girls after they'd settled Ashleigh at the dinette, moaning softly, head on her arms.

They'd shed their khakis and red Serendipity Ranch polos

for clothes they'd scavenged from Nora's small wardrobe: her running shorts, rolled up to just beneath their butts and T-shirts scissored into sleeveless crop tops.

From what she could gather from Mackenzie, thus attired and having helped themselves to her wine and whiskey, they'd sashayed forth into the rendezvous with her cash tucked into their bras in search of beer and boys, both of which had taken them about five minutes to find.

'Blake? Jake? Something like that? Here with his parents and bored out of his skull just like us. And his friend, Adam. He went right for Ashleigh. Adam and Ashleigh.' Mackenzie giggled. 'They were so cute together.'

Dear God. Boys and drunk girls. A nightmare scenario.

Mackenzie must have sensed her thoughts. 'Don't worry. I kept an eye on them. Told him if he hurt her, I'd cut his nuts off with rusty scissors and that he'd better believe me because I'm a runaway juvenile delinquent.'

Oxygen fled Nora's body. Her voice, when she found it, was high and thin.

'You told him that? D-d-did you tell him from where?'

'Nooooo.' Mackenzie's eyes were heavy. Whatever she'd drunk and smoked was catching up with her. 'How stupid do you think I am?'

Pretty fucking stupid. A thought she kept to herself. The damage, whatever it might be, was already done.

Somewhere in one of the other Airstreams were two teenage boys who knew about the existence of two teenage girls and that at least one of them was a runaway. Any family who invited a second teenage boy to the rendezvous likely was traveling with one of the super-sized Airstreams, the kind tricked out with all the comforts of home, including television. (Her own much smaller one also had come with a TV, which she'd removed as soon as taking possession of the keys.)

The kind of people who could afford one of those probably were the successful types who prided themselves with keeping up on the news. What were the chances that the boys had glanced – or would glance – at the TV while a newscast was running? One with the image of two girls with long flowing hair whose facial features nonetheless resembled those of the buzz-cut, hard-partying pair they'd just met?

'We've got to get out of here.'

'Whaaa?' Mackenzie slumped against Ashleigh.

'We've got to go.'

'Go where?'

Good question. She was out of options. She'd hoped to wait at least a day before returning to the library to see if her emails and forum posts had yielded any response, but it was too late for that. It was time to throw herself on the mercy of the police.

Portland was at least an hour away, a few minutes more factoring in the need to stop for gas and a TracFone. She'd call Artie on the way.

'Mackenzie. We have to leave *now*.'

'Whyyyyy?'

The only benefit to the girls' near-incapacitation was the somnolence fast overtaking them. If she told them that Vance and Allen were prowling the rendezvous, no telling what sort of unmanageable panic might erupt.

'Never mind. The truck's almost out of gas. I need to get a phone. My money. Where is it?'

'Ah. Sorry about that. We sprang for the beer. Here's the rest of it.'

She reached under her shirt – Nora's shirt – and fumbled at her bra. 'Wait a minute . . .'

Nora's fingers tattooed the tabletop. The girls could sober up on the drive. With luck, they'd be coherent when she pulled up to the police department.

'Sonofabitch.' The blurriness fled Mackenzie's voice. 'That fucking bastard.'

Her hand emerged empty from her shirt.

Nora stared at the slightly grubby palm, the fingers with the raggedly chewed nails, as though willing a wad of green-backs to appear in their clutches.

'Mackenzie?'

The girl's lower lip wobbled and her eyes filled with tears, transforming her instantly from worldly-wise teen rushing toward adulthood to a scared six-year-old.

'Ms Best? Nora? Don't be mad. Please don't be mad.'

'No.'

Mackenzie, misunderstanding, hiccupped a small sob of relief.

'No,' Nora said again, as Mackenzie's words confirmed her fear. '*All* of it's gone?'

'Don't worry, Nora. I'll find him. I'll get it back.'

'No,' Nora said a final time. 'We need to get as far away from those boys as possible, and as fast as possible.'

They already had the last of her money. If they'd figured out that Mackenzie and Ashleigh were the two missing girls in the news, would they also go after the reward?

Nora's gaze roamed Electra, taking in the two girls with their butchered hair, wearing her own butchered clothing, one of them nearly passed out and the other only in slightly better shape. Mooch and Murph crept out from beneath the dinette and leaned against her.

She took a breath. 'I didn't want to tell you this. But they're here. The transporters. Vance and Allen. I saw them.'

Mackenzie – cool, smartass, imperturbable Mackenzie – yelped and curled into a ball.

Ashleigh, her stomach seemingly empty just minutes before, threw up again.

'We don't have time for this,' Nora snapped.

Yet, she herself took a moment, caressing Electra's aluminum wall. For the last few months, the trailer had been her primary home, a reliable shelter through the storms crashing over her life. She flattened her hand against the wall so hard her skin whitened as she tried to avoid the inescapable conclusion about the only path left to her.

'Mackenzie, can you please clean up Ashleigh again while I pack a few things and then help me get her and the animals into the truck?'

They'd be more nimble and far less recognizable without the trailer. Leaving Electra would give her at least a fighting chance to get to Portland undetected. Besides, she could go farther on the remains of the gas without the drag of the trailer.

Mackenzie uncurled and helped Ashleigh, her movements slow, automatic.

Nora stared narrow-eyed at her, this girl who'd picked the lock to the trailer in the few seconds that Nora had her back turned; who'd thought to squirrel away the paints that disguised the airplane decal; who'd cut her own hair and Ashleigh's and fashioned a new look from Nora's own clothes.

'I don't suppose,' she said, 'your particular skills include knowing how to siphon gas?'

FORTY-EIGHT

How'd the saying go? Every time one door closes, another opens?

Nora felt as though she were in some sort of mirror version of optimism. All her doors were slamming shut, the most recent propelled by Mackenzie's reply.

'You can't siphon gas from cars anymore. Not easily, anyway. They did something to them so it doesn't work that way.'

Nora took some comfort in the scorn in her words. Mackenzie was coming back to herself. Good, because Nora needed all the help she could get.

'How do you even know that?'

Mackenzie stripped off Ashleigh's soiled shirt, retrieved a clean one from Electra's closet and eased it over Ashleigh's head.

'My dad told me. I guess he and his friends used to siphon gas back in the day. Turns out he was a bit of a juvenile delinquent in his time, too. Only his parents didn't send him off to some fucking, fancy-ass reform school. Guess they just figured he'd outgrow it. Which he did. Wish my mom had been the same way.'

She'd packed more information into those few sentences than Nora had heard since her arrival at Serendipity Ranch. Any other time, she'd have quizzed the girl, eager for more insights. But this was not the time.

'The truck's sitting on empty,' she said helplessly.

'I could go look for one with the keys in the ignition,' Mackenzie volunteered with puppyish enthusiasm. 'I'll bet half the cars here are unlocked and half of those have the keys in them.'

Nora's jaw hung open. She snapped it shut. 'Thanks, but I'm already in enough trouble without a grand theft auto charge.'

'But it'd be me! I'm still a juvie!'

'Absolutely not. There's a town ten miles away that should have a gas station. I can probably get that far and find enough pocket change for a few gallons instead of using my credit card. Let's just get going. It's going to be light soon.'

Nora stuffed food for the animals into a duffel, along with a change of clothing so she'd have something clean to wear when – if – they let her out of jail.

Mackenzie coaxed another glass of water into Ashleigh. 'Can you walk?'

The girl hunched and gagged.

Nora held her breath.

Ashleigh coughed, swallowed, and raised her head. Her eyes swam red in a face the color of a freshly bleached sheet. 'Sure.'

Nora and Mackenzie exchanged long looks. Each took one of Ashleigh's hands and pulled her to her feet, then braced themselves on either side of her.

They'd just reached the door when the knock sounded on the other side.

Ashleigh, so limp seconds before, writhed in their grasp.

'Let me go! Don't let them get me!'

'Ashleigh!' Nora hissed. 'Do you want them to hear us?' At which point, Murph let out a deep-throated bark.

Nora wrapped her arms around Ashleigh.

'We almost made it,' she murmured into the girl's hair. Although, they probably hadn't. Her harebrained escape plan had been little more than a pipe dream. But it was better than nothing, which is what she had now.

She envisioned Vance and Allen's hulking figures on the other side of the door, their leering faces, the hunger in their voices when they spoke of the girls.

Whatever happened next, she'd insist upon staying with the girls. That way, the transporters couldn't do anything to them.

A new knock rattled the door.

'Nora. *Nora*. Are you in there?'

'Oh, my God.' Ashleigh recognized the voice first. She bounded upright.

'Nora. Let me in. It's Luke.'

The girls nearly fell over one another to get to the door.

Luke slipped through, stopping just inside as his gaze took them in.

'Oh, thank God. You're all here.'

The girls collapsed against him. 'You came!'

He directed a small, tight smile at Nora over their heads. 'They borrowed someone's cellphone and called me. I got in the car as soon as I heard their message. I've been driving all night.'

Nora tried to pull the girls away from him but they clung fast.

She tugged harder. 'Why did you call him of all people?'

'Because he's the only one besides Miss Hanford we trusted, at least until you came along.'

Disgust tinged with pride – they trusted her! – coursed through her. Luke must have done one hell of a number on them. Now he had them in his clutches, an arm around each girl, tussling with her for their possession.

'Nora, we've got to get them out of here. The transporters are out looking for them. If I could find you, so can they.'

Swooping in like some sort of savior, probably planning to get the girls away from her for his own nefarious purposes, Nora thought, taking perverse pleasure at the effect of her next words.

'Too late. They're already here.'

The girls wailed in unison.

'Quiet!' Nora put her finger to her lips.

'Turn off the lights,' Luke advised. 'We don't need to draw any more attention to ourselves.'

'They don't know we're in this trailer,' Nora said. 'They've been going up and down the rows. It's only a matter of time before they come back again. We were just on our way out. But the truck doesn't have any gas and I'm out of money. We were just leaving when you showed up.'

'I can do you one better,' Luke said. 'Let's just take my car. I'm parked near the entrance. I'll go get it.'

'No!'

The girls and Luke stared open-mouthed at her vehemence. She scrambled for an explanation.

'I'm already in trouble for sheltering them and . . . well, a lot of other things at this point. No use dragging you into that mess. If you can just spot me some gas money, we'll be on our way. Maybe you can keep a lookout for Vance and Allen, divert them somehow if you see them.'

She held her breath, setting it free in a near-gasp when he nodded.

'Good plan. I'll follow you, just in case.' He patted his pockets. 'Damn. I left my wallet in the car. Let me go get it.'

He let go of the girls and closed the door soundlessly behind him.

Nora checked an impulse to bundle the girls and animals in the truck and leave without him. She ranked Luke only slightly lower on the danger scale represented by Vance and Allen. But she needed whatever money he could give her. At least she hadn't told him where she was going. She took grim satisfaction in imagining his likely reaction when she pulled up to the police station in Portland.

Which reminded her that she still had no idea where it was. She could ask to use his phone and look it up. And, text Artie while he was at it.

The tap at the door came sooner than she'd have thought possible. He must have sprinted all the way through the campground and back.

She unlatched the door.

It flew open with such force that it knocked her to the floor.

One of the transporters loomed over her, stun gun in hand. She lashed out with her feet but he laughed and caught at them as the other lunged gleefully toward the girls, and that was the last thing she saw before the device buzzed against her neck.

FORTY-NINE

Darkness.
Motion.
Pain.

Nora let the sensations come to her one by one, each informing her situation, and the hopelessness of it.

She was in a moving vehicle, prone on a hard metal floor, staring at a barely visible metal wall. A van, then. Light leaked in through the windshield.

She angled her head toward it, only then feeling the tightness against her cheeks. Tried to open her mouth.

Couldn't.

Duct tape.

Her shoulders burned. She tried to move them, only to discover her arms wrenched behind her back, duct-taped at the wrists. She bent her left knee. The right moved with it – her ankles, too, duct-taped.

The girls!

She tried to call their names, forgetting about the damnable tape. Her voice emerged as a weak moan.

'You hear that?'

A voice from the front of the van.

'They're waking up. Good. More fun for us.'

The girls, oh, the girls.

She lifted her head and turned it the other way, her eyes adjusting enough to the low light to stare straight into Mackenzie's, wide with the sort of terror that mirrored her own.

A whimper sounded from the far side of the van, letting her know that Ashleigh at least was alive.

The sensation beneath her changed, the vibrations intensifying, the engine sounding louder, the van climbing a hill.

Probably the one not far from the rendezvous site. Nora didn't know much about stun guns, but thought of them as a short-term device, probably incapacitating the three of them just long enough to get them into the van and haul ass away from the rendezvous.

Now what?

The girls would be delivered to Ennis, who would probably spin some convincing lies to their parents about how Nora had lured them away. But first . . .

The van slowed with a jolt. Nora tumbled against Mackenzie as it took a sharp turn and lurched forward for a few more seconds before stopping at a downward sloping angle. The emergency brake creaked.

They must be on the bluff, the lights of the rendezvous and the safety it represented maddeningly within view below, its participants blissfully unaware of the horror taking place above them.

'What are we doing?'

Nora, too, very badly wanted to know the answer to his question.

'Checking to see if this is high enough.'

The engine cut off. The doors opened, the men's voices floating back to her in the sudden silence.

'Shit. It's high enough but look at that slant. She'd just roll down and probably land alive. And we can't use the old place. Jesus, remember what a pain it was dragging Carolee all that way? We'll have to find somewhere along the road. Maybe one of those bridges we crossed. They were pretty high.'

'But how would she have gotten there?'

The silence went on long enough for the temperature of Nora's blood to drop far south of freezing as the two men considered the problem of her own demise.

'Shit. We'll have to go back and get her truck. I'll follow you in it and leave it by whatever bridge we use. It'll look like she just parked there and jumped.'

Admiration tinged the laughing response. 'Good one. But first, let's get paid.'

The front doors slammed shut. Their footsteps crunched across gravel.

Get paid? What did that mean? And where were they going for it?

The back doors flew open and Nora had her answer.

FIFTY

The men crawled in on all fours, dark forms looming in the gloom, smelling of sweat and something animal.

Mackenzie humped away from them, kicking with her bound legs, her curses sounding as muffled moans behind the duct tape. Ashleigh, perhaps even more worrisome, neither moved nor made a sound.

Gone catatonic, Nora thought, diving deep inside herself where whatever was about to happen would take place far, far away. She knew something about that. The thought of Ashleigh being in that state broke her heart.

'No,' she tried to shout. 'Take me.' She knew they wouldn't – at least not at first – and it didn't matter anyway because the tape rendered her words unintelligible, but she had to try.

'Christ. Get her out of here.'

Rough hands reached under her arms, hauling her across the floor, through the space between the front seats, dumping her half across one of them with her legs draping the console and her head hanging over the edge of the seat. Blood rushed to it. She tried to writhe into a more comfortable position, but gravity worked against her as she tried to jerk her torso upward against the van's downward angle.

'Now, where were we?'

Was that Vance? Or Allen? Did it matter?

She heard a laugh. The metallic ratchet of a zipper. Mackenzie's moans of protest rose in pitch.

'You think you're hollering now, girl? Give me a minute here.'

They were going to rape Mackenzie. And Ashleigh. And lie about it afterward because they knew full well no one would believe a couple of runaways with an already-checkered history. And then, when they were done with the girls, they'd throw her off a bridge and say she was just one more suicide in an unfortunate string.

Nora allowed herself a split second of bitter recrimination for failing to protect the girls.

But she could show them one last mercy.

'I'm sorry,' she said into the duct tape. The movement pulled a layer of skin from her lips. 'I'm so sorry,' she said again.

She kicked her bound ankles against the emergency brake and squeezed her eyes shut as though the inability to see the van's tumbling rush over the bluff would somehow ease all their deaths.

FIFTY-ONE

'Nora. Her name is Nora. Nora Best.'

Luke, his words tight with fear.

'Ms Best? Nora? Can you hear me?' A different voice, female.

She turned her face toward it and opened her eyes. Light blasted them closed again.

'Hey. Angle that away from her face, would you?'

Something jabbed at the back of her hand. She jerked, but was held firm.

'IV's in.'

'Hold still, Nora. We're trying to help you.'

She opened her mouth. *She could open her mouth.* The tape was gone. The tape that had been put there by . . .

It came back to her in jagged bursts. The men. The girls. The sickening series of bounces down the bluff, her body ricocheting off the walls of the van until the final crash when the sound of their moans, masculine and feminine mingled in a single agony, rose above the slow ticking of the engine. And then . . .

But the girls. *The girls.*

She must have spoken. Or someone – Luke, probably – saw what she was trying to say.

'Mackenzie and Ashleigh are alive. They're fine.'

'They'll *be* fine,' someone corrected, and Nora opened her eyes again, this time to a much-reduced glare that allowed her to see the face of a young woman in a dark uniform with a stethoscope around her neck. 'There's just enough angle on this hill that you basically rolled down. If it had been a straight drop, you'd all be pancakes right now.'

'Gail.' The other paramedic, the one busy taping the IV line to her arm, tore away a final piece of tape with his teeth and pressed it tight to her skin. 'She's a trainee,' he said to Nora. 'Needs a little work on her bedside manner.'

'It's fine,' Nora whispered in her new, hoarse voice. 'I'm glad we're not pancakes. But what about . . .? What about . . .?'

Her hands performed a St Vitus' dance at the thought of Vance and Allen. She turned her head and gagged. A plastic kidney bowl appeared beneath her mouth, but nothing came up and she pushed it weakly away.

'Those men?' she finally managed to say.

Gail's lips tightened and she shook her head. 'They didn't make it. A goddamn shame, if you ask me. If ever two people needed to stand trial—'

'*Gail!*'

But Gail was on a roll. 'Couple of bastards. Pants down around their ankles, and the girls all taped up the way they were. Thank God the van went over the edge before they could do anything more. Idiots were too stupid to set the brake – hey!'

Nora jerked in their grasp.

'Are you OK?'

She nodded, not trusting herself to say anything more.

She and the girls were alive. Vance and Allen were dead. Did it really matter how the van had come to roll off that bluff?

Not only were the girls alive, but like Nora their injuries consisted largely of concussions and deep, whole-body bruises. According to the doctors, their restraints may have kept them from even more serious injuries.

'We just bounced around like so many sacks of potatoes,' Mackenzie said with enthusiastic authority. 'They said that if we hadn't been all taped up, we'd probably have tried to brace ourselves and ended up breaking our arms and legs or even our necks like . . .'

She snapped her fingers.

Nora jumped, sending her wheelchair rolling back a few inches from Mackenzie's bed. They'd put the two girls together in one room and Nora next door in a hospital in Portland.

'I was on my way to Portland anyway. Not exactly how I planned to arrive,' she told a police detective, who seemed unimpressed with the irony. He'd just started in with his questions when a nurse stuck her head into Nora's room and said she could see the girls.

'I'll wait,' he said, as the nurse helped Nora into the wheelchair. 'Twenty minutes, maybe?'

Nora opened her mouth to suggest the next day, but the nurse answered for her. 'That should be fine. We don't want to wear the girls out. Ms Best will be back soon.'

Both sets of the girls' parents were flying in, and the girls were under strict instructions not to talk to police until they – and their lawyers – arrived.

Charlie Ennis had shown up at the hospital with impressive speed but, as related by Luke, did an about-face upon being informed that none of them wished to speak to him.

'He was arguing with the woman at the nurses' station when he got a phone call,' Luke said. 'I think it was from your parents' lawyer, Mackenzie. I didn't know a white man could turn even whiter. Or move that fast.'

At Nora's insistence, Luke likewise had been barred from visiting until Mackenzie and Ashleigh had sworn up and down – 'on your dog's life!' – that he'd never once made an improper move on either of them, or any of the others.

'We'd have heard about it, Nora. Nothing happened at that place that we didn't talk about. We all knew about the transporters. But any trash talk about Mr Rivera, that was just Director Ennis trying to smear him, the way he did Ms Hanford when she stuck up for Irene.'

Someone tap-tapped on the closed door, then pushed through it without waiting for an answer.

'Ashleigh! Oh, my God, Ashleigh.'

A blonde woman brushed past Nora and nearly fell across Ashleigh's bed, her hands patting the girl's face and body as though to make sure she was really all there. She turned on the man who'd followed her in.

'Bruce, you sonofabitch. I told you we never should have sent her there.'

He looked so stunned, mouth hanging open, eyes filling with tears, that it took Nora a moment to place him. She studied the woman to make sure. Yes, that was her.

'I know you.'

The woman looked at her and recoiled. Nora kept forgetting about her eyes' swollen technicolor splendor; the shapeless mass of her nose disciplined by an ungainly metal splint.

The woman shook her head so emphatically her gold teardrop earrings struck her cheeks. 'I don't think so. Who are you, anyway? Are you the kidnapper? How are you allowed to be anywhere near them?'

Against medical advice, Mackenzie sat up.

'Ow,' she said, and fell back against the pillow. But her voice was as strong as her body was still weak.

'She's not the kidnapper. She's the one who saved our lives.'

FIFTY-TWO

Nora did indeed know Ashleigh's parents.

It took a few minutes for them all to confirm Ashleigh's memory of Vance and Allen hauling her away that morning in Indiana.

'If I'd known, I'd never have taken a job there.'

'And if we'd known, we'd never have sent Ashleigh there.' Tears wore tracks through Katherine Blanchard's carefully applied make-up. She shot another poisonous look toward her husband. Nora guessed it would be a very long time before he shared the marital bed again.

'I wanted to tell you. But I could never make it out of First Rung,' Ashleigh said, her voice still weak. 'You have to be

Third Rung before you can even write to your parents, and Fourth before you can talk on the phone, and even then everything's monitored.'

'Besides.' Mackenzie broke in with the voice of authority. 'Even if she'd told you, Director Ennis would have just called it "manipulation". And you'd have believed him.'

The accusation winged its way toward Ashleigh's parents, but Nora guessed its true targets were still somewhere in the skies between Cambridge and Portland. She wondered if Mackenzie's parents would be as remorseful as Ashleigh's.

'No,' Katherine said. 'Your father took a call from our attorney when the plane landed. It seems as though Irene Bell's parents are contacting other parents about signing onto the suit they're filing.'

A suit! Nora had nearly forgotten the note she'd put on the message board approximately one thousand years ago, although it was barely more than twenty-four hours earlier.

Another tap sounded on the door. Nora expected to see Mackenzie's parents, but instead it was the detective, holding up his wrist and pointing to one of those outsize and absurdly tricked out watches that triathletes used.

'I suppose I should go,' Nora said, hoping they'd urge her to stay.

But they merely nodded agreement and Jeffrey Blanchard mumbled a shamefaced thanks. Katherine surprised Nora with a quick hug that wafted expensive perfume. 'Is there anything we can do for you?'

'No, thank you. Wait . . .' Nora remembered the turreted mansion in Indiana; took in Katherine's whisper-soft cashmere sweater and the gold bracelets circling her thin wrists; the pumps with the vertiginous heels and red soles that marked them as something far out of Nora's price range, even at the height of her career.

'A phone,' she said. 'I really, really need a phone.'

FIFTY-THREE

Detective Alex Eberle was young, ostentatiously fit – the watch apparently not just for show – and so poker-faced he gave Nora the willies.

'Let's go over again why you think Irene Bell and Carolee Hanford were killed rather than committed suicide.'

His bristling flattop seemed all of a piece with his tone.

'Because of what Vance and Allen said in the van. That they'd pushed them off the cliff near the trail, and that they were going to drop me off a bridge and leave my truck beside it, so everyone would think I'd killed myself, too.'

Her voice shook damnably at the memory, foiling her efforts to maintain at least a façade of calm.

'Vance and Allen are the men in the van?'

'Yes. Like I already told you.' Nora tried to keep the irritation from her voice.

'The ones who died when the van went off the edge,' he continued implacably. 'So they can't corroborate your story.'

'They probably wouldn't anyway, right? I'd imagine it's a rare murderer who admits to the crime.'

Nora tried a smile. It fled before his blank look.

'Lucky that you three survived the crash that killed both of them.'

'Yes. I'm grateful.' Nora chose her words carefully. What was he getting at?

'I mean, sounds as though you just had a concussion.'

'Not exactly just.' Nora had held herself very still during their talk, wary of the pain that flashed through her head at each abrupt moment. She brushed her fingertips against her forehead, wincing at even that light touch. 'I'm sorry. I'm feeling faint. Do you mind?'

He snapped his notebook shut.

'To be continued.'

* * *

But it wasn't.

Reporters, who might otherwise have slotted Nora's email into a file of Stories To Be Checked Out Later, descended en masse upon the story, the account outlined in her emails bolstered by the lurid details of the van's crash, as well as the photos of conditions at the ranch she'd finally been able to send.

So many parents yanked their children from Serendipity Ranch and so many of the instructors quit that the program shut down. The story went national, with an emblematic photo of the ranch's elaborate gate framing the burned-out lodge across the clearing. It took Nora a moment to recognize the blotch of scarlet by the ranch gate as one of June Ennis' scarves, probably tossed through a car window by a jubilant girl as her parents drove her away.

Further scrutiny of the fire in the lodge got lost in all the hubbub. 'That's a good thing, isn't it?' Nora nudged Ashleigh during a surreptitious coffee break in the hospital cafeteria, before the girl's parents flew her home, where they'd lined up round-the-clock care from nurses and physical therapists, as well as visits from a psychiatrist specializing in teen trauma and PTSD.

'Of course we started it,' Ashleigh said. 'We were pretty sure Irene hadn't committed suicide. And then after you found Ms Hanford – we were terrified one of us might be next. It looked like they were picking off anyone who'd told them about the transporters. We figured the fire might be a distraction. Remember when you saw Sofia helping Mr Rivera change out the smoke detector batteries? Every time he handed her a dead one, she gave it right back to him, pretending it was a good one. Oh, and we used some of Mackenzie's Benadryl on the instructor on bunkhouse duty that night, just like we did with you.'

Nora blinked. 'That's quite the impressive criminal enterprise.'

Ashleigh lifted a shoulder. 'So's rape. And murder,' she said matter-of-factly.

'Point taken.' Nora studied her. Ashleigh sat up straighter as she described the planning that led to the fire, her eyes sparkling, features animated, so different from the cringing, easily intimidated girl she'd met upon her arrival at Serendipity Ranch. No doubt Ashleigh would benefit from the intensive therapy her parents had arranged – Nora wished they'd thought of it before sending her to Serendipity Ranch – but she had the feeling Ashleigh would be fine, regardless.

Ashleigh dug her fork into a piece of cake that Nora placed before her. 'Think of it as a reward for putting up with all of that cold oatmeal.'

'God, the oatmeal.' Ashleigh made an initial show of pushing the cake away, then ran a finger through the icing and popped it in her mouth. 'They got away with everything for so long. The shitty food, the punishments, the isolation. They probably thought they'd get away with this, too. I wish I could see their faces now.'

Each day since the accident had brought new information, news organizations competing to break the latest story about Vance and Allen's criminal pasts, about the farcical nature of the Organization for Adolescent Programs, about a slew of laws proposed in the legislature, as well as in other states, to provide true oversight for such programs.

Ashleigh finally abandoned all pretense and dug into the cake with her fork. 'Honestly, we were surprised they hadn't killed Luke, given that he knew about the transporters, too. I told him and he went to the Ennises. That was right before you found Ms Hanford. We were so afraid he'd be next.'

Nora knew Ennis had, in his way, planned a far worse fate for Luke, one that would have ruined the rest of his life, the same way he'd tried to blackmail her into staying. How else to retain staff?

'So weird,' Ashleigh continued, 'that the transporters died in the crash and we didn't. Just dumb luck, I guess.'

'Yeah,' Nora said. 'Just dumb luck.'

FIFTY-FOUR

Four months later

The morning light woke Nora a little earlier each day now; it was only February but spring was on the way. Montana would still be buried in snow, the cold so crystalline that the very air appeared on the verge of shattering. Here in the Pacific Northwest, bulbs pushed green shoots through damp black earth and there was an exuberance to the seagulls' constant cries that made her smile. But on this day, she blinked into darkness, as the sunrise – or what passed for it here, a gradual lightening of the ever-present shroud of mist – was apparently still distant.

Nora edged an arm from beneath the blankets and reached for her phone, careful not to wake Mooch, curled into the crook of her neck. At least Murph now slept on a fleece pad on the floor, his arthritic joints no longer permitting even the low leap onto Electra's bed. She muted her alerts at night, but something must have been flagged as urgent.

She scrolled to the most recent alert. It was from Artie.

'Call me.'

Her hand shook so badly it took three times to tap in the number.

'What's so urgent, Artie?'

'Why are you whispering? I waited until a decent hour to call.'

Nora held the phone away from her ear to check the time. It was seven in the morning, nearly midday for Artie.

'Luke got in late last night. He's still sleeping.'

He'd spent the previous day in Seattle, nearly three hours away, completing some of the coursework required for school counselors in the state of Washington. An unexpected benefit of the publicity about Nora's role in saving the girls had been job offers at a middle school in a town on the peninsula that had hosted the Airstream rendezvous. Nora was enrolled in a program that allowed her to teach, under supervision, while working toward her certificate.

'It helps us attract and retain teachers in rural areas like this one,' the principal said of the program. 'People think it's charming when they first arrive. But the more time they spend here, the more trips they start taking to Seattle and Portland and even Vancouver. After a while, they don't come back. It's just too quiet here. Our teachers stay two, maybe three years, then . . .'

His hands rose in a fluttering motion, a bird flying away. The look on his face left no doubt he expected them to follow suit.

'Quiet,' Nora had assured him, 'is just what we're looking for.'

She and Luke were still feeling their way, gentle with one another, cautious, slowly shedding suspicion and betrayal. The fact that, unlike at Serendipity Ranch, they'd both passed extensive background checks before being accepted into the school's program did much to soothe their lingering unease. At least there'd be no surprises on that front.

'If Luke's still asleep,' Artie said, 'you might want to brace yourself.'

Nora stiffened. He had to be calling with news about Charlotte's lawsuit. But other than the embarrassment of further publicity, how could it possibly hurt her? She'd given up on getting the insurance money long ago and if she had to sell Electra and the truck to comply with a settlement, so be it.

She had Luke, the animals, a small but steady income. She'd found to her surprise that working with younger children suited her, their eyes still round and innocent, their incessant questions about innocuous subjects a relief after the unrelenting defiance of teenagers. And, after having her life threatened twice within the last few months, a mere lawsuit seemed like the least of her worries.

'Hit me,' she told Artie, 'I can take it.'

'Charlotte's dropping her suit. Seems she's uncomfortable with the optics of challenging the hero teacher who saved two girls.'

Nora dropped the phone.

'Nora? Nora?'

She retrieved the phone and held it to her ear.

'Are you there?'

'Artie. Talk.'

'This frees up the insurance money. The company should be cutting you a check in a matter of days.'

Seconds earlier, she'd thought herself impervious. Now she buried her face in the comforter to muffle a quick, hard sob of relief.

Luke jerked awake, lunging from the bed. 'What's wrong?'

She pulled him back, murmuring reassurance. She'd only recently begun to appreciate the extent of his PTSD from Iraq – the shouting nightmares, the defensive crouch upon being startled from sleep. It frightened her nearly as much as it did him, but she was learning to cope, speaking quietly, calmly, until he came back to himself.

'Shhh. Everything is fine,' she whispered. 'So fine.'

He curled tight against her, the shakes slowly easing.

'Uh-oh. Sounds like I woke up Luke. Sorry.'

Her phone dinged.

'I've got another message coming through. Artie, thanks for calling. And thanks for everything. You made my day. My month. The rest of my life.'

His voice, usually all dry efficiency, went soft.

'You deserve a break, Nora.'

'Yes,' she said. 'I do.' But he'd already rung off.

Then she looked at the incoming message. 'Break's over,' she muttered.

'Remember me?'

'How could I forget? What are you doing calling at this hour, Detective Eberle?'

'I'd given up trying to get through to you at a normal time.'

Luke, who'd finally started to relax, stiffened anew.

She turned and looked into his eyes, wide and wary as her own, and just like that, she was back in the van amid a jumble of bodies, somehow tossed into the rear during the long rotating tumble down the bluff.

Moans. Her own. One of the girls, but oh, God, not the other. And, voices.

'Fuck. Fuck! What the fuck!'

'My arm,' one of the men whined. 'I think it's broke.'

Nora opened her eyes but her face was mashed against the hard ridges of the back doors.

'Forget about your arm. We gotta get outta here before somebody finds us. Shit, shit, shit. Quick, get the tape off those girls.'

'I can't. I just told you. My arm's broke. Anyhow, why?'

'Because, dumbass, dollars to doughnuts half that fucking campground heard this and called nine-one-one. What's it gonna look like, they find them all taped up like this?'

'She still out?' A hand roughly jostled Nora. She held her breath. 'Good.'

Hands fumbled at Nora's wrists and ankles, then moved to her face. Flesh tore away with the tape. She bit her lip against a cry and let her arms fall limply to her side, hoping her feigned unconsciousness persuaded.

The van's back doors flew open.

'Get your hands off her.'

He loomed in the van's open door, a shadow. He clicked on a flashlight and swept its beam across the van's interior.

'Luke. Hey, man.' Vance sat back, an arm across his eyes against the glare.

The flashlight jerked. Nora cringed away as the light hit her face.

The light swept the van again, more slowly this time, lingering on Mackenzie's shirt, pushed up to reveal her bra, Ashleigh's shorts pulled down to her knees.

'Jesus Christ.'

The tone of it. Nora heard it. So did the men.

'Fuck it. I'm outta here.'

The man lunged for the door, cradling his broken arm.

Luke caught him easily, twisting the bad arm behind his back, then moving so fast Nora couldn't tell what happened, only that the unearthly scream ended in a crack.

Luke let him go and he collapsed with a thud.

His partner rose to a crouch, then made a break for the door with the quickness of a striking snake, shoving Luke aside.

Nora's hand shot out, finding his ankle. Her other hand joined it, holding tight even as his boot slammed into her face.

'Luke!' she gargled through the blood filling her mouth. 'I've got him.'

The man's legs lashed the air. Nora jerked like a fish on the end of a line as the men grappled and grunted.

Another crack. Another thud. Silence.

Then, a siren's rising wail.

'You're unconscious,' Luke ordered. 'Hold still.' She heard a tearing sound and then he pressed fresh tape over her mouth and wound more around her wrists and ankles.

The van's doors slammed shut and Nora fell back into the darkness.

Nora put her phone on speaker so Luke could hear it.

'To what do I owe the pleasure, Detective?'

Luke elbowed her and shook his head, his message clear: cut the sarcasm.

'We've finished the investigation into the wreck that killed Vance Norcross and Allen Givens.'

Nora's heart banged bruises against her ribs. Luke held her tighter, burying his face against her back.

Words raced through her mind: Accessory. Manslaughter. *Homicide.*

Eberle cleared his throat and spoke in stilted cop phrases. 'It appears the motor vehicle incident indeed could have caused the injuries to which Mr Norcross and Mr Givens succumbed.'

'Wait,' Nora said. 'Are you saying . . .?'

'That the investigation's over? Yes. You sound surprised.'

He was crazy if he thought she'd take the bait.

'Of course that's what happened,' she said. She tapped off the speakerphone and was saying goodbye when he spoke again.

'Wait. Remind me of something.'

'I'm late for work,' she began.

'This will only take a minute. The Serendipity Ranch

employee who arrived just after the EMTs got there. What was his name?'

Goddamn him and his games.

'Luke Rivera,' she said after his long silence indicated he was prepared to wait her out.

'He'd served in Iraq.'

'I believe I knew that,' she said cautiously.

'Did you know he was part of a special unit? They call them the Raiders now. Sort of like the Navy Seals or the Army Special Forces.'

'Detective, I really have to go.'

'What I'm saying is, he has some very particular skills. You should ask him about it sometime.'

Nora lost patience. 'What are you really saying, Detective?'

'Vance Norcross and Allen Givens were bad guys, Ms Best. But we have a justice system for a reason.'

'The same justice system that held Charlie Ennis accountable?' she blurted.

Because of course – of *course* – Charlie Ennis had somehow weaseled out of criminal charges. Yes, Serendipity Ranch had been shut down and there were lawsuits aplenty, but documents had magically appeared that seemed to cast blame for its worst practices on Carolee Hanford. The level system, the punishments, the isolation room – all of them outlined in long memos touting them as 'best practices' and signed with her name. Carolee Hanford, who was dead and couldn't defend herself.

She hadn't even been able to implicate the Ennises in Carolee's death. The van she'd seen in the middle of the night at the ranch, the one presumably carrying a kidnapped Carolee, really had delivered flour as well. June Ennis – who expressed loud and tearful shock at the 'revelations' about Vance and Allen – had the invoices as well as several sacks of flour, to prove it.

The alumni forum buzzed with the news that the Ennises had used the insurance settlement from the fire to buy property in neighboring Idaho and were busy touting their new program on a website loaded with testimonials from parents who, Nora imagined, had been granted hefty breaks on tuition.

'Thank you for your call, Detective Eberle,' she said icily and clicked off.

'What was that last bit about?' Luke sat up. Nora pulled him back down beside her. 'Go back to sleep. You need it. You got in so late.'

'I probably should have spent the night in Seattle, but I wanted to get back to you.'

She nestled against him. 'I'm glad.'

'What else did Eberle want?' he persisted.

'He said you're a Raider. Like the Seals?'

He ran a hand through her hair. 'They didn't call us that back then, but yeah. Something like a Seal.'

She glanced over in time to catch a crooked grin. 'Only better.'

'He said you had special skills. That I should ask you about them.'

He pulled back so he could look her in the eye.

'So ask.'

She shook her head. 'I don't need to.'

That night in the van, clutching Vance's ankle, hanging on for dear life despite the battering her face was taking, knowing her only hope lay in keeping him caught long enough for Luke to gain purchase, to deliver that life-taking, life-saving *crack*.

Knowing exactly what he was doing and what she was, too.

'You got a problem with it?'

She pulled his too-warm face to hers, her words like a vow in his ear.

'No. No problem at all.'